"The moment I first truly saw your face, I knew you were the one...."

Giles stopped in midsentence as a fiery blush rose like a tide from Vera's throat to the roots of her hair.

Her fury was greater than her embarrassment. "Surely you cannot expect me to believe such nonsense. You threatened to throttle me on the spot, and I saw in your eyes that you meant it. If that is your idea of wooing, I cannot wonder that you have no respectable woman to wife."

Giles was appalled. "God's teeth, will you let me finish, woman? You have not the slightest understanding of what I am asking of you."

She lifted her face to him, pale and set. "Are you not asking me to be your mistress?"

"I am not!" he roared. He leapt up from the chair like a scalded tiger. "Do I look like a madman?"

Dear Reader,

Welcome to another great month of Harlequin Historicals. These four selections are guaranteed to add spice to your summer reading list.

Garters and Spurs, from popular author DeLoras Scott, is the tale of Fargo Tanner and his search for the man who killed his brother. But when clues lead him to lovely Sara Carter, Fargo finds himself doubting his intentions.

In the last installment of the TEXAS series, Ruth Langan tells the story of *Texas Hero* Thad Conway, an ex-gunslinger who just wants to run his own ranch—alone. But prim schoolmarm Caroline Adams is determined to change his mind.

When impoverished Sir Giles of Rathborne hatches a scheme to enrich his coffers in *The Cygnet* by Marianne Willman, he turns a young bandit into a missing heiress and falls under her spell.

As a secondary character in *Sweet Seduction,* the first book in the NORTH POINT series, Barbara Johnson was a woman of exceptional courage and depth. Now, in *Sweet Sensations,* author Julie Tetel gives Barbara her own story in which she enters into a bargain with a mysterious drifter in order to keep her family safe.

July also marks the release of our Western short-story collection—*Untamed—Maverick Hearts* with stories by Heather Graham Pozzessere, Joan Johnston and Patricia Potter. Whether you like reading on the beach or by the pool, Harlequin Historicals offers four great books each month to be enjoyed all year round!

Sincerely,

Tracy Farrell
Senior Editor

The Cygnet

MARIANNE
WILLMAN

Harlequin Books

TORONTO • NEW YORK • LONDON
AMSTERDAM • PARIS • SYDNEY • HAMBURG
STOCKHOLM • ATHENS • TOKYO • MILAN
MADRID • WARSAW • BUDAPEST • AUCKLAND

Harlequin Historicals first edition July 1993

ISBN 0-373-28781-X

THE CYGNET

Books by Marianne Willman

Harlequin Historicals

Vixen #7
Rose Red, Rose White #29
Tilly and the Tiger #55
Thomasina #103
The Cygnet #181

MARIANNE WILLMAN

is an established author in both the historical and
contemporary romance genres. She was born and
raised in Detroit, and she now lives close by with her
family.

As a child, Marianne haunted the local libraries, and
she still manages to read volumes of history, as well as
fiction of all kinds. When her hobby of collecting
antique inkwells finally forced her to acknowledge that
she wanted to be a writer, she gave up her critical-care
nursing career and turned to writing. She's been busy
ever since.

To John (E.J.) and Lowell Montgomery Clark,
the best brother and sister-in-law in the entire
world—and for Kristen, Karin and Marc. Thanks
for the love and the laughter.

Chapter One

The thunder of hooves, scarcely softened by the thick leaf mold of the forest floor, sent a tremor of danger through the air. Even the bold ravens abandoned their perches on the ancient oaks, bursting upward through the leaves in a dark cloud, up and up into the bright blue sky.

The men causing the commotion paid no heed. Sir Giles of Rathborne—adventurer, rogue and the fiercest knight in all Christendom—raced on horseback beneath the gnarled branches in a black fury. His sun-bronzed complexion was deepened by the flush that covered his high cheekbones, and his dark eyes shone with anger.

God's eyes, the woman was intolerable! Giles ground his strong, white teeth. He had sailed the seven seas with Sir Francis Drake aboard the *Golden Hind,* risking his life a hundred times against the sea's might and the Spanish navy for the glory of England and her queen—only to be sent away from court by Elizabeth's royal decree, as if he were a mannerless rustic!

His chances of the queen sponsoring his sailing expedition to the Orient had withered and died between one heartbeat and the next. Worse still, he had even lost the chance to set sail with Hawkins for the West Indies. His frown deepened. If his half brother had not died an untimely death, leaving Giles the reluctant heir to Rathborne, he would even now be on the Spanish Main. The sedate life of a landowner might have suited Morse, who was ten years his senior, but it was not for him.

Giles spurred his horse and plunged deeper into the leafy gloom. His rich scarlet cloak flamed out behind him and the wind tousled his thick black hair. There was no other horse alive that could keep up with Caliph when the bit was between the gelding's teeth. Already the rest of his party had fallen far behind.

His close friend and comrade-at-arms, Francis Finch, called out after him, "Giles, wait! Wait before I lose myself in these accursed woods!"

It was no use. As Giles's horse sped beneath the lofty oaks, Francis nudged his bay to greater speed. "The fool! He'll kill himself."

"Not 'im," a weary veteran with a grizzled beard interjected. "Knows every inch of this countryside, from here to Rathborne. Grew up like a wild thing, 'e did, roaming the woods and meadows to escape the old man's strappings."

Francis sent him a quelling look, but the man went on with the ease of an old retainer. "Rides like a centaur, 'e does. Never known Sir Giles to be thrown by any four-legged creature on God's green earth. 'Tis the two-legged, female kind that 'ave been 'is bane."

Francis reined in. "Ah, then. No need to kill ourselves keeping pace with him when he's in the devil's own fury. As if we could."

The men-at-arms sighed with relief. After three years on the high seas they were more at home on a pitching deck than the backs of galloping steeds.

"If you're proven wrong, we shall still arrive in time to pick up the pieces and carry them home in a sack," Francis offered smoothly.

The men cast looks at one another but took the hint. Francis spurred his mount forward and they fell in behind him, sure there would be more than one broken neck before they ever reached Rathborne. And Sir Giles had gained even more ground on them. His scarlet cloak was a ribbon of moving color along the high road.

Francis sighed. Although they were close to Giles's home they had agreed earlier to stop at The Green Man in Paddiston for the night. The beds were clean and soft, the ale like nectar and the innkeeper's daughters saucy and willing. Or so Giles had promised. Francis had looked forward to finding a cozy armful to warm his own bed. He only hoped that Giles would remember to stop at the inn. Why, the way he was riding, he looked as if he would stop for nothing short of heaven or hell!

In fact, Giles had forgotten their arrangements. He galloped beneath the spreading branches of gnarled old trees, unaware that he had outstripped the others in the futile attempt to outstrip his anger. In his mind's eye he was still seeing the queen as, surrounded by glittering courtiers, she had frowned at him from the end of the corridor.

"I see, Sir Giles, that you have inherited your late father's penchant for enticing young maids into secluded corners," Elizabeth had said scornfully.

By God, that had stung!

The smirks and stifled laughter of her party been nothing in comparison. He had known that, as Elizabeth's new favorite, he had provoked jealousy. She inspired fierce loyalties, and not only because of the power and prestige her notice could bestow. Although not a great beauty, she had something far more alluring—all the fabled charm and fascination of her mother, Anne Boleyn, combined with the wit and piercing intelligence of bluff King Hal.

Her wrathful image was clearly imprinted in his memory. Elizabeth had looked forbiddingly regal in a gown of ivory silk seeded with pearls and small gold beads. Every inch Gloriana, she'd had a dainty diadem of gold, amethyst and pearls crowning her redgold hair. At such times, when her displeasure was aroused, she was very much her father's daughter. Henry VIII had married six wives—and beheaded two of them.

The queen's eyes had been hard as polished topaz. "We think your time would most certainly be better spent attending to your distressed estates, Sir Giles, than to simpering in corners with our ladies-in-waiting!"

Remembering, Giles squared his jaw in anger. The single ruby earring he wore glowed like a drop of blood against his skin. Curse it, he had never wanted the burden of owning Rathborne, with its unhappy memories. And he had not been *simpering* with anyone, he had been merely removing a speck of dust from the Lady Jocelyn's eye with the corner of his linen handkerchief.

It had not been *his* fault that that comely maid-in-waiting was a protégée of the Earl of Leicester and had therefore reignited the queen's violent jealousy. Nor that Lady Jocelyn had a rosy little mouth, a delectable figure and the most wondrous hazel eyes he had ever seen—dark lashed, flecked with gold and sparkling with invitation. Why, what man of flesh and blood would not have succumbed to the lure in their lambent depths?

Giles let Caliph have his head as the wood opened to wild meadowland. Women—the devil take them! All the trouble in his life had come through them. Female wiles were nothing but traps to catch the unwary bachelor. A woman would deny her own feelings and spurn the honest love of a poor knight to marry a snaggletoothed ancient with a title and coffers of gold. As Laetitia Lattimore had done to him three years earlier.

Or hound a sweet and innocent wife into decline, as his father's cruel mistress had done to his own mother.

His dark brows knit together in a fierce scowl. Romantic love was for fools. When this business at Rathborne was finished he would return to the life he loved. The sea would be his only mistress.

Feeling cynical and wise and hard of heart, Giles of Rathborne pounded down the road on Caliph's strong back. He was, at that moment, completely unaware that Destiny could make a fool of any man, be he ever so wary.

Only a few hours' ride away, one of England's great houses lay basking in the afternoon sun, surrounded by its lawns and meadows. Beyond the proud, glinting windows of the relatively new Tudor front, the original remains of Rathborne Castle brooded in the shadows of its long decay. Sudden shouts and curses broke the pastoral tranquility of the scene. The disturbance came from the vicinity of the kitchen gardens.

"Stop him!"

"Young knave! A pox on you!"

A slight youth in a padded jerkin and trews of light brown homespun dashed out the open kitchen door with a leather sack in his grubby hand. Moments later two stout women rushed through the same portal, puffing mightily and waving their long iron spoons. The youth easily eluded the matrons.

The women cursed as their quarry scampered past the rows of late squash and slipped easily over the walls of the kitchen garden. An old gardener took up the chase but was unequal to the task. He picked up a bit of broken rock from the wall and threw it at the running target. Then there was nothing but a trill of laughter as the fugitive ducked into the orchard and out of sight.

The cries of the women and the barking of a dog became muted as the youth, still grinning, skipped into the shadows of the encroaching woods. The way was rugged, scored by the ditches of ancient embankments long covered over with grass and concealing shrubs. The path, such as it was, posed no problem to someone so familiar with its secrets.

From time to time the lithe figure doubled back or took to the trees, weaving through rush and bramble. As the thief ducked beneath a hawthorn branch, a twig caught the dull brown cap and tore it free, revealing a mass of bright gold hair. A slim hand quickly replaced the hat, thereby concealing the telltale tresses once again. A few deft twists and turns in the escape route seemed in order to elude would-be pursuers. It was a wise fox that outsmarted the hounds.

Once through the stag meadow in the forest's center, the thief entered the trees once more. A thorny hedge, taller than a man, grew unchecked here; the youth skirted it, then ducked under a concealed opening in the briars and marched into a hidden camp.

Several men sat together, fletching a new batch of arrows with grouse feathers. Instantly alert, they reached for their knives and crossbows, then sank back in relief. "Be easy," one said. "'Tis only Vera."

"God's eyeballs!" their leader, a grizzled man of middle years with a wrestler's physique, exclaimed to his companions. "She makes no more noise than a butterfly." Pride and exasperation warred in his voice.

Vera stooped down beside them, her blue eyes alight with pleasure at the compliment. "Aye, you have taught me well, Tal. In more ways than one, as you will see. I have brought us a fine supper." She opened the worn leather sack she carried and produced two fat capons, roasted to a turn, and a fruit pie still warm from the oven.

Tal's mouth watered at the sight and smell of the good food, but he frowned at his adopted daughter. "I will not take food from the mouths of those we have vowed to protect. Some honest yeoman's family will go hungry to bed for your work."

Vera pushed a bright lock of hair from her eyes and laughed. "Only that corpulent swine of a steward. This was to be his supper."

"Jesu, girl, you have not been inside Rathborne!"

Despite Tal's horror, the others looked at Vera admiringly. None more so than Garvin, Tal's second in command, and young Hewe.

Vera shrugged, secretly delighted at their reactions. "Only Rathborne's kitchens. It was no great feat. The two portly wenches in charge mistook me for a new serving lad and set me to work. I took my turn at the spit, where four fat capons were roasting over the fire."

"You did not dare!" Hewe breathed in awe.

"I did." A dimple peeked out at the corner her mouth. "The opportunity was too good to pass up. And when the capons were done, one of the good dames told me to remove them from the hearth—and I did." Little lights of mischief danced in Vera's eyes. "After removing them from the spits, why, I removed them from the house as well. With this pie for good measure."

There was general laughter over her exploit, but Tal was concerned. He noticed that she had kept her face in profile to him. Taking her chin, he turned her to face him. The mud Vera had daubed over her delicate cheekbone did not fool him one whit. Beneath the drying streaks a dark stain discolored her skin. "How came you by this bruise?"

She flushed and her hand flew up to hide her cheek. "'Tis nothing. One of the gardeners threw a rock in my direction. I was looking the opposite way and ducked too late."

Seeing that he was upset, she gave him a saucy grin. "Come, Tal, admit that I escaped from that accursed convent school in the nick of time. Another month and I might have forgotten everything you ever taught me!"

"A few inches higher," he growled, "and you would be food for crows or a drooling idiot."

Vera twisted off a piece of the capon. Her mouth grew sulky. "You would not say that if it had been Ferris who stole the food. You would call him a brave lad."

Tal watched her gnaw on a wing and wipe her greasy fingers on her trews. What she said was true, up to a point. The fact remained that in her sojourn at the convent, Vera had blossomed into womanhood. The long, padded jerkin hid her ripening figure and a stranger would have taken her for one of the lads. Indeed, she was becoming more like one every day. And there was the rub. His conscience pricked at him. This was not the kind of life to which she had been born.

When he had taken to the woods with his companions, outlaws all, Vera had been little more than a cub. At the time Tal had had no other choice, and he had expected their exile to last only a few months.

Vera had taken to the scheme immediately. She had shucked off her petticoats and adopted boy's garb willingly. Soon she had proved as adept as any of them at searching out food or keeping watch. A good thing, too, for the few months of refuge in Rathborne Forest had stretched into years.

During that time Vera's abilities had kept pace with those of the youths her age, and her quick wits and budding leadership counterbalanced what she lacked in sheer strength. By her thirteenth year she could draw a bow and hit a target with greater accuracy than any but Tal and Garvin themselves. Anything Hewe and Ferris could do, Vera tried also. She had climbed the highest trees, swum the fastest river currents and put herself in danger time and again, to prove that she was as good as any among them.

That was one of the things that had worried Tal the most and resulted in him shipping her off to the convent, in hopes the nuns would teach her things. Female things. Because when all was said and done, Vera *was* a female.

He took the drumstick she offered him and bit into it. The meat, though done to a turn, tasted like tallow in his mouth and was as difficult to swallow. Tal sighed again. Vera deserved better than this rough exile. Most of all, what would happen to her if he was killed or wounded or otherwise unable to look out for her? Especially now in these hard times, when the hated steward of Rathborne had turned so many out of their shops and cottages. It gave him nightmares.

Vera looked up and was startled by the somber lines of Tal's face. She wiped her chin with her sleeve. "What gloomy company you are today."

He did not answer directly. "How old are you, child? Nigh to fifteen summers, are you not?"

Vera wished she did not have to answer. She knew, with a sudden sinking in her stomach, what was coming. "Nearer to seventeen," she said at last. She didn't clarify which side of seventeen.

Tal chewed over this information. God's teeth, where had the years gone? He steeled himself. "Come, Vera. Most maids your age are already married. Have you no hankering for a little whitewashed farmer's cot with a husband and wee ones of your own?"

"Jesu, no!" Vera was aghast. "Why would I choose such a life over this? Weaving and sewing and baking. Setting the hens to lay and minding the hogs. Fie! And what need have I of a husband?"

She became aware of many glances flicking her way. The easy camaraderie of her youth had been slowly changing, slipping away through her fingers. Because of her sex, because she had had the misfortune to be born female, they were beginning to treat her differently, as if she were some dainty piece. Well, she would soon put a stop to *that* nonsense.

She rose and challenged Hewe, Tal's skinny-shanked nephew, to a wrestling contest. He raked his hand through his straight, flaxen hair. "We're not children anymore, to scuffle in the dirt together."

Vera was greatly annoyed. "What, are you afraid that I will best you? Come, Hewe. We used to wrestle like pups when we were younger."

Hewe's face and neck reddened. "Aye. Much younger. That was before you were grown into a woman. It would not be seemly now."

Vera turned to a gangly lad of fifteen. "Then you, Ferris."

But Ferris scratched his scrawny arm and declined as well. Vera felt a wall closing about her, shutting her off from all that was most dear. All because she was a woman born. The games of her youth were forbidden, the fast friendships awkward and strained. Her eyes prickled with unshed tears, but she would be damned to hell if she would let them see her weakness. "Cowards!" She turned and ran away, into the forest.

The sun lowered, casting dark shadows through the trees. There were places thick with undergrowth and others where ancient oaks grew, the ground beneath their arching limbs clear of all but leaf mold. Her favorite place was a certain mossy bank beside a meandering stream. She threw herself down and was horrified to realize her eyes were full of tears.

Vera dashed them away angrily. She would not turn into a woman, no matter what changes nature wrought in her body. *She would not!* She would not stay near the cook fire and simper at babies while the men were out on the hunt, having wonderful adventures that she was barred from sharing. Womanhood meant the end of her happy life with Tal and the band forever. Did they not understand? She might look different, but inside she was still just plain Vera.

That had always been good enough for Tal and the others. She wiped at another tear with the back of her hand. Why was it not so now?

She was glad she had not told them her real objective at Rathborne. The lesser one had been to see the famous plaster ceiling in the great chamber at Rathborne; the more urgent one, to find the steward's tax books so that proof of his cruel tactics might be presented to the queen. She had failed this time, but Vera had not given up her quest.

The sun was westering and she knew she should head back to camp, but a stubbornness was upon her. Vera settled back into a mossy depression between the high roots of an ancient tree and looked up. The treetops were silhouetted against a bright sky streaked with mauve and rose and orange, like Sister Johanna's skeins of embroidery silk. A hawk soared high above, wings gilded by light. The graceful bird slowly rode the air currents that rose from the valleys that flanked the wooded hills.

Voices disturbed the peace. She recognized Tal's first, and then the answering tones of Garvin. "I have done wrong by Vera. I see it now," Tal murmured. "As a doting foster father I let the girl have her head, and treated her as I did my younger brothers."

"Aye, she's bidding to be a rare handful. She needs a husband to tame her," Garvin replied. "It was one thing to run free like a boy in her younger days, but now it might bring trouble. Hewe is fair besotted with her. Ferris, too, if I'm reading him aright. And more than one of the men from the other camps looks to her with lust in his eye. The girl's ripe for tumbling."

Vera was too furious for speech. Her whole body shook with rage. How dare they discuss her in such a way!

Garvin was not done. "If matters were settled with Rathborne, I would ask you for her hand myself. God knows I have loved her well for many a day. When the tyrant is removed and we can return to our former lives, I shall build a little cottage down in the wold on the land my father cleared. I swear to heaven that I would protect Vera from all harm, were she my wife."

"Aye, and you would be my choice of a proper mate for her—if matters with Rathborne were settled." Tal sighed. "When they are, you must speak to me again. I hope it may be soon. Meantime, what am I to do? Unless we have gold to purchase weapons, we can never hope to rid ourselves of this foul steward who has blighted our land. As for Vera, I took her to the convent as much for her safety as anything else. The nuns could not tame her, either. If I take her back she'll likely run away again and join us before sundown."

Aye, Vera vowed silently, *you may be sure of it!*

She could tell by the soft crackling of leaves that they were turning away toward the river, and strained her ears to hear. Garvin was speaking.

" . . . near Salisbury. The farm is small but the land is rich indeed. My sister's husband is a good man. I am sure they would take Vera in until I can claim her hand in marriage. With so many children to care for, they would find another pair of hands welcome. I think Vera would learn to love it. There is so much to be done, not like the convent, where there is naught but prayer and penance. Why, Vera could make herself useful in a hundred ways—spinning, cooking, tending the animals."

There was a long pause while Tal thought over the other man's words. Garvin persisted: "A woman in camp is a danger to all. Vera would be safe with my sister, and she could learn what a goodwife needs to know to keep a proper house. You know in your heart that I am right in what I say."

"Aye," Tal said, his voice filled with relief. "That would be the best solution for all. Consider it done! I shall talk to Vera in the morning."

They wandered away. Vera stared blindly at the shadows of the forest, shocked and trembling with indignation. She felt hurt and terribly betrayed. Between them, Tal and Garvin had parceled out her future for her without even a by-your-leave! After all she had gone through in the past two weeks—making her way north from the convent to Tal's encampment, begging and stealing food to stay alive, sleeping in haystacks and ditches along the way! Arriving wet and weary and footsore but with her heart bursting with joy...only to find herself unwelcome in the only home she had ever known. And they meant to send her away again. Forever.

She drew her dagger and flung it in one smooth motion. It whistled through the night air and buried itself to the haft in a tree trunk. Some of her anger flew with it, and she was relieved to see that she had not lost her touch.

Since coming to the forest with Tal in her eighth year, she had tried to outfight, outrace and outwit the boys her age—and she had succeeded. She had done it all for Tal, to be a credit to him and to prove she would be no trouble to him. To be, as far as she could, the son he had yearned for and never had. And now, because she had been born a female, he meant to trade her away to Garvin's family as if she were a spavined horse.

As for Garvin, that slow-moving ox! Why, she would sooner marry Ferris or... or Hewe. Garvin's idyllic dreams of a little house in the wold were a nightmare to her. Vera's dreams were filled with adventure and derring-do, not with spinning and laundry and having a sniveling horde of someone else's brats at her apron strings.

If she ever owned an apron, which was, she thought with a scowl, highly unlikely.

A dark shape came padding out of the gathering twilight, then bounded toward her. Vera grabbed the shaggy creature and turned her face away from its slobbering tongue.

"Down, Wolf, you mangy cur. Shh! You'll give my hiding place away."

The hound gave her face a final lick, then settled down beside her protectively. His loyalty and love moved her. Here, at least, was one faithful soul who had never betrayed her trust. Aye, and never would. He had guarded her through many a dark night. Then he pricked up his ears. Vera heard the faint whistle a moment later. Wolf gave her a look of apology and bounded off between the trees.

Vera was wounded to the quick. Even Wolf had deserted her. She clenched her hands into fists. Nothing had changed but their perception of her, if only she could make them realize it. Somehow she must prove herself to be more useful to them as a member of the band then imprisoned behind convent walls or slopping the hogs for Garvin's sister. She had endured her exile at the convent as long as she could, for Tal's sake, but all that praying and chanting was enough to try the patience of a saint.

Which, Vera knew very well, she was not.

And being told she must give up hunting and fishing had been the final straw. Vera admired the mother superior, who was cut from the same cloth as Tal—a good leader, generous with praise, yet taking no nonsense from subordinates—but she had no desire to emulate her. The quiet world of women held no appeal for Vera. As to the learning, of which Tal thought so highly, she considered it a waste of time. As far as she could see, reading and writing did not feed hungry bellies or clothe the poor against a winter's chill.

Deep in thought, she slapped absently at a fly and missed. The warm breeze was soft against her cheek and dried the sheen of tears whose existence she would have denied to anyone. Yes, by St. Stephen's bones, she would think of a plan to prove that she belonged here with the others. It would have to be something spectacular. Something so daring it would take their breath away.

Something so significant that they would never, ever even think of sending her away again.

As if in answer to her silent prayer, she caught the distant drumming of approaching hooves.

Chapter Two

Vera scrambled toward the rise of land that overlooked the road to Rathborne. A breeze ruffled her pale locks; she tucked her hair behind her ears, glad she had cut it, no matter how much she had shocked Tal. There was a certain place high on a rocky outcrop that gave a commanding view of the surrounding country. She clambered across shelves of limestone until she reached the summit, dismayed to find herself a bit breathless.

Only a few months of soft living at the convent, and look what pitiful shape she was in!

She reached the cleft of a gigantic rock and shielded her gaze against the glare of the setting sun. The road swung wide to avoid the marsh and she strained her eyes for a view. Across the wet meadow a cloud of rooks flew up, signaling riders from the highway. As the party came round the curve she caught sight of the crimson-and-blue banner bearing the Rathborne arms.

Her stomach knotted. This was dire news, indeed: the new Lord Rathborne had come to take up residence—and wring whatever else he could from the starving people under his control. Then anger rose within her, banishing all fear, and an idea began to take form in her mind.

Now the riders were approaching a clearing, the one in the lead far ahead of the others on his magnificent black gelding. The ground rose up for a goodly distance, then swung sharply down to follow the course of the river, before plunging into the the dark woods surrounding Rathborne.

Vera wrung her hands tightly. This was her chance. Her violet eyes sparkled with growing excitement. Here for the taking was the gold that Tal sought. And it would serve the double purpose of helping their cause while proving her worth to the band.

The sun swam in a blaze of gold above the far horizon. There was no time to waste. She scrambled down to the river. Hewe and Ferris had shucked their garments and were splashing in the shallows. Norbert, a gangling lad with peach fuzz on his chin, was down by the reeds, trying to spear frogs with a sharpened stick. The firewood they had been gathering lay stacked beside a heap of boulders, forgotten.

Vera whistled the blackbird's song that was her signal. They looked up. Hewe blushed as fiery as the western sky and ducked into the water until only his head was showing. Ferris followed suit. They were embarrassed, partly because this grown-up Vera had found them cavorting like boys and even more so that she had found them shirking their tasks.

All to the good. In all their youthful escapades she had been the leader. Vera saw no reason it should be different now. She was sure she could enlist them in her adventure with familiar ease. The important thing was not to reveal her entire plan just yet. She had no illusions about her friends. What she intended was a bold feat; they would not have the nerve to follow through with it.

She jumped down beside them.

"Still playing at boy's games, I see, when you should be doing the work of men."

Hewe lifted his shaggy head. He was stolid, unimaginative and desperately earnest. "There's naught else to do."

Ferris threw down his stick in disgust. "Tal, Garvin and the others have gone off to the tavern to spy out the lay of the land—or so they say. They made us stay behind."

Vera placed her arms akimbo. "That is because they think of you as mere boys. You must prove to them that you are men—if you dare."

Their heads came up like dogs sniffing an intriguing new scent. "Dare what?"

Ah, she had them now. Vera grinned. "Adventure calls, my friends. A party of horsemen approaches. A rich party, by the jangle and gleam of gold and silver." Her dimple flashed again at the corner of her mouth. "Mayhap that gold and silver would do us far more good than it will them."

Hewe sent her a doubtful look. "Tal would hide us to a fare-thee-well if we set ourselves to such thieving."

"Our situation is desperate. The people are starving. Tal may hold to his fine scruples, but he would not turn away from the gold that would buy us food and weapons to fight our cause. And those fine riders would not even miss it." Vera shrugged impatiently. "But I should have known you would be too afraid to follow me."

She turned away. "I will do it myself then, since you are such cowards."

Her words rankled them. Both were still trodding the unstable ground between callow youth and early manhood, and they were as eager to prove themselves to their elders as they were to win Vera's approval. "Tell us your plan," Hewe said at last.

After a few questions and her ready answers, they began to see Vera's side of the matter. "We shall surprise them all with our daring," Ferris vowed, still smarting at being barred from the tavern.

"Aye," Hewe said. He had seen the looks Garvin had been sending in Vera's direction. It would be well to let Garvin know that he was not the only man in the band who aspired to Tal's foster daughter.

The air was glowing with the sunset's splendor in the west, but to the east it was already taking on the luminous blue of approaching twilight. "We must make haste," Vera said. "Ferris, I shall need your belt. Norbert, bring the firewood, and Hewe, you must fetch that big branch that fell in the last storm...."

They gathered round eagerly as Vera outlined her strategy.

Twilight lit the meadows, but deep within Rathborne Forest, night was already falling. Giles slackened his pace. He knew his way, but seven years was a long time to be away from his land. He did not want Caliph to come to harm from stumbling over a fallen branch or a boggy patch in the road.

Vera watched from her perch in one of the tallest trees as he tried to calm his restive mount. With his trim beard and high cheekbones, he was a handsome fellow—she had to give him that. He seemed wide of chest and shoulder, as well. Padding, no doubt. She had heard from the serving wenches who used to work at The Green Man that some fine fellows stuffed their hose and doublets with wool or sawdust to obtain a more manly form. Prancing popinjays!

Vera tensed as the rider came toward her hiding place. He was armed with a sword and dagger, but she doubted if he knew how to use them well. Fie! she thought, as she took in his fine velvet clothes, embroidered with gold and jewels. And that ruby earring dangling from his lobe. She grinned. So this was Giles of Rathborne—a strutting peacock with no bite worth speaking of! Well, she'd pluck his tail feathers before he knew what she was about.

She leaned toward Ferris. "No harm must come to that horse. I shall fetch a good price for it at the bridle fair. Enough to last us through until the New Year."

Her confederate goggled at her. "Horse thieves are pilloried and hanged."

"Only if they are caught."

And she had something far more dangerous in mind. A tight smile played over her full lips. Lord Rathborne would pay for all the misery he had caused—and pay very well, indeed. She waited until the last possible moment, then gave the signal.

The rider came toward her hiding place. The horse stumbled, neighing wildly.

Giles struggled to prevent the great creature from falling and killing them both. The horse reared in panic but Giles hung on. "Easy! Easy, now!"

It was several seconds before he managed to regain control. He jumped down to check Caliph for injury. As he bent to examine the gelding's near front leg, he realized that the stumble had been no accident. Dead branches had been dragged across the way and hidden beneath a scattering of dirt, leaves and grass. If he had not been quick, he would have gone flying over Caliph's head. It was a miracle both horse and rider had not broken their necks.

Hewe, wanting to outshine Ferris, dropped down from an arching limb into the rider's path well before the appointed time. He held a stout cudgel in his broad hands and brandished it wildly. Vera could have slapped him. Now their intended victim was apprised of the threat he faced.

Drawing his sword, Giles shouted a warning to Francis and the others. "Brigands! *À moi, François! À moi!*"

Vera glanced down the road. A second horseman came into view in the distance, riding hard. He was unfamiliar with the twisting path that led deeper into the woods. As the trees closed in, he slowed his pell-mell dash. Vera smiled grimly. She raised her hand and let it drop in a swift, chopping motion. Ferris's nerveless fingers picked at the strip of soft leather that had previously formed his belt and was now an integral part of their trap. He finally worked the strip free and a great branch went flying across the path of the lead horseman.

"Jesu!" Giles held Caliph as the mighty beast reared. This attack had been well planned. Another figure, quick and slight, jumped down from the shadow of the trees and raced for the horse's bit. Giles belayed his sword right and left with vigor.

"Have at me then, you miserable cowards!"

The deadly steel blade cut a swath too close to Vera for comfort. Hewe lunged to save her and Giles caught him in the shoulder with the tip of his sword. A dark patch spread over the homespun jerkin as he fell to the ground. When Ferris attacked, Giles kicked out viciously. His boot slammed into the youth's midsection, knocking the wind from him.

Vera lunged, but was sent sprawling with a painful whack to the buttocks from the side of Giles's sword. When she rolled onto her back he lowered the blade and held it two inches from her heart.

There was still enough light to make out his attackers' faces. One sniveled in fear and Giles grimaced. They were naught but young lads with peach fuzz on their cheeks. Why, the one glaring up at him with angry, defiant eyes had not a single whisker of which to boast.

Francis Finch joined him, sword in hand. "Well, well, what have we here, Giles?"

"A band of children playing at Robin Hood, or so it seems. Young gallows apes!" He sheathed his weapon in disgust.

"What do you intend to do with them?"

Giles rested his fists on his hips and surveyed the erstwhile bandits. Their daring amused him. But, by St. Stephen, he would not have them attacking travelers on his land! He must put the fear of God into them.

"If I were feeling generous, instead of tired and angry, I should probably give them a good hiding and turn them loose. At the moment I'm debating whether to take them to Rathborne and throw them in the dungeon to rot, or whether to hang them from one of these oaks and be done with it!"

Vera lay still, but her mind was working at full speed. She had seen the blood on Hewe's jerkin. Jesu. She took a shuddering breath. She had gotten Hewe and

Ferris into a terrible predicament. Now it was up to her to get them out of it.

"I beg mercy for my friends, Lord Rathborne. 'Tis all my fault and none of their doing. I was making a hunting blind in the tree and dropped my wood. They did only mean to protect me."

The tip of Giles's sword pressed into her. "Building an arrow blind in the growing darkness? And on my land?"

There was no answer for this. Giles looked over at Francis. His comrade saw the twinkle that was hidden from the others. "Brigands and liars. I believe I shall hang them here and spare us the trouble of taking them with us."

Vera decided to cause a diversion in hopes that her friends might escape. Her fingers closed on a sharp rock and she tensed her muscles to throw it. Suddenly the forest came alive with yips and yaps and bloodcurdling cries. Then the sky seemed to fall down around their ears, and the dusk was filled with hurtling shapes.

"Tal!" Vera shouted in relief.

Giles wheeled around. Five, no, six men—who were, however, unarmed but for the longbows they carried, useless at such close quarters. No great threat to two men who were mounted, armed and well versed in the arts of war. And with solid reinforcements on the way. He could hear the rest of his party approaching now.

He grinned and leapt for the saddle. Francis had engaged one of the bandits, but was hit by a stone from a slingshot. While he cursed and steadied himself, Giles charged their leader. Caliph responded eagerly; this was a dance the mighty horse knew well, and he reveled in its pattern. Charge and dodge—*slash!*—retreat and charge and dodge.

The tallest bandit swung his blackthorn staff at Giles's shoulder, but missed as his target ducked low, then came up with all his might to bisect the heavy pole with a swoop of his keen sword.

Another fellow moved in from the left, while a third, meaning to bring down Caliph, came from the right with a long stick, its tip hardened by fire.

Giles turned toward him with murder in his eye. Any fool raising a hand against Caliph would answer to his master instead. Sword gleaming with dying light, Giles swept down upon the man. The assailant gaped in fear, then broke into a run toward the opposite side of the clearing.

Vera ran into Caliph's path, shouting and waving a branch to frighten the beast. She would not let Garvin be trampled beneath those slashing hooves.

Cursing again, Giles reined in and the black horse reared up. They were a formidable sight. Vera ran off, glancing over her shoulder only when she reached the safety of the oaks. The clearing echoed with Giles's harsh laughter. "Cowardly villains!"

The words were no sooner out of his mouth than Caliph's ears pricked and the horse sidled abruptly. The arrow that had been intended for Giles's heart whistled past and landed in an oak, quivering with the force of its flight.

Horsemen erupted into the clearing as Sir Giles's men-at-arms arrived on the scene, and in no time the bandits were routed. Francis headed off the elusive archer and Giles dismounted and went after him. It was useless. The man had disappeared into the forest, leaving no trace. The others melted away into the gloaming.

When Giles returned to the clearing his fury had reached the point of combustion. This was Rathborne land.

"God's teeth," he vowed, "I shall see every one of them hanged from the Druid's Oak."

Francis's gray eyes were filled with glee. "How unkind of you, Giles, when those primitive knaves provided us with the only true test of mettle we've had—excepting for the queen's displeasure—since we set foot again on good English soil. I thought it a splendid little melee!"

Giles wiped his sword clean. The wounded man was gone, but could be tracked with hounds. "I did not sail round the world at the risk of my hide, only to come home and waste my energy scrapping with such a raggle-taggle band."

His friend laughed. "You would fight the devil himself for a chance to tweak his tail. Come, admit that it stirred your blood to draw your sword once more, even against such a miserable foe."

Francis spoke true, although Giles merely shrugged his broad shoulders and gave the signal to ride on. For just a moment, when the brigands had first attacked, he had felt the thrill of combat and the wild singing of his blood. Then he had assessed the situation. Except for that murderous archer, the entire affair had been as exciting as attacking a tiltyard dummy with a wooden spoon. And that was likely to be the best sport he would find at Rathborne for many a day.

Jesu, he thought wearily, *but I am not made for this life which has been thrust upon me all unwillingly.*

He set Caliph to his paces, alert for further signs of trouble. They were almost to the place where the road veered from the woods once more when he spied movement among the branches ahead. Once alerted, it was no great task to make out the shape hidden there; it appeared to be the slight youth. Giles sensed no danger, merely curiosity. Well, by God, he was equally curious.

They reached a place where the trees grew so thick that little of the fading light penetrated their canopy of leaves. The ground was covered with thick leaf mold and almost bare of undergrowth. It was the kind of place where even a civilized man felt invisible presences. "This is an ancient place," Giles said. "The druids worshiped here."

Francis crossed himself quickly. The rest of their party drew together a short distance behind. Only Giles seemed unaffected by the atmosphere.

"I have been thinking of taking down these woods," he said conversationally—but loud enough to carry.

Francis was startled. "You have? By St. Stephen, why? Surely they provide good hunting and a feast for your table."

"Yes. These woods have stood here since before William the Conqueror sailed from Normandy. Deer and pheasant and boar abound, and the meadows they enclose are thick with the nests of game birds." His dark eyes narrowed. "But I have no wish to provide a nesting place for brigands, as well."

Francis heard the odd note in his comrade's voice and went on the alert. Something was afoot.

Giles rubbed a gloved hand over the scar along his jaw. The great cabochon ruby on his middle finger glowed with inner flame. "Perhaps I'll bring in sheep. There's a fortune to be made these days in good English wool."

"To be sure there is—"

Suddenly Giles rose in the stirrups, drawing his sword as they reached a low-hanging bough. He waved it over his head like a magician's wand, and conjured up a prodigious trick.

There was a rattle of twigs and leaves and a soft cry of alarm. Then a slight form tumbled from the limb like a fledgling from its nest. Giles observed the youth in baggy jerkin and trews who sprawled in the dirt. Defiant violet eyes stared up at him for the second time.

"Ah," Giles murmured silkily, "I had expected acorns from oaks, but it seems that I have harvested a brigand boy instead. And a clumsily familiar one, at that."

Apparently the lad had had the wind knocked out of him. He lay in a pile of last year's leaves, gasping like a trout in a creel. He was an unprepossessing thing, with dirt streaking the side of his face and twigs and bits of bark caught in his shoulder-length hair. Giles leapt down from his mount and prodded the boy with the point of his sword.

"Up with you, my fine young villain."

Vera tried to rise. Her legs were shaky. She had seen the blood on Hewe's shoulder as he had fled into the forest. Tal and Garvin had been right after all; she had brought them more trouble than any of them had dreamed.

She looked up at Giles with the wariness of a cornered animal. By the saints, he was a fierce-looking, black-visaged creature! So might the devil himself look. He certainly fit with her image of Rathborne's hated lord. She brushed back the hair from her eyes.

The point of the sword pricked her again. "Come along, boy, the night is falling fast. Has no one taught you manners? It is not polite to keep your betters waiting."

Gritting her teeth, Vera struggled to her feet. Only a dozen yards separated her from the darkened woods that were her home. Once within them she could easily lose any pursuers. But with that sharp sword at her breast, the yards might have been miles. She gathered her wits and used them.

The defiance slipped away from her posture, replaced by a cringing servility. She tugged her forelock like a villager hauled up before a magistrate.

"God grant you ease, kind sirs. I am only a simple peasant lad, searching for birds' eggs among the trees. . . ."

"That you are not," Giles said grimly. "You are my prisoner."

Francis was surprised. Surely this green lad was no threat to them. He eyed Giles keenly. What was his old friend up to now?

Vera tried to swallow around the lump in her throat. The butterflies in her stomach had suddenly developed wings of lead. Her voice came out tight with fear. "Prisoner! I have done nothing, my lord."

"That is for me to decide." Giles prodded again. "To the horse with you. Step lively."

A tremor ran through Vera's limbs. The thought of being this man's prisoner made her knees turn to pudding. Here was a complication she had not foreseen. Tal's wise words came to her mind: *Never show fear, for it only serves to sharpen the wild beast's appetite.*

She lifted her chin and regarded Giles. In the gathering shadows he looked cruel and handsome, every bit the scoundrel. "Wh—where . . ." Hell and damnation, her voice squeaked like a pup with its tail caught in a door! She cleared her throat. "Where are you taking me, my lord?"

Giles smiled grimly. "Why, to Rathborne. Where else?"

Vera almost recoiled. She summoned all her will-power not to do so. "Wh—what do you mean to do with me?"

"Feed you to the hogs, belike, if it pleases me. Or perhaps I shall throw you in the dungeon and leave you there forever."

Fear was like a cold wind through Vera's soul. Those who entered Rathborne's dungeon were heard from no more. She would have to chance an escape, even if she risked a sword in her back. A quick end was infinitely preferable to a slow one within dungeon walls.

She pretended to look down, but her eyes gauged the distance from the tip of Giles's sword, now lowered, to the closest cover. It was a forlorn hope, but she had to take her only opportunity for freedom. A marshaling of strength, a leap forward . . . and she came crashing down with a sharp yelp. The leaves had hidden the entrance to a small animal's burrow. A hot agony ripped through her ankle and little red lights of pain danced before her eyes. Vera nursed her injury and cursed beneath her breath long and colorfully. Her attempt to escape had caught her captors by surprise. If not for fortune's evil tricks she might have reached the trees.

Giles stood over his prisoner. The lad had a mouth like a sailor! A cunning little rascal, he thought, but badly rattled. He hunkered down. This was no ruse. The boy was white-faced. "Hold still," he ordered.

He prodded Vera's tender ankle. She bit her tongue against an outcry and tasted blood. At least she had not shamed herself with tears, she thought bitterly.

"Nothing broken," her captor announced. He took a square of embroidered linen from his doublet, folded it and wound it beneath the arch of her foot and twice around her ankle. Immediately the pain subsided to a dull ache. Vera was impressed. She was also spurred on by renewed hope; she might yet make a break for the deeper forest.

Giles rose and held out his hand. "Shake a leg, young gallows' bait. We ride for Rathborne Castle."

Vera grimaced as he brought her to her feet with a powerful tug of his arm. But the saints, the man had the strength of an ox! She concealed her amazement and tried her best to look pitiful.

"I swear, my lord, I cannot take a step upon it."

Francis Finch was hoodwinked by Vera's playacting. "Indeed, Giles, his hurt seems genuine enough."

"Do not be a fool. The ankle is merely twisted. This little ruffian means to feign injury and then run off at the first chance."

Once more Vera put her weight upon her foot, which ached like fury but seemed to have sustained no real harm. But it would not do to let these fellows know as much. She gasped and fell down with a convincing howl. "'Tis broken."

Giles stood over her, his fists on his hips. "Is that so? Then, my fine lad, you'll ride in style."

He motioned to one of his men. "Tie his hands and toss this young knave up before me. And watch that he does not try to steal your dagger and stab you in the back with it."

Vera cursed silently as a thong bit into her wrists, binding them together. Her faking of a greater injury than she had actually suffered had done her more ill than good. At least on foot she would have escaped more easily. Now, if she did manage to get away, it would take a good hour and more to chew through the leather thong and free her hands. God knew what wild creatures she might meet in the interval. Wolves and boars came instantly to mind.

Giles watched with satisfaction. He had read the young rogue's face as if it were a page in one of his books.

Giles swung up on Caliph's back. A moment later he secured the wriggling lad in front of him on the saddle. "Hold tight." With a nudge of his spur, Giles sent his gallant horse off at a brisk trot. It turned to a breath-robbing gallop once they reached open land. He laughed to himself. No chance of the boy trying to jump down now, when they were moving at such great speed.

And, by God, once they were at Rathborne he would find out everything there was to know about the bandits infesting his lands, if he had to beat the truth out of the boy.

Vera had never been on a horse like Caliph before. It was both frightening and thrilling to travel at such great speed. The beast was as huge and powerful as its master, all hard muscle and supple sinew beneath the elegant trappings.

The twilight glow had left the sky and a thousand stars shone brightly far above them. The mysterious qualities of the night had always intrigued Vera. Now the blackness closed in upon her like the folds of a velvet cloak.

Vera clung to the saddle as best she could, jouncing along until her teeth rattled—and wished to God she had never set eyes on Giles of Rathborne.

Chapter Three

The full moon rose, bright as a new shilling. As they crowned the gentle ridge, the uneasiness that had been growing in Giles bloomed into alarm. There were no shocks of grain in the fields. The few fences visible were in disrepair.

He reined in suddenly. Had he lost his way in the darkness earlier? Surely this was where The Green Man had stood. He looked for the huddle of buildings that had stood on Chipping Hill since time immemorial. There was nothing but a grove of trees that whispered in the wind, and an odd shape that proved to be the ruins of a chimney.

"Wait here," he said, and dismounted, leaving his wary young captive atop Caliph.

He had not been mistaken. This was—or rather, had been—The Green Man. His boots scuffed the flags that had once floored the inn's taproom. A few charred beams littered them. He prodded a piece of a wooden bench with the toe of his boot. The seat looked as if it had been attacked with an axe prior to the fire. The heavy smell of burnt wood lingered.

He went back to Caliph, but instead of mounting he queried sharply. "What happened here?"

"Your steward sent his bullies to The Green Man," Vera said curtly. "That is what happened here."

"Insolent cub! This is none of Rathborne's doing. I have known John Tapper all my life."

Vera shrugged angrily. "Ask anyone in the village. If you can persuade them to overcome their fear of your retribution."

"You are speaking nonsense. No one in these parts has reason to fear me, except those who break the law."

"Yes, the law of Lord Rathborne," she countered coldly.

"Jesu," Giles murmured to Francis, "I have saddled myself with this young fool, who is either a liar or a madman."

The cavalcade started out once more. In no time at all Vera recognized the darker shape on the horizon: Rathborne. She knew of people who had entered the walls of that evil house, never to be seen again. With every surge of Caliph's strong legs, her trepidation grew.

Giles reined in sharply. A muscle jumped at the corner of his jaw. He had not seen Rathborne in seven years. It looked splendid by moonlight.

The house itself was set like a jewel amid vast parklands and almost ringed by a curve of the river. The moonlight turned the dark water to a ribbon of electrum flashed with diamonds. The pale glow gilded the remnants of the original castle and glazed the massive oriel windows of the Tudor addition with pure silver. It was all as Giles remembered.

But as they descended and crossed the stone bridge spanning the river, the illusion created by moonbeams and distance was dispelled. A closer look, even in the half-light, exposed the sorry plight of a once-noble estate. What appeared to be open windows on the third floor were, in fact, missing ones. A great owl flew in and out with the ease of long residence, and starlings had nested in the eaves. The ledges were white with birdlime. The dozen chimneys were in need of pointing and the one that served the old chapel seemed in danger of falling under its own weight. A missing section of lead over the eaves warned of water damage and roof rot.

Giles felt a knot of helpless anger in his stomach. The queen's rebuke was understandable, if she knew even the half of it. There was much work to be done here. And not enough gold or silver in his portion with which to pay a tenth. What had his half brother been thinking of, to let Rathborne come to this?

"God's teeth, but this place has suffered under Morse's hand."

Giles had scarcely known his much-older sibling, who been their father's heir. Indeed, he had scarcely known their father, being the product of a most unhappy marriage, the only offspring of two people as suited to one another as oil and water. By the time Giles was born, both Morse and John of Rathborne had been away, fighting the French for possession of Calais. When they finally returned, Giles had been up in the wilds of the borderlands, with his mother's people.

When his father's doxy pressured him to wed her, the foolish man had accused his wife of adultery and had branded Giles a bastard. His father's perfidy had broken his mother's heart, but it had hardened his own.

Some time later Giles was reinstated as a legitimate successor but the damage had been done. He had neither seen nor spoken to his father since.

As for the two half brothers, their lives had been separate, their few meetings distant and polite. Giles had wished Morse well, without the slightest trace of envy for the vast lands he had eventually inherited.

With good cause, from the looks of things.

Francis stared at Rathborne's forbidding facade, unable to hide his dismay. He shook his head. "Egad, Giles! You assured me of comfortable quarters and a fine supper. Why, I doubt that there is an aired bed, a swept chimney or a winsome wench within those crumbly walls."

"We've slept in worse places in our travels," his companion replied. "And the inside may be in better condition." Nudging Caliph forward, Giles led the cavalcade toward the house.

Francis tried to put on a good face, but he knew that his stay in the country was liable to be an uncomfortable one. Thank heavens it would also be short.

Rathborne and his men seemed to have forgotten Vera. She was jolted to the bone and weary from riding in such an uncomfortable position. With her hands tied she had to balance herself carefully to keep from falling beneath Caliph's hooves. She held herself quiet and still and remained alert for a rescue that would not come. It was the rule that if any of the band were caught, they were on their own. Still, she had been ready.

Giles was in a foul mood as they rode beneath the great elms that lined the avenue. Or what passed for an avenue. The straight track was rutted and weed choked. Halfway to the house their way was barred by an elm felled by lightning; no attempt had been made to clear it away.

Francis glanced at his host but said nothing. Giles was a boon companion, always ready with a laugh, advice or a helping hand—but he had a fiend's temper when crossed. And, seeing the disrepair and decay all about, Francis had no doubt that that formidable temper was simmering like a kettle on the boil.

Giles set Vera down first, then dismounted, let his groom take Caliph to the stables, and frowned at the heavily ornamented entrance. The brass was tarnished and the door hung slack on its hinges. There had been great waste under his father's rule here, and greater folly. The money that had been spent on his young and greedy harlot should have been put to better use.

His men dismounted and led their horses to the stables. Giles opened the massive door and pushed his captive through, then strode into the great hall. Vera was astounded. The interior of the house was in as bad shape as the outside. The rushes stank. Cobwebs draped the carved beams and the window glass was begrimed with soot. Pigeons perched on the rail of the minstrel's gallery as if it were their permanent roost. As she watched, one flew out where a leaded pane was missing.

"Aye," Giles said bitterly. "I have seen hovels better kept than this. When last I saw it, Rathborne was the fairest house in England."

He cupped his hands. "Hello the house!"

A door opened upstairs. After a moment, a gnarled woman in a gown of faded satin came to the landing. Giles was relieved to see her. Irme Wyndom was an elderly cousin who, for as long as he could remember, had kept house for his father. Except for a few more creases in her wrinkled face and more iron in her hair, she was unchanged.

"Good day to you, cousin."

Irme stopped on the stairs and gasped in shock. Giles laughed shortly and went to the foot of the stairs. "You need not be alarmed, I am not a ghost."

"Oh...Giles! We heard you were lost at sea!" A work-reddened hand fluttered to the small ruffle at her throat. "But I knew you were alive and that you would come home one day."

Giles frowned. "Who told you so?"

Irme rushed on without answering. "Oh, if only you had given notice of your homecoming, I should have had a meal prepared and waiting. Your steward is gone to Turnley Manor and I doubt there's so much as a currant in the house."

"I sent a messenger three days ahead of us."

"Alas, he has not come near Rathborne. He might have come to trouble in the forest."

Giles cast a wry look at Vera. "That is something I can well believe."

More like, Vera thought, the messenger had deserted rather than ride up to Rathborne's gates, once he had heard tales of it. As for there being no food in the house, Vera knew that was an utter falsehood. Her stomach growled loudly.

Giles sent her another wry glance. "Hungry, lad? 'Twould seem that you have come visiting at an inopportune time. Perhaps my good cousin may find a few crusts of bread to tide us over till the morrow."

"She is lying," Vera announced baldly. "There is meat aplenty in the cold larder by the well. I saw it myself when your fat pig of a steward brought up a beef roast and a side of bacon yesterday."

Irme's skin took on an angry flush before blanching so strongly she looked bloodless. "'Tis true that there is meat in the cold larder, my lord. However, Heslip keeps the key to it on his person at all times."

Giles turned to his men. "One of you go and break off the lock." A red-haired man went away to do his bidding and Giles swept an increasingly angry gaze around the dusty hall. "What has happened here?"

His cousin came down the staircase hurriedly. "Now, Giles, I suppose you will want an accounting of things. After your father died, your half brother Morse—God rest his soul, for he was kind to me—took over. Things were already in a bad way, to be sure...."

Irme brushed away a tear. "If he had not succumbed to the fever, I am sure Morse would have set all to rights. But with you gone on the high seas and almost given up for dead, Morse's steward took over the running of Rathborne. After that, well . . . What has transpired in the past two years under Heslip's rein is enough to curl one's hair. I have tried my best to keep the place from wrack and ruin, to little avail."

"Rest easy, cousin." Giles took her poor hands, red and callused from scrubbing, in his own. "I know the fault is not yours. I see the evidence before me."

He introduced Francis Finch to her. She flushed again, this time pink all the way to her hairline when he bent low and smiled. But when Irme saw the slight, towheaded figure peering from behind Giles, she gawked in surprise.

"And who is this young person?"

Giles swung around. He had almost forgotten the boy's presence. "This sorry cub?" He laughed without humor and eyed the youth. "My new page, mayhap. Or a bag of bones to feed the sows. Send a servant up with water for my bath. This young blackguard can assist me with it."

Vera swallowed hard. The very thought of seeing Sir Giles stripped brought a hot blush to her face. She used her wits. "Nay, my lord," she said, scratching fiercely along her flank. "I am half-eaten by fleas and lice. You would not want my little beasties to take up abode in your bedchamber."

"There is truth in the lad's words," Francis said, looking askance at Vera and stepping away from Giles rather sharply. One could not be too careful. After all, Rathborne had come the past few miles with the wily creature squirming before him.

Giles tugged his neatly trimmed beard, a cynical smile playing over his lips as he eyed Vera. "Very well. Though I have not seen you scratch even once before, I shall take your word for it."

He turned his attention to Irme. "Take this poor excuse for manhood to the serving women and have him scoured and rid of the fleas and whatever else may inhabit his sorry person."

Vera's eyes lit up at that. This would likely prove to be her last good chance to escape, and she would have to make the most of it. If she failed, her secret would be discovered—and it would be the worse for her. If she read this surly lord aright, the man had a hard and dangerous look to him.

The serving wenches, however, would be another matter entirely. If she could not slip away from them, she had indeed better give up the forest life and take to slopping hogs for Garvin's sister.

Irme signaled her and Vera turned to follow, all false meekness and downcast eyes.

"Not so fast with you," Giles said, stepping between Vera and the door. There was challenge in his voice and face. "You see, my fine young scoundrel, I am not as witless as you think me to be."

He turned to the captain. "Bevins, post a guard to watch this youth at all times so that he cannot run off at the first chance. If he escapes, it will be on your head. Lady Irme, when you deem this ruffian presentable, he is to be brought directly to my chamber."

Vera cursed her luck. Lord Rathborne was a formidable foe. He had guessed her intentions even as the plans were forming in her own mind. She sent him a dark look.

Irme was pleased to have direction in her life once more. "Now that Rathborne has a master again," she said, "all will soon be set to rights. And the great bedchamber is in order." A smile touched her withered lips. "I kept it in preparedness for your homecoming."

She reached out to grab the lad's sleeve, then thought better of it. Sir Francis was right. God only knew what pestilence he might carry.

In the silence that followed, Vera's stomach rumbled once more, this time like distant thunder. Irme looked at her in sharp disapproval. Vera saw another opportunity for possible escape. "God's toes," she said boldly, "but I cannot help it. I have had nothing to eat and am fair famished."

Giles threw back his head and laughed. Vera was surprised to see how much younger he looked when he did so. "Feed the lad first," he said. "I doubt that young scrawny-shanks has had a good meal since he was weaned."

This time Vera lowered her lids to hide the gleam of hope in her eyes. Irme started out of the room and one of the men prodded Vera with the butt of his spear to propel her forward. She marched off, wondering what diversion she might create in order to best escape. She was relieved to be free from the keen scrutiny of the Lord of Rathborne. The man saw far too much.

Giles took Francis into the Great Chamber with its famous hanging ceiling. Moonlight frosted the tall windows of clear glass inset with colored panels bearing the Rathborne coat of arms. The effect was of a lattice of light and shadow across the marble floor. The place smelled musty, but seemed in fair repair.

"We shall be cozy here once the fire is built up." Giles crossed the floor toward the carved chimney breast. He started a fire with his tinderbox. The first flame flickered and grew, seeming as small in the huge opening as a candle in a cavern. Giles fed the fire, adding some large logs once it caught well. Then he rose and looked around.

His first impression had been deceiving. Giles cursed aloud. From the plaster ceiling hung cobwebs so large and long that they swayed in the drafts. Leaves and dirt had blown in through the broken panes of one window and had piled up across the room. The chairs and table that should have stood in the center were missing, as was the old court cupboard that had belonged to his mother.

Francis was staring about mournfully, thinking that this was not at all the way he had hoped to spend the evening. Giles strode to the door and shouted for a servant. A nervous-looking fellow appeared from the direction of the kitchen. "My lord?"

"What has happened here, that the Great Chamber is uninhabitable?"

The man trembled at his master's roar. "'Tis difficult to keep up so large a house with so few servants," he said quickly.

"Why were none hired?"

The man's trembling went into his voice. "L-lady Ir-Irme asked the s-steward if she m-might not bring in village m-maids, my lord. He s-said it was a waste of g-good c-coin, and forbade it."

"I see." Giles's dark brows drew together in a straight line. "And he ordered the chamber closed up."

"Y-yes, my lord."

"Very well. You may go." When the servant had disappeared toward the kitchens once more, Giles looked at Francis and shook his head like an angry bear. "By God, the steward will answer for this when he returns! I'll string up Heslip by his fat thumbs."

He led Francis up the staircase. "Likely the master's bedchamber will be in better order. It belonged to Morse, and our father before him."

At the doorway Francis held back. "Perhaps you would rather go in alone."

Giles gave one of his characteristically impatient shrugs and began to push open the door. "Do you fear I'll be overcome with weeping? Calm yourself. John of Rathborne had no love for me nor I for him. I reminded him too much of my mother, whom he cast off when a young doxy caught his eye. He told her their marriage was annulled, although I discovered after his death that he had lied in this."

Francis glanced at his friend. "And this...er, doxy?"

"She ran off with a wealthy merchant while my father lay dying, God rot his soul."

He entered the room. The floor was swept clean of rushes and the bed linen and rich blue hangings were fresh. Firewood was carefully laid beneath the wide chimney breast, which was carved with the Rathborne arms. The chamber had the appearance of a shrine. Giles suppressed a shiver. He crossed quickly to the windows, clean and intact, and threw open the casement. A warm breeze blew in, chasing away the chill.

A small alabaster bowl caught his eye. Giles touched it tenderly. "This was hers. She died in an almshouse when I was but a weanling." And he had been by her side, weeping and inwardly cursing his father, when she had breathed her last.

Giles seated himself in a leather chair and waved his companion to its twin. "God's teeth, but I am famished. I hope that we find the kitchens in a better state than the rest of this benighted pile of stones, or we shall go cold and empty to our beds."

The words were hardly uttered when the door to the landing swung open. A shy girl with copper hair, and more freckles than a man could count, entered bearing a tray. She dropped a curtsy and deposited the tray upon the table, then hurried out again as if the devil were at her heels.

"Have we grown horns and monstrous faces?" Francis snapped. He was used to admiring glances from maidens young and old.

Giles took up his ale. "No doubt they are fearful that I'll require them to attend to their tasks once more, rather than idling about while the place falls down around their ears." He took a refreshing gulp and swallowed. "And so I shall. 'Tis a sorry day to see such wrack and ruin. And brigands in the woods, as well!"

He swore softly. "I shall have my work cut out for me."

His companion was sympathetic. "The life of an estate owner is not for you, Giles. You were born for adventure."

"Aye, 'tis a strange homecoming," he mused, growing more morose. "I had never thought to be master here. Nor wanted it."

Morse's untimely death, following so closely on their father's, had thrown Giles's life askew. He was nonplussed by the results. It was an odd joke of fate that he had inherited what he had always despised.

"Let us talk of pleasanter things. Tell me more about this meek little mouse who has caught your eye at court."

Grinning, Francis told him of the young, beautiful and very married lady who had begun to send him notes and trinkets. "One evening I heard a tapping at my door, and when I opened it I scarce could believe my eyes. It was the lady in question, wearing a dark cloak and nothing at all beneath it—"

His story was interrupted by shouts and shrieks from the staircase. Giles jumped up, threw open the door and went out to discover the source of the commotion. Francis was right on his heels. They found a strange scene unfolding: Irme, her embroidered cap knocked askew above her wispy hair, was wringing her hands and screaming like a banshee. To add to the confusion, several of Giles's men were gathered at the foot of the steps, shouting and jostling one another.

"Stop her!" someone cried.

Giles overrode their din. "What is the cause of this unseemly racket?"

Irme pointed with a shaking finger and stepped aside. Giles drew in a sharp breath. A fair-haired girl in servant's garb was hanging from the railing of the balcony of the minstrel's gallery some fifteen feet above the stone floor below. She seemed about to jump. Giles was there in three bounds, leaning over the balcony to grasp her wrists. Not a second too soon, for she let go at that exact moment.

The onlookers gasped, but he took her weight easily and hauled her up toward him. The girl struggled for all she was worth. Her nails dug into his flesh until they drew blood. "Let go!" she cried.

"Jesu! Hold still, you she-devil, before you dash your brains out on the stones below! Here, Francis, give me a hand!"

Still she writhed and kicked, but together Giles and Francis drew the girl over the rail to safety. She was praying under her breath...or so Giles thought; then he realized that she was cursing. Fluently, and rather inventively.

Giles reacted quickly, sure the creature was either mad or in the grip of hysteria. He slapped her once across the cheek to bring her to her senses.

"Oh!" Vera recoiled, white with anger and cradling her cheek. Then she slapped him back so hard that his ear rang.

The naked fury of her assault stunned him for a fraction of a second. She darted away and through the only door that offered escape. Before she could bolt the latch, he slammed past her into the chamber. When Vera twisted and tried to flee, he caught her around the waist. If he had not dodged quickly, she would have disabled him with a knee jab to his groin.

He tightened his hold. "You will not escape me, you little firebrand."

He stood her against the wall and took a good look at her. She was tall, with hair as fine and shining as spun gold. A dark bruise graced her left cheekbone and her right one displayed the mark of his hand. Her mouth, beneath a small, straight nose, was clamped shut in an obdurate line. She was barefoot, and wore a shapeless brown garment cinched at the waist by a length of twine. Her eyes—so dark a blue they verged on violet—smoldered with outrage.

A pretty wench, if unusually mettlesome. He was not used to interfering in domestic squabbles, but it behooved him to settle the disruption immediately. Giles looked from her to his cousin, who had crept into the room, and back. "Enough of this nonsense!" he roared. "I demand to know the reason for this disturbance!"

His tone was hard and brooked no disobedience. Irme trembled. Vera was made of sterner stuff. She only clenched her fists and glared at him.

Irme took a deep breath and brushed back a strand of gray hair that had loosened from her coif.

"My lord," she said agitatedly, "I have done as you said—taken the young person off to be fed and bathed and dressed in clean linen, but now..."

She broke off helplessly. Giles could barely rein in his impatience. He was hungry and tired and in no mood for digressions. "And what has that to do with anything?"

Irme sent a fearful look at her charge, scrubbed and simmering with outrage in her borrowed female garments. The older woman stretched out her arm and pointed an accusing finger at Vera.

"Well, my lord, here that young person is."

A hush fell over the assembly. All eyes were suddenly on Vera. Irme continued in a rush: "But as you see, 'tis not a *he* at all, my lord, but a *she*. And I am wondering what you expect me to do with her next."

Chapter Four

Giles glared in astonishment. "What witchery is this?"

Even as he thundered out the words, he knew the scene before him was neither magic nor jest. One look at the girl's violet eyes convinced him. There was no doubt that the grubby boy whom he had brought in as his prisoner had been transformed into the furious young woman facing him. It was one of the greatest shocks of his life.

"If I did not see this myself, I would never have credited it!"

Francis Finch was equally amazed. "I am doubly surprised, Giles. In truth, it is difficult to believe that anyone could mistake so lovely a maid for a filthy boy. Especially, I might add, a man of your vast experience," he added with a twinkle in his eye.

Chagrined, Giles could only join in his friend's merriment. "Yes, I am sadly out of practice. But remember that I have spent the greater part of the last three years aboard ship, with only the mermaids to sing me to sleep."

"Except for the last two weeks at court, when you were kept busy dividing your favors between Lady Jocelyn and the fair Laetitia Lattimore."

Giles eyed Vera in her dull brown dress, her face unbecomingly blotched with anger. "An unequal trade, you must admit."

She fairly bristled with outrage. "Scoff at me, will you, you arrogant swine? I shall give you something to remember me by!"

Her fury amused him; his guard was down. In the twinkling of an eye Vera whipped a dagger from beneath her gown and launched herself at him.

His reflexes were sure. Giles deflected the blow with a sinewy arm and sent the dagger spinning away. The bright blade slashed through the edge of the bed hangings and impaled itself in a carved panel. Irme shrieked and fell into a swoon, while Giles twisted Vera deftly and pinned her arms behind her back. Francis had already drawn his small sword.

"Stand back!" Giles roared. "I have her fast."

He dumped his prisoner on the bed without further ceremony. Vera scrambled to the opposite side, baring her small, white teeth. "I shall fight you tooth and claw," she snarled.

Giles laughed, which only angered her more. "By God," he said, "'tis a wild little vixen I've brought in from the wood!"

"Tread warily," Finch warned. "She may have another dagger up her sleeve."

Giles, sweeping a thorough glance from her head to her toes, saw no need for caution. He grinned. "I'll be damned from Land's End to Dover if she has anything on beneath her dress at all."

Irme had roused from her swoon. Giles helped her to steady herself and gestured to his friend. "Take the lady to her chamber, if you will, and see that a maid is with her. I shall handle this interrogation alone."

"Aye," Finch said slyly, "and so would I, were our positions reversed. She is not so uncomely as she looked at first, with her face all twisted with venom." He took Irme's arm and escorted her to her room.

Giles signaled to his men, who had taken up stations on either side of Vera. "Leave us, but guard the door. I will deal with the wench alone."

Giles closed the door behind them and thrust the bolt home. Vera tensed. The only sound in the room was her own quick breathing. Her captor once again surveyed her from head to toe. There was a peculiar, assessing look in his eye. Vera thought she knew what was coming. The room was dominated by tall windows on one wall and a huge curtained bed facing it. Her heart beat violently against her rib cage.

Giles came toward her with a menacing smile. "And now, madam, we shall settle this between us. It was most unwise of you to attack me—twice in one day."

Vera edged away from the bed toward the window. "There's no help for you there, sweeting," he told her. "The drop from this tower is sheer to the paving stones of the courtyard. There would not be enough of you left to plant in a thimble."

"Much I care!" She lunged desperately, but Giles was too quick and her injured ankle, twisted again in their recent fracas, betrayed her. Vera fell to the floor with him atop her. His solid frame knocked the breath from her; she was unable to move or speak.

Giles was surprised to discover her figure so rounded and womanly beneath her overlarge garments. She

made a pleasant cushion between him and the floor.
Moonlight streamed through the open casement, gild-
ing her hair and highlighting the proud curve of her
cheekbones. There was something distinctly familiar
about her features. Something that had nothing to do
with her masquerade.

He pinned her face between his hands, frowning.
Had he seen her before, on his one and only visit to
Rathborne to visit Morse, after their father's death?
"Who are you?" he demanded. "By what name are
you called?"

Vera wanted to twist her head away from his scrutiny. Instead she stared up at him, intense curiosity almost replacing her fear. Jesu, there was a vital
masculinity about him that rattled her. This was a man
used to command. She must be careful to reveal nothing. Half-truths would do. "I am Vera. I own no other
name."

Giles was suddenly aware of their undignified position. Rolling free, he held out his hand and helped her
to her feet. She puzzled him. She was half-wild, as
Francis had noted, yet her skin was fine and soft as
peach bloom and her speech was not of the lower
classes. "Where are you from, Vera, and who are your
kinfolk?"

She replied warily, "I am from nowhere, my lord.
My parents are dead and I live in the forest, like the
vixen you called me. I beseech you, my lord, to set me
free. You can want nothing from a simple maid such as
myself."

He was too wily to be fooled. "Never let it be said
that Giles of Rathborne holds a grudge against a mere
woman. In truth, I have taken a liking to your spirit. If

you have no family and no home, it behooves me to offer you one."

He took her hand and held it firmly when she tried to draw back. "You shall stay at Rathborne, Vera, and make your home here."

"Have you taken leave of your senses?" she answered.

He dropped his voice suggestively. "Not in the least. You are a comely maid. I am certain that I can find some employment for you...."

A shiver ran up Vera's arm. She had a fair idea of what his terms of "employment" would be, and she had no desire to be his unwilling mistress. "Please let me go, my lord. You can want nothing from the likes of me."

His dark eyes shone with golden lights. "Ah, so you prefer this Tal to me, is that it?"

"Nay, my lord. I have a home with Tal and he will be sore worried if..." Too late, Vera saw the trap he had sprung.

Giles felt the telltale jerk of her fingers in his. He smiled grimly. He had heard her call out that name during the attack upon him and had taken a chance that had paid off handsomely. "So I was right. Tal, is it? A fine name—for a murderous brigand living on my estate lands."

Her eyes brimmed with unshed tears at her unthinking betrayal. "Please, my lord. He is no brigand. He has been a father to me all my life...a simple wood-cutter, living in the forest and paying his due to Rathborne."

A likely story! Giles slanted a glance her way. "I see. You are fond of Tal." She nodded. "And," he went on, "you would do much to save the life of this . . . simple woodcutter?"

Misery was chiseled in every line of Vera's face. She bit her lip to hide its quivering. "I—I would do . . . anything, my lord."

Her loyalty to her bandit colleague—whether father, brother or lover—was commendable. He could use it to bend her to his advantage. "Then perhaps we might come to an agreement. . . ."

Giles leaned forward and cupped her chin in his hand. Vera flinched at his touch, then became still. He lowered his mouth to hers and tasted salty tears. Her lips were warm against his. A rush of unexpected desire filled him, sending the blood coursing hotly through his veins.

"Do you fear me, Vera?"

"N-nay, my lord."

He placed his hand over her breast. Her heart fluttered beneath his callused palm. A gallant little creature, he thought, and slid his arm possessively about her waist.

Vera felt the heat of his hard body, the strength of his hand. It robbed her of breath. She must show no fear, yet her traitorous body was wracked with trembling.

"The bed is soft," Giles murmured. "Will you lie with me, Vera?"

Her answer was barely audible. "Yes . . . my lord."

Now her whole body shook as if with the ague. At the same time that her lips consented, her eyes was darting about the chamber, searching against hope for any possible escape route.

Giles threaded his fingers through her short locks and dragged her head back. Her mouth was ripe for kisses. For a moment the thrill of desire and the ache of loneliness warred with his conscience. He kissed her throat where the pulse beat so erratically and felt her struggle to keep from crying out in alarm.

"Sweet liar," he said softly. "At the first opportunity you would slay me while I slept." He released her. "I have no need of forcing my favors upon unwilling maidens. Fear not, little Vera. I will not harm you."

She closed her eyes in relief. Safe, at least for now. God willing, she would think of some way to escape her captor. It was urgent she warn Tal that his name was known at Rathborne.

Giles stopped, as if belatedly remembering something.

"By the way, my men apprehended one of your forest friends. He has been put in chains and thrown into the dungeon. A talkative fellow. I am told that he has offered to disclose everything I wish to know. By nightfall tomorrow the whole band will be in my custody."

Vera quelled her panic. Her face fell into desolate lines. "It must be Hewe, then. Ready to sell his soul to the devil to save his scrawny hide." She lowered her head and one hand crept up to dab at her eyes. "That white-livered cur." Her voice broke.

Giles was torn between triumph at how easy it had been to break her spirits, and an odd sort of guilt. Qualms of conscience had never bothered him too much in the past; he was an adventurer by trade and could ill afford such niceties.

"You are correct. The man called Hewe has agreed to cooperate fully with me, and suggests that you do the same."

Vera laughed in his face. "Fool! Did you think I would be duped by your falsehoods? Your men could no more capture Hewe than they could a shadow—they are as quiet as wounded stags, thrashing about in the brush." High color painted her cheeks. "And I know that Hewe is not in your custody. He would rather plunge a dagger into his heart than surrender to his sworn enemy."

Her trickery infuriated him. She had certainly jumped to the man's defense. Perhaps Hewe was her lover then, and not this Tal she had mentioned.

Giles summoned the guard without another word to her, but he personally escorted Vera down the staircase and through the Great Chamber. His arm linked hers like an iron band. When they crossed through the open doors at the far side she felt a wild spurt of hope that he meant to release her. Then they crossed the small grassy courtyard toward the shadows of the ancient keep, and her heart sank.

The dungeons of Rathborne, long whispered about in fear, were said to be haunted by the ghosts of those who had perished within. Vera gave a little shiver. To be shut away from the light, perhaps forgotten among the moldering bones, was more than she could bear. But she must be brave. Tal had raised her to value courage above almost all else.

The evil pictures her mind conjured were mercifully wrong. Giles stopped before a small door on the ground floor. "Your bower, my lady."

Vera found herself thrust into a low-ceilinged chamber. She rubbed her arm—egad, the man was strong—and looked around. Three narrow unglazed windows, little more than narrow openings, were set in the wall behind her. Evidently this keep was some sort of storage place, built against the outer wall of the early fortifications. From the smell, animals had likely been housed here.

Giles stood framed in the doorway, his wide shoulders blocking the light. "I trust you may find your new home comfortable. Before the lock is turned, I shall offer you a bargain, madam. I will give you your freedom in exchange for the names and secret hiding places of your friends."

Vera's chin went up. "Judgment Day will come sooner!"

He shrugged. "As you wish. You will have plenty of time to think it over. Sleep well."

As he started to close the door she rounded on him. "I shall never change my mind. And I shall not close one eye beneath this accursed roof. It is a wonder that you can, my lord, knowing that you are hated far and wide."

That brought him up short. "Hated? Who has reason to hate me?"

"Do you expect us to love the man who is our oppressor?"

Her insolence infuriated Giles, but it was the last word that stuck in his craw. It had been hurled at him with such bitterness. "*Oppressor?* What nonsense is this? I have oppressed no one."

"Are you not master of Rathborne?" Vera taunted, her vivid blue eyes darkening to steel. "Are you not the man who turns widows and children out of their cottages to starve? Who burns the fields of men who refuse to pay excessive taxes into your bottomless coffers? For shame, Sir Giles. I wonder that you can abide your own company."

The vehemence of her unjust accusations stung him. "You are mad! I have been three years on the high seas. I have oppressed none but the Spanish fleet."

Vera's skin flushed with the heat of her anger. "You are master of Rathborne," she repeated. "Whether you are here or elsewhere, what is done in these parts is done in your name. And if you doubt my word, you may ask any chance-met soul from here to Ripley Wold."

Giles glared. Her allegations held the ring of truth. "I shall. You may be sure of it."

She lifted her chin and turned away from him in stony silence. After a moment she heard him move toward the door, which then shut behind her with gloomy finality. Vera heard the rasp of a bolt ramming home. A wise woman never overlooked the obvious. She tried the handle. There was no budging it.

With a sigh of frustration, she examined her quarters more carefully in what little light came through the windows. The room was furnished with a few rudimentary necessities, including a rough bench, a straw-stuffed pallet and a blanket of undyed wool. The one way out was through the door, which was sturdy and thick. and could be opened only from the outside....

Francis Finch was still abed when Giles rode out the next morning. Vera's accusations had disturbed the Lord of Rathborne. His steward had not come back from Turnley, so Giles intended to see to the situation himself. He was dressed plainly, without emblem or badge of rank, not wanting to reveal his identity as the new lord just yet.

Dew beaded the grass and the sky had a clear, fresh look that usually brought a sense of peace to his soul.

Today it failed. Giles had not gone far from the manor house before he realized that all was not well on the estate.

The orchards had not been trimmed or cleared, and the banks of the river were littered near the weir with an accumulation of branches and debris from the high waters of spring. A rising wind whipped at his cloak as he checked the pastures. The rain would come by afternoon, he thought. He found the grazing cattle too lean and some had open sores. Every new discovery made his heart sink a bit lower. There was far worse to come.

Past the river's bend, Giles recalled several freeholder's cottages. In the unhappy days of his youth, before fleeing Rathborne with his mother, he had often escaped to one or another of these cheerful, albeit small homes, where he played with the younger sons of the family. He would pay a call to Tom Cooper and his fair wife, Joan. They would tell him what was amiss.

After rounding the bend he reined in his horse. Where the whitewashed houses had stood there were only blackened ruins and the ashy smell of smoke. The fires had been recent. His mouth thinned to a severe line. No doubt this was the handiwork of the thieves and robbers who had attacked his party in the woods.

He dismounted to look for clues. A thrush sang overhead as he went toward the last cottage. A boy of perhaps eleven, scrawny in his plain brown homespun, came out of a thicket. He stopped when he spied Giles and turned as if to flee.

"Hold!" Giles called out. The boy froze in place like a frightened fawn. His eyes were the color of moss and wide with fear.

"I mean you no harm," Giles told him. "Do you know what happened to these cottages?"

The boy gnawed his knuckle. "'Twas turrible. They was burned out this Eastertide, 'cause they would not give up their money to the men."

"And the people who dwelt here—the Coopers and the rest—what of them?"

"Some went to the village. Where the others is, I do not know, sir."

"Do you know aught of these bandits who burned them out?"

"Bandits? No bandits did this. 'Twas Lord Rathborne."

Surprise and anger rose in Giles, but he fought them down. The boy was obviously frightened, and he did not want him to bolt just yet. "Lord Rathborne did nothing of the kind. He has been away at sea with Sir Francis Drake."

"'Twas his steward that ordered the burning. Aye, and carried it out." The boy indicated the ruins of the last house. "I saw him throw the first faggot on that one with me own peepers. And he was wearing the Rathborne badge, so 'tis all one and the same."

"God's death," Giles muttered, biting back his fury. He flipped the boy a copper. "Go home and spread the news that Lord Rathborne has come home. There will be no more burned-out homes, and those with just grievances need have no fear. They may come to the courtyard a sennight from this day to state their cases. I will listen with an open ear to their complaints."

The boy stood openmouthed in shock, then gathered his wits and scampered into the woods. He had not taken in much of what Giles had told him. Who would be so foolish as to believe it?

Giles glanced at the sky. Dark clouds massed on the horizon, blotting out the sun. The boy bolted across a field and over a style. By the time he reached his home all he remembered to tell anyone was that Lord Rathborne was back, and that he was fiercer by far than Heslip.

The copper coin lay safely hidden in the little pouch inside his jerkin, along with some shiny pebbles and a holey stone. Better to say nothing about that, in case his older brother snatched it away from him. Better to say nothing at all.

When he returned to Rathborne, Giles's spirits were as leaden as the skies. There were years of work here, and the sorry state of things brought home plainly that he could not leave them to a steward's care. His adventurous plans had turned to ashes, like the ruins of the cottages.

Instead of sailing the high seas again, he would be immured at Rathborne, trying to right the rampant neglect. Instead of listening to the song of the wind in the sails he would be listening to his tenants' grievances. Instead of watching for Spanish ships, he would have to settle for watching the hay and wheat and barley grow.

He took a shortcut through the Long Gallery to the wing where his rooms were. The gallery had once been famous over the length and breadth of England for its beauty and richness. But when Giles threw open the doors, he stopped in dismay. Light filtered in through the grimy panes of the tall windows; the floor was thick with dust and the carved paneling dull for lack of polishing. Cobwebs hung from the beams, stirring gently in the disturbed air, and the ornate plaster of the ceiling showed patches of damp. Even the stables had been better kept than this!

His strong jaw clenched and unclenched. He wished to God that he had never heard of Rathborne, much less belonged to it by blood. The necessary repairs would gobble up his share of Drake's successful enterprise. The Spanish gold and silver, with which he had planned to build and outfit his own ships, was as good as gone.

The long windows, here, too, centered with colored glass in the Rathborne coat of arms, ran down the entire south wall. Built as a place to take exercise in inclement weather, the gallery, like so many other rooms, had become a display place for family portraits. The wall opposite the window was filled with them, in all sizes.

Giles spied Francis Finch there, examining them idly, and stalked down the gallery, his eyes glowing like coals. Francis stifled a yawn.

"Bored to death already?" Giles asked. "They are an unprepossessing lot. Neither heroes nor villains among them."

"But some fine portraits, for all that." Francis indicated one. "This one, for instance."

Giles joined him. His heart lurched painfully. "My mother," he said gruffly. "Clarice Hammond."

It was a full-length painting. She gazed down from the canvas, as fair and sweet as he remembered. Her hair was a shade between auburn and red and her dark eyes mirrored his own; but while his were sharp and wary, Clarice Hammond's eyes were soft and gentle.

It was only now, as he gazed upon the painting with wiser eyes, that he saw the sadness in their depths and noted the lines of strain in her even features, which had been captured by the artist's sure hand.

"Six months after this likeness was painted my father repudiated us both and installed his whore here."

Francis was subdued. "I plead ignorance as my excuse. I did not mean to open old wounds."

Giles was not offended. "I will have the portrait carried down to the Great Chamber and hung there. Meanwhile, this talk of portraits has given me an idea. There might be, among these canvases and painted boards, a treasure that would bring a tidy sum."

"Aye, you may be right. If you remember, not so many years ago a painting of Henry VIII was discovered at Burlington House. The Earl of Leicester paid a marvelous sum for the portrait and presented it to our queen."

Giles remembered it well. The earl's star, dimmed slightly by his secret marriage to Lettice Knollys, had for his clever act been polished and set back in the firmament of Elizabeth's favor. "Let us hunt for painted treasure then, while the light still holds."

They moved down the wall, examining the pictures one by one, but found only time-darkened paintings of dour men and simpering women, alternating with a handful of indifferent landscapes and several family portraits. "Ah well," Giles said. "It was only a thought."

As they headed for the double doors at the far end, the sun came out from behind a bank of towering clouds. The gallery was flooded with warm, golden light. Giles found his eye drawn to another portrait, half-hidden by an arras. He pulled the tapestry aside.

The portrait depicted a slender woman dressed in the garments of an older generation. Her fair hair was parted in the center beneath a cap of blue velvet sewn with pearls. A little girl sat on the woman's lap, clutching her mother's hand.

"A charming portrait," Francis remarked. "Who are they?"

"Allys de Breffny was cousin to my father. Until he met the fair Allys, Sir Lyle Stanton populated the countryside with his bastards. The marriage changed his ways. They had only one daughter, who bid fair to rival her mother in beauty and grace. When her parents died of lung fever within ten days of one another, my father petitioned the queen for wardship of Lady Verena. She was raised here at Rathborne."

That surprised Francis greatly. John of Rathborne had not been known for his works of charity. "It was kind of him to take the child in."

Giles gave a bitter laugh. "Kindness had nothing to do with it." He frowned at the portrait. Something nagged at the back of his mind.

"Lady Verena was a great heiress. Had she lived, she might have saved Rathborne from its current state of neglect. The greater part of the Stanton estates had originally belonged to Rathborne, from the time of the Conqueror. They were stolen by trickery and false accusations during the reign of bluff King Hal.

"You see, my grandfather was unwise enough to seduce a maid who had attracted the king's roving eye. He escaped with his life at the loss of one-half his lands, which were given to Sir George Stanton for services rendered. Some say, for pandering for the king."

Francis was puzzled. "Then how could she have saved Rathborne?"

"When Elizabeth came to the throne and adopted the role of peacemaker to bring her divided kingdom together again, she learned the truth of the matter. Although our land had been taken through trickery she could not restore it to us outright. To take away the estates from their current owner would have pitted powerful enemies against her and threatened that fragile peace.

"Since the queen could not legally give Verena's estates back to Lady Allys, she agreed to make Lady Verena a ward of my father, thereby giving him the freedom to draw upon the bottomless coffers of her vast estate. He planned to marry her off to Morse, thus keeping the fortune in Rathborne hands."

"Poor child," Francis said, still looking up at the young Verena's haunting face. "How did she die?"

"No one knows. While I was still in Northumberland a terrible plague decimated the countryside. At Rathborne, two died for every one that survived. Amid the turmoil young Lady Verena disappeared, along with her nursemaid. My father made inquiries. The nursemaid died in a pesthouse run by a religious order. No trace was ever found of the girl."

"A terrible pity."

Outside, the clouds moved across the sun, shifting the light across the painted surface. The interplay of sun and shadow made the portrait seem to come alive. Giles was intrigued. It almost seemed that Allys was smiling at him from her portrait. Odd, he had never noticed how tall the lady had been, but her pose beside the doorway made it obvious, now that he looked more closely. And her face seemed terribly familiar—yet not in the way of a portrait that has been viewed in the past and forgotten.

It was, Giles thought with a frown, more as if he had seen her recently, and in person.

He stared at her regal figure, her finely molded features and deep blue eyes. So deep in hue that they were almost violet.... Realization hit him like a thunderclap. It was no wonder that the high cheekbones, straight nose and shapely mouth looked exceedingly familiar. He had seen them earlier that day, mirrored in Vera's face.

"Jesu!"

His sudden exclamation startled Francis. "What is it?"

"Can you not see what I see? Come closer and tell me that I am not a complete fool."

Francis approached the painting. "God's teeth!" he breathed. "If you are a fool, than I am one as well. The resemblance is uncanny!"

A surge of excitement ran through Giles, like the sensation of challenge and danger that had come when he stood aboard the *Golden Hind* and spied just over the horizon the top of a mast flying the Spanish flag. The outlaw girl, who was presently enjoying the hospitality of the old cow byre, bore more than a passing resemblance to the woman in the portrait—and to the small girl at Allys's side. The height, the oval face, the great violet eyes ...

Giles rubbed his jaw. An outrageous idea was forming in his mind. It brought with it the wild rush of excitement that accompanied danger and great risk. It was a feeling he knew well and savored. He threw back his head and laughed.

There was something in his voice and demeanor that sent a ripple of apprehension down his friend's spine.

"I mislike that look in your eye, Giles. What deviltry are you planning?"

"You will know soon enough," Giles replied softly. The air fairly crackled with his barely contained excitement. "But first, there is another matter that I must attend to first. Are you in the mood for a bit of fun, Francis?"

"When have I not been?"

"Excellent. Join me in the kitchen garden at sunset. Come quietly." Giles winked. "And come armed."

It was cold in the stone byre where Vera was kept prisoner. As the sun set, the air grew chill and the damp penetrated her bones. She wished in vain for her warm, padded tunic and trews instead of this stupid dress. Dresses were useless things, no good for riding or hunting. "When I get out of this scrape," she vowed, "I shall never wear a dress again."

If not for her misadventure, she would be sitting around the fire now with Tal and his band. Given events, she feared that her foster father would be in a rare fury. Once she escaped—and Vera had no doubt that she would, eventually—Tal would surely send her off to Garvin's sister. After this episode, she could hardly blame him.

A single tear trailed down Vera's cheek. Tal was the only father she had ever known. More than that, he was her first and greatest hero. And in repayment, she had betrayed him to his enemy. She dashed the forlorn tear away with her sleeve. Somehow, some way, she must escape and warn him.

In her folly and pride she had made two grave errors. The first was mistaking Sir Giles for a court peacock and attacking him in the forest; the second, letting him gain possession of her dagger in his chamber. If only she had bided her time, she might have used the weapon more wisely. A feint, and an upward thrust between the ribs as the blade drove home and . . .

Despite her anger at Lord Rathborne, Vera doubted she could have killed the man. Not unless her life had truly been in danger . . . and she doubted that he meant to harm her, despite his silken threats. Her cheeks burned with remembrance of his kiss. His touch.

Vera realized that her fingertips were at the base of her throat, stroking lightly where he had pressed his lips. She almost imagined that she could feel the tickle of his beard against her tender skin. His hand, warm and possessive against her breast . . .

Fie! What was she thinking? She rubbed her mouth with the back of her hand, trying to wipe away the imprint of his touch. Sighing again, Vera pulled the warm wool blanket more tightly around her and lay down upon the pallet. Her lids were heavy and her eyes burned from lack of sleep. She needed to be fresh and prepared when the moment for action presented itself. She surrendered herself to sleep.

Something awakened Vera abruptly. For a moment she was disoriented and did not recognize her surroundings. Her fingers reached out and scraped against mortared stone. The reality of her imprisonment hit her all at once, and for the first time she knew an overwhelming despair.

The chamber was dark once again as the bottom of a well shaft. There was only a faint glimmer of starlight from up near the ceiling. She heard a muffled sound, but could not tell its source. A hungry rodent, no doubt. The noise, which seemed to be coming from below the right-hand window, grew louder. A very *large* rodent.

She sat up straight. An owl hooted nearby. Tal's signal—for it was too early for such an owl to be about yet. Could she have imagined the sound?

Hope and trepidation swept through her. None among their band would attempt a rescue—unless the chance of success was almost assured. What chance would they have at Rathborne? They would not even know where to find her. On the other hand, Rathborne had few servants within its walls and was poorly manned. She had managed to discover as much before she had been recaptured in the bedchamber. And the byre was in the old castle, away from the main residence.

Another hoot sounded, this time unmistakably Tal's. She had to let them know where she was kept. Vera looked up. If only she could signal her whereabouts to them! The bench was not high enough for her to peek out, even on tiptoe. Unless she stood it on end.

The bench was so heavy it seemed to be fashioned of iron, but she managed to drag it underneath the narrow windows. Balancing it on end was more difficult. Vera managed to climb atop it, but the side was uneven and wobbled precariously.

Pressing her face against the crumbling stone, she peered out, straining her eyes. She could make out shapes moving along the edge of the woods, then skittering away into the darkness. Soon the shadows began to gather close to Rathborne's walls. Relief made her weak. Yes, they had come to rescue her! And she would never, never do anything foolhardy again.

Then the area beyond them silently filled with men and armor. She realized Tal had been led into a trap. "Run!" she cried. "Run before they surround you!"

It was too late. Torches flared. The two groups engaged swiftly while she watched in horror. Lord Rathborne's men were in fighting trim and had the added advantage of superior weapons. Vera screamed a warning to Hewe, but he went down as the flat of a sword caught him across the stomach.

She flinched and her bench suddenly teetered and swayed. Instinctively she caught at the window ledge—and found herself dangling helplessly six feet above the floor. The bench crashed to the stones below. Her fingers slipped. She dug in her short nails, feeling the sharp bits of mortar sting her hands, and slipped again. She hung on by her fingertips, clawing at the stone for support.

The door was flung open just as the ancient mortar crumbled away beneath her touch. Vera heard her name called out. She fell with a cry and landed, not on the hard floor, but in a strong pair of waiting arms.

"Tal!" she gasped in relief. "I knew you would come!"

He picked her up and tossed her over his shoulder. She bumped along, head down, and it took her awhile to realize she was being carried not to the woods, but into the house again. They pushed through a door and up the dimly lit stairs until she found herself in a small bedchamber.

When she was finally set on her feet, she was face-to-face with Giles of Rathborne.

He smiled grimly. "I hope your disappointment is not too great, lady. I am sure you would rather it was Tal who took you from your prison chamber."

"A thousand times more!" she exclaimed bitterly.

He brushed a cobweb from her face and she slapped at him. Giles caught her wrists in his strong hands and forced them down. "Easy now, my fair firebrand. I would not want you to hurt yourself. Not after the great favor you have done me in drawing your bandit friends into my net."

A dull misery filled Vera's chest. "You lie."

"See for yourself."

He led her to one of the windows overlooking the front of the house and pushed the velvet curtain aside. Torches filled the scene with lurid light. Tal, Hewe, Garvin and Ferris were bound with ropes and chains. A long weal marred Hewe's bony cheek and one of Garvin's eyes was swollen shut. Ferris looked small and frightened and very, very young. Tal's swarthy face was set and white, making him look suddenly old. Vera felt sick at heart.

Giles let the curtain drop. "Your friends will sleep snug in the dungeons of the old keep tonight. Meanwhile, you little wildcat, try me no tricks—or I will have them hanged from yonder tree at daybreak."

Her breath hissed in on a smothered gasp. "They only came to save me." Her tongue was so dry it stuck to the roof of her mouth. She lifted her head and met his gaze levelly. "Do with me what you want, my lord. But please, I beg of you, set them free."

Giles felt a pang of conscience. She was in sore distress. Then he remembered that this violet-eyed wench had attacked him twice and accused him of terrible crimes against his people; that her comrades had made Rathborne Forest unsafe for travelers and had attempted to steal away his prisoner. That his future and that of all the people dependent upon Rathborne might well lie in her hands. Haste could ruin everything.

He went to the door. "Perhaps I shall hold you to your word. We will speak of this again in the morning. Meanwhile, I hold your friends' lives in ransom for your cooperation. Heed my warning, and they may yet go free."

He left, closing and locking the door behind him. Vera went back to the window and lifted the curtain, but the courtyard was dark and empty. She turned away and paced the floor restlessly, wringing her hands.

The lock on the door was scarcely necessary. With her friends in his custody, Lord Rathborne held her captive more surely than the strongest chains and bars.

Chapter Five

By the following day, two more buxom matrons had been hired from the village to help make Rathborne livable. Only the promised payment and the chance to be the first with gossip about the new lord had lured the women to the estate.

The entry hall had been cleaned and the Great Chamber swept of debris and prepared for use. When Giles entered at late morning, a fire crackled in the hearth and golden sunshine poured through the windows, which had been cleaned by two of the gardeners. The room looked altogether welcoming. Two goblets flanked a flask of wine and an inlaid chessboard and ivory playing pieces were set on a small table. Francis was busy at the larger table, but looked up from the maps he had been perusing.

"Am I in error? I thought that we were to play at shuttlecock this morning?"

"There is still time," Giles said. "I was out catching rats. Or rather, one fat one."

Francis lifted his eyebrows. "I can hardly imagine you at such a task. What have you really been up to?"

Giles grinned. "I see I cannot fool you. I have been to Turnley and brought Heslip, the steward, back in chains. He is imprisoned in the stone byre. I had thought of putting him in the dungeons with the bandits, but decided against it. They might strangle him, and I wish the man to be brought to public trial.''

"A brilliant scheme, Giles. As brilliant as your calculations for our proposed voyage. I have planned out the entire route. Two ships, four months at sea, and we could fill our coffers with the treasures of the Orient. If," he said, stroking his blond mustache, "we had two ships and you were not bound to this place."

Giles straddled a chair and stared into the flames. The fire highlighted red tones in his dark hair and exaggerated deep, unhappy lines around his mouth. "The chance of me leading the expedition is highly unlikely, under the present circumstances. I had hoped to draw upon the resources of Rathborne to finance our venture. That was before I rode out and saw firsthand how matters lie."

He tilted his head and surveyed the ceiling of carved plaster. Each square and knobby protrusion had been filled with a relief of molded fruits or flowers, their contours highlighted with gold leaf. In one corner leaking rainwater had made bubbles in the plaster, like the lesions from some scrofulous disease.

"God's wounds, where will I find the skilled craftsmen to restore this? And where, the gold to pay them for their labors?"

Francis had no easy words of comfort. He set aside his instruments and poured wine into the goblets. Giles did not notice; he rose and paced the floor as if it were the deck of a ship. "What I have seen and heard today has curdled my blood in its veins. Once this was the fairest estate in all of England. My grandfather, for all his philandering, was a just man and well loved in the district. He treated his tenants and bondmen fairly. Harvests were bountiful and provision was made for lean years. Not one soul went to bed hungry or in fear.

"My father and half brother were stamped from a different mold—and their steward as well." He eyed his comrade grimly. "Which you have certainly realized by now."

Francis was renowned for his tact. "I have noticed that all is not well here," he murmured politely.

Giles gave a bark of bitter laughter. "You should have been a diplomat, my friend. Your golden tongue would have earned you far more than your share of Drake's booty. I have seen stables better kept. Aye, and crypts more filled with merriment."

He paced to the fireplace and back. Everywhere he looked there was need and want. "Curse Heslip for his greed and negligence! When I saw how he had let this place go I was bewildered, then angry. When I learned today what had been done to the people...my people," he amended after a hesitation, "I was heartsick."

"Surely you can borrow against your estates?"

"There are already encumbrances against the property." And he was in danger of losing the lands that supported Rathborne. But though Francis was his oldest and dearest friend, Giles could not bring himself to disclose how near to ruin he stood.

Unless he went ahead with the mad scheme that had formed in his fertile brain. He paced in silence a few minutes. Never let it be said that Giles of Rathborne was a coward, afraid to take a risk when so much was at stake. By the saints, he would do it! Giles turned back to Francis.

"We may find our treasure closer to home. If all goes well I shall have those ships outfitted and ready to sail this spring, with the first fair weather."

"What, have you decided to steal the queen's jewels?"

"In a manner of speaking." Giles tugged at his beard, a habit he had when he was deep in thought. Francis watched him with growing apprehension.

"God's eyes! What deviltry do you have in mind?"

"I have decided to try my hand at sewing," Giles said mildly. He flashed a wide grin and suddenly looked younger. "Making silk purses out of sows' ears."

Francis stared. Giles laughed, but a moment later his face was still and stern. "I told you of the wench Vera's accusations."

"Yes, but—"

"They are truth. While I have been plying my sword right merrily in the West Indies and along the coast of Alta California, my tenants and freeholders alike have been fined, flogged and taxed near to extinction."

"You cannot be held accountable. You inherited this great pile of stones but two weeks before we set sail with Drake. In all conscience you must not condemn yourself for what your steward has done in your absence."

Giles refused to shift the blame elsewhere. "Heslip is indeed a villain—and his loathsome acts began during the months of Morse's final illness. If I had traveled up to Rathborne when the news of his death first reached me in London, I would have discovered the facts for myself. Instead I put off my obligations for fear Drake would lift anchor without me. And three more years passed."

His eyes were hooded. Those responsible would be dealt with swiftly, but it would take a great effort to win back the faith and loyalty of those who had suffered.

"Go back to your maps, my friend. If my plan works we shall have those ships in good time. Meanwhile, I have my work cut out for me here."

"Sewing those silk purses you spoke of?"

"Aye. And by supper tonight you shall see the results of my handiwork."

Giles would say no more and left Francis wondering.

Giles went to the chamber where Vera had spent the night. The moment the door opened she sprang up, glowering. This had certainly not been the first time that she had slept in her clothes, yet in the warm morning light—and with her captor stunning in red and black, his beard freshly trimmed—she felt clearly at a disadvantage.

"I have not had a morsel to eat since yesterday," she snapped in lieu of greeting. "If your intention is to kill me, my lord, I had rather you used a quicker method than starvation."

He folded his arms. "I see that imprisonment has not smoothed your rough tongue, or taken away your appetite. Somehow I had imagined that you would refuse all meat and drink."

Vera sent him a look that one would give a small and not particularly bright child. "It would be foolish of me to pine away from hunger when I may need my strength to escape."

Giles was taken aback by her honesty. "You are a bold creature!"

"I was brought up to speak the truth whenever possible."

"And lie when it became impossible?"

She did not deign to answer. Giles took a turn about the room. "Who is this Tal, and why does he live in the forest with his men, like wild creatures?" He whirled suddenly and caught her by the arms. "No lies, Mistress Vera. I would have the truth!"

Vera remembered the touch of his mouth to hers and broke away. "Keep your hands from me, sir, and I shall tell you. Tal is the son of an architect and builder. Through study and skill he became a master carpenter and builder himself, with a fine home and a wife. Then he ran afoul of your covetous father. I do not know the details, only that he did no wrong to incur such wrath.

"Tal was thrown into the very dungeon where he lies at this moment. He was released six months later to find his home burnt to the ground, his crops destroyed and his tools and land confiscated. He took to the forest and was joined by others who had suffered at the hands of John of Rathborne. They vowed to live free until such a time as justice could be done. At first they were few. Now they are many. And they live in fear, with prices on their heads."

She sat on the edge of the bed, her face averted. Her profile was lovely, Giles thought suddenly, and wondered that he could notice such a thing when his soul was so tormented. He squared his jaw.

"You said harsh things to me, Mistress Vera. I was stung by your angry accusations. And I am appalled to learn that you were right. The people hereabouts are in sore straits."

"How *noble* of you to notice," she flared. "However, if you had come anytime in these past three years, my lord, you would have learned of it that much sooner."

He folded his arms. "If the situation was so dire, why did the people not petition the queen?"

Vera shot him a wry look. "They have, to no avail."

"Now *that* is an outright lie. Elizabeth has great love for the common people and a sense of justice. She would not have tolerated it."

"Messages were sent on three separate occasions. The queen sent word that it was none of her affair."

Giles straddled a chair and faced her. Her eyes seemed alight with blue flames. "And who delivered these messages and brought back such a false reply?"

"Sir Albert Sprocket of Fairfield Hall."

"Poor fools! Sprocket is third cousin to Robert Heslip. Your messages were never delivered. That false reply was surely given by Heslip himself."

"Jesu." Vera sighed. "We did not know."

Giles knew that her distress was genuine. "It seems, Mistress Vera, that the affairs of these people are very close to your heart."

"Aye, my lord. Like Tal, I have pledged to lay down my life in their defense."

He braced his hands on the back of the chair and rested his chin upon them, assessing her intensity. Her loyalty to her friends was of prime importance in his scheme. It seemed genuine and unshakable, as was his affection and concern for those he had sailed and fought with for the past three years. But behind her bold words and convictions were the soft body and heart of a woman. She was an enigma.

"A commendable if foolhardy sentiment. I cannot imagine that your dying would do anyone much good.

While your living might prove to be a boon to all concerned.''

Vera felt a prickle of anxiety between her shoulders. She tried, unsuccessfully, to read the expression in his fathomless eyes. ''I do not understand your meaning.''

Instead of answering, he got up and stood before her. Vera, for all her height, suddenly felt rather small.

Giles examined her face carefully. Her resemblance to the females in the portrait was more than uncanny. It might be a coincidence of coloring or something in the shape of her mouth; the possibility that the likeness was not happenstance nagged at him.

''Tell me, Mistress Vera, what do you remember of your earliest days?''

His change of subject puzzled her. His mind, she thought, was quick as lightning, darting here and striking there. Vera frowned, thinking back in time.

''I remember my grandfather's cottage . . . a small place near Brampton Mill. And I remember chasing the geese with a stick, to keep them out of the garden. That was before he died and I went to live in the forest with Tal.''

Giles relaxed. These were not the memories of a well-born lady. He had been foolish even to consider the possibility. But he had not lived through many a scrape by overlooking the obvious. And it was well known that Lyle Stanton had peppered the countryside with his bastards.

Giles was not a man to waver over his decisions; a course of action, once determined, was carried through with dispatch. He ran the plan through his mind once more, looking for weak spots, and grinned. It would do.

He knew well what Francis would say of his mad scheme, but a combination of careful planning and trusting his intuition had gotten him this far. Ignoring the hesitant voice of caution, he went with gut instinct.

He took Vera's hand in his and held it when she tried to snatch it back. "I might be of a mind to free your outlaw friends and grant them pardon. But first I would require something of you. Will you make a treaty with me, Mistress Vera?"

Distrust was mirrored in her wide violet eyes. *I would as soon make one with the devil,* they said as clearly as any words. But this was no time to sport her colors. Vera swallowed and pulled her hand away. "First, my lord, I would know your terms."

Clever little wench. He met her cool gaze levelly. "They are simple. For my part, I will repeal all unfair taxes levied by my steward. Secondly, property unjustly confiscated—including cottages and fields—will be restored. Last of all, if you cooperate, I will rescind the price on the heads of your outlaw friends and declare them free men again."

She appeared dazzled. Giles moved in with what he felt was his strongest bargaining point. "As for you, sweeting, you will go from the drab plumage of a cygnet to the glory of a swan. You shall give up the rude life of the forest for a life of ease and luxury, wearing fine gowns and a fortune in jewels."

Vera drew in a shaky breath. She could hardly believe her ears. Could she trust him? A part of her wanted to, very much. Another part held back. Heaven knew, she had no cause to rely on his word. Her inner struggle was fierce. She smoothed a fold of her dress with her fingers, staring at the dull brown fabric as if she might find an answer there. There seemed to be no real choice.

"It seems a lopsided bargain, my lord. You are a man of rank and power... and you are handsome and do not lack in address, when you desire to be pleasing. Why... why have you chosen me, of all others?"

"No other woman could play the role. But now that I have seen your face in candlelight and sunlight, I know that you are the one..."

Giles stopped in midsentence as a fiery blush rose like a tide from Vera's throat to the roots of her hair. He realized that he had not explained her role at all. Egad!

Vera's fury was greater than her embarrassment. "Surely you cannot expect me to believe such nonsense. You threatened to throttle me on the spot—and I saw in your eyes that you meant it. If that is your idea of wooing, I cannot wonder that you have no respectable woman to wife."

Giles was appalled. "God's teeth, will you let me finish, woman? You have not the slightest understanding of what I am asking of you."

She lifted her face to him, pale and set and very vulnerable. "Are you not asking me to be your mistress?"

"Jesu, I am not!" he roared. "Do you take me to be a lunatic?"

Vera's emotions were mixed, but relief predominated. She skewered him with a sharp glance. "Having had no experience of lunatics, I shall leave that last question for others more qualified to decide."

Her quick rejoinder caught him by surprise. Giles's eyes narrowed. "Your claws are as sharp as your tongue! Beware, lovely Vera. There is nothing as distasteful in a woman as shrewishness."

"Oh? And I can think of *nothing* more distasteful than being your mistress."

It was his turn to be taken aback. Despite his prowess with women, Giles had no conceit, but the disdain in her voice cut him to the quick. He glared at her. "You need not sound so revolted. I am not a vainglorious man, but I must tell you that no lady has ever refused my addresses."

Vera smiled coolly. "Perhaps the court ladies have stronger stomachs."

An angry tension filled the air. They bristled like two wary hounds, each looking for the other's weakest spots. Then Giles strode across to the stone hearth and stared at the flames until he had mastered his temper. It was not an easy task. By St. Swithin, he had fought duels over less!

He waited until his blood no longer boiled, only simmered. His eyes still snapped with anger when he faced her once more, but his tone was calmer. "Come, Mistress Vera. Let us declare a truce. No good will come from us baiting one another. We have matters to discuss."

She was still wary of his motives. But if Lord Rathborne meant what he had said, she would be a fool not to listen. She crossed one leg over the other and leaned forward, as if she were still dressed in boy's garb and living in the forest. "Very well, my lord. What is this 'bargain' that you propose?"

He smiled grimly. "I intend to pass you off to an unsuspecting world as a female of gentle birth. I believe that you might learn the outward form of acting like a lady—at least, for the short time that that will be necessary."

She sat very still while he told her of how he meant to restore Rathborne and repair the damage caused by Heslip's reign of terror. Then he told her the story of Verena, the missing heiress. "I could petition for the return of Lady Verena's properties. With the monies from them I could work miracles here."

He tipped up her chin with one finger. The sunlight caressed her cheeks and lit the depths of her eyes. He felt a catch in his throat and desire stirred in his loins. Giles dropped his hand.

"There is enough of a resemblance between you, the girl in the portrait and her mother's likeness that the ruse would work."

The plot seemed outrageous to Vera—but what a reward she would reap if they were successful. "How long must I carry out this impersonation?"

Giles leaned closer. "You do not understand. You would not be impersonating the Lady Verena, you would *become* her! And in time you would become a very wealthy young woman in your own right."

The visions Vera had conjured vanished like fog on a summer's day. "God's eyes, you are indeed a lunatic! I might learn some things, but I could not carry off such a masquerade for any length of time. Nor would I wish to!"

She waved her hand disdainfully at the rich velvet hangings of the bed and window, the colorful carpets and tapestries. "I am near to suffocating with all these...these *things!* I need air and light, my lord. Most of all, I need freedom. Without it, I would die."

Unexpectedly, Giles believed her. "You need not stay at court. You would make your home here at Rathborne until you married."

Vera sent him a look that would have withered fruit on the vine. "I do not want a husband," she said shortly.

Giles felt his advantage slipping. "Very well. We will have to think up something plausible. Perhaps Lady Verena must disappear again, this time forever. Meanwhile, there would be months of grooming you for your role—gowns to be made and fitted, lessons in music and dancing and the art of conversation. All things, in fact, that would prepare any lady to take her place at court."

He frowned at her masculine posture. "And the first step is for you to sit like a lady, with your feet modestly planted on the ground. Only a tavern doxy would assume so unladylike a pose."

She rose, her back straight as a spear, and fixed him with a haughty eye. "If you wish me to act the part of a lady, you must show me the proper respect. I doubt that tavern doxies are considered a suitable topic to discuss before a gently bred woman."

"Aye, that's it!" Giles beamed at her. Who would have thought that this wild little creature could display such ice-edged dignity? "Where did you learn such tricks?"

She frowned. "In a most respectable place. For a while I lived and studied with the good sisters at the Convent of St. Agnes. They taught me to read and write."

"A lucky day for us both," he murmured. "Now, Mistress Vera . . . er, Lady Verena, do we have a bargain?"

Her hands clenched and unclenched. "I have no reason to trust your word, my lord."

"Then I shall give you one." Giles led her to the window. "I believe you will recognize these fellows."

A wagon and a team of horses were pulled up in the courtyard below. Two men in Rathborne livery rode on the front board, three others on the back, and Francis Finch stood nearby. But it was the four men inside the wagon who caught Vera's eye, although they could not see her: Tal, Garvin, Hewe and Ferris, bound hand and foot like hogs to the market. Fear filled her heart. She clutched the stone window ledge desperately, for fear her trembling legs would not hold her upright. This was the sorry result of her foolhardiness.

Her throat was so dry her words came out in a whisper. "What—what do you mean to do to them?"

Giles saw that he had her now. He put his warm hand over hers and felt its trembling. "That is for you to say. Accept my proposition and they will go free, as a gesture of my good faith. Reject it . . ."

Vera's face went paper white. She had no choice. None at all. "Very well, my lord. I accept your bargain. But if you play me false in any way, you will not sleep safely beneath your own roof, unless it be with one eye open and a dagger at your side."

"What a bloodthirsty wench you are!" He lifted her hand and pressed it between both of his. "I give you my word as master of Rathborne that your honor will be safe under my guardianship, and that I will keep my promises."

Next he gave her quill, paper and ink. "You will write a note to this Tal, telling him that you prefer a life of ease at Rathborne to living like a creature of the forest."

Her hands trembled and the first draft blotted the paper excessively. Giles made her copy it over. When the ink had been sanded, he summoned a guard. "Take this to the man called Tal."

Vera sat with head bowed. Her neck arched like a cygnet's and she looked tender and vulnerable. Giles felt a pang but hardened his resolve. "Come to the window with me. You must smile and wave, to convince them you stay of your own free will."

At Giles's signal, Francis told the prisoners to look up. Giles put his hand on Vera's shoulder. Tal hissed through clenched teeth and Hewe paled. The guard brought Vera's note to Tal and held it so he could read her words.

Vera trembled at the disbelief in Tal's eyes, the pain in Hewe's and Garvin's. It froze the smile on her face. The wagon started up, its iron wheels loud on the cobbles, then soft on the lane that led away from the house toward the wooded hills beyond. Vera watched them go, half-paralyzed with fear. What if Lord Rathborne were lying?

But after what seemed like an eternity, the wagon reached the green tongue of woods slanting down a hill and turned around. She saw the flash of knives and feared the worst, then realized that the Rathborne men had only cut the bonds holding Tal and the other three.

The four outlaws stumbled away from the wagon, stiff from their former immobility. Tal rubbed his ankles, then motioned to the others to hurry. The last glimpse Vera had of them was as they disappeared among the trees and became one with the forest. Soon they would be safely back in their hidden camp.

A bright tear spilled from her eye and trembled on her dewy cheek. Giles wiped it away with the back of his hand. "Do not be afraid, mistress. I shall keep my word. I give you my solemn oath on it."

She dragged in a shaky breath, embarrassed that she had let him see her weakness. "I shall hold you to it."

"At dagger point, no doubt!"

"You may be certain of it."

A smile creased his dark face, transforming his features. The weight of ages seemed to have dropped from his shoulders. "I'll see that food is sent up to you immediately."

"More bribery," she said. "However, I shall accept."

"By New Year's Day this will be behind us. We shall look back on this moment as a very good day's work."

His confidence heartened Vera. She had no way of knowing that Giles had never been so wrong.

Chapter Six

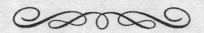

Giles and Francis took their midday meal in the Great Chamber. Giles was in high spirits, which had nothing to do with the excellent wine he had found in his cellars. When the dishes were cleared away he proposed a toast: "To fortunes lost and found again. To riches, fame and glory."

Francis raised his cup in salute. "God knows, I am heartily in favor of all three. But tell me, what is this great plan of yours that will replenish your coffers with gold?"

Giles took a healthy swallow. The wine warmed his blood. "It has to do with the little bandit maid. When I return to court at Christmastide, I shall take her with me."

Francis nearly dropped his wine goblet. "You will *what?*"

Giles threw back his head and laughed. "The idea is not as farfetched as it seems. If I had stewardship of the Stanton estates, I could restore Rathborne before it falls to ruin. Then, my duty done, we could return to a life of adventuring. With two fast ships at our command."

Francis began to understand; his hair stood on end. "Giles, can you be such a fool as to claim that this bandit wench, this Vera is one of Stanton's bastards?"

"Oh, no. A bastard cannot inherit, as well you know." Giles laughed softly. "My plan is bolder by far. I intend to take that grubby ragamuffin called Vera and turn her into a lady. Lady Verena Stanton, to be exact."

"You *are* mad!"

"I have never been more sane. Or more in earnest. I shall announce to the queen and court that I have found the missing heiress to the Stanton estates, living simply in a nearby village with a couple—conveniently deceased, of course—who never guessed at her true identity."

Francis was appalled. "That blow you took to your head during the Spanish attack has addled your brains."

Giles clapped him on the shoulder and grinned. "Come, we have work to do."

The floor of the Long Gallery had been swept of dirt and broken glass, and the mellow wooden flooring had been scoured and waxed to a fare-thee-well. The windows had been cleaned, a task that had taken two men and four boys half a day. Once the extra help had gone away, Vera's lessons began. They had been at it now, by her calculations, for something close to eternity.

"By the saints," Giles exclaimed in frustration. "If you kick my shins or step on my feet once more, I shall resort to wearing armor."

Vera gave him a sullen look. She tried hard, but it seemed to her that Lord Rathborne found fault with everything she did. "It was *you,* my lord, who insisted that I wear this stupid farthingale beneath my dress."

"Accustom yourself to it. You will spend many a long day in one soon enough."

Perhaps the rest of her life, he thought, grinning to himself. Heaven knew, once the girl realized what luxury and excitement there was in store for a wealthy heiress, she would turn her back on the forest forever. "Let me see you walk across the floor once more."

Vera saw the smile and thought he was laughing at her. She would show that prattling oaf. She took a deep breath and crossed the gallery for the fifth time in as many minutes. Giles watched her critically. "No, no! Walk like a lady," he chided.

"I *am* walking."

"You are striding about like a farm boy. *Glide!* Like so." He held out his hand and took a few airy steps. Irme tottered into the room and stopped short in alarm. Vera burst into laughter.

Giles saw nothing humorous in the situation. "We have been at this for three hours and, by God, we shall not stop nor rest until you cease galumphing about."

"But I am hungry," Vera complained.

"You are always hungry. I vow that you must have a tapeworm. Cross the chamber once more—and *glide!*"

Lifting her skirts as delicately as she knew how, Vera started across the floor again. Her attempts at gliding ended when the toes of her dainty shoes caught in the collapsible framework that held her full skirts out in a circle. Dignity abandoned, she went sprawling in a tangle of farthingale, legs and lace-trimmed under-skirts.

Giles uttered a round oath, Irme retreated and Vera flopped about like a trout on a riverbank. She only hoped that she had not revealed her bare backside in the mishap. The red that flooded Giles's face told her that she hoped in vain.

She floundered around until her back was to the wall. Francis Finch entered, almost colliding with Irme. An impish smile split his face and he had to smother his laugh behind his hand. "Things do not seem to be going smoothly. Perhaps I may be of assistance?"

"You?" Giles folded his arms across his wide chest. "Be my guest, Francis. I am as near to wit's end as a man may be and still be sane."

Vera backed into a corner and levered herself up by grasping the edge of a table. "I'll not quarrel with that. This whole scheme sprang from a lunatic's mind. It is no use, my lord. You had best let me go back to the forest."

"Oh, is that what this extreme clumsiness is about?" He faced her across the width of the table, his face as red as hers. "I should have known that, once your friends were free, you would go to any lengths to foil me."

Vera glared at him. "Extreme clumsiness? How can anyone be expected to move gracefully in such a barbarous outfit! This tight-fitted bodice makes it difficult to draw in a breath and this stupid farthingale...it is like trying to walk while wearing a gigantic basket."

She tugged at the offending contraption and the straps that held it tore free. It collapsed, showing a good deal more of her neatly turned ankles beneath the layered petticoats than any lady would ever dare. "This is nothing short of torture. I refuse to wear such a ridiculous thing."

He took a step toward her. "You'll put it back on or I shall do it for you."

Francis ended the standoff. He bowed to Vera without the slightest hint of mockery and extended his hand. "Come, Mistress Vera. Take my arm and stroll about the chamber with me."

She was about to refuse, but saw that accepting would annoy Giles. Schooling her features, Vera let Finch take her hand. She almost attempted a curtsy, but was afraid she would go hem over head again. "I shall be delighted, Sir Francis."

It was, Giles thought, almost a miracle. At first Vera was self-conscious and awkward; but as she moved about the gallery on Francis's arm her rigid limbs relaxed, her movements became graceful and effortless, and her feet—the same ones over which she had tripped a few moments ago—danced across the floor like a breeze over a pond. He retired to the boxed window seat, brooding.

Giles's way with the fairer sex had never failed him in the past. And yet this little outlaw maid seemed impervious to his charm. Not, he had to admit, that he had extended much charm toward her. The past three hours had been a severe trial of his temper.

Vera gazed up at Francis Finch with gratitude. He was a handsome fellow with a ready smile and easy manners. They had not gone ten steps before he coaxed her into a light mood and after a few more she laughed aloud. "Fear not," he said, casting a glance in Giles's direction. "I shall protect you from yon fierce-visaged dragon. Now, Mistress Vera, imagine that you are a swan gliding on the river...head high and proud, moving gently with the current. Ah, yes. Now, follow the river's bend just so..."

Giles rested his arm upon his knee, frowning. Vera was the most obstinate young woman it had ever been his displeasure to meet. His instructions to her had been disdained, his example ignored and his orders scorned. And yet here she was, tripping about the room on the arm of Francis Finch as if she had known him her entire life, and smiling all the while.

He slapped his palms against his thighs and rose. "Now you have it at last! By St. George and the dragon, I knew you could not be as stiff and awkward as you seemed."

The words were scarcely out of his mouth when Vera slowed, stumbled and halted in place. It was, Giles thought, as if she had forgotten his presence until his voice had broken the spell.

His surmise was almost correct. Vera sent him a poisonous glance. Although she had enjoyed Finch's light banter and frank encouragement, she had always been acutely aware of Giles watching. She had wanted to prove him wrong for calling her clumsy. Finch's support and mild distraction had eased her embarrassment.

But it had taken only a handful of words from the master of Rathborne to make her feel like the disheveled ragamuffin he had once called her. She wished she had never given him her solemn vow to play out this fool's charade.

At first she had been reluctant to be a part of his outrageous plan. So much could go wrong. She was no lady, and despite his attempts to turn her into one, she knew that Giles was beginning to doubt that she was capable of pulling it off. She could read as much in his face. Suddenly she wanted to prove him wrong—in every way.

Vera straightened her spine again and became in her mind the swan once more. She pictured herself gliding serenely past the castle and beneath the stone bridge that spanned the river...past the clustering willows and into the still, deep pools...past the black-visaged oaf glowering at her from the window seat.

She tripped again, tried to keep her balance and ended with the bottom hoops of her farthingale caught over the back of a low chair. She could not move a step without taking the chair with her. The oaf gave out a bark of laughter.

Francis came to her rescue, averting his eyes as he freed her. Vera was mortified. She dipped him a jerky curtsy, sent a look of loathing toward the master of Rathborne and fled the room.

Giles glared at her retreating back. All his hopes of saving Rathborne went with her.

He crossed to the window embrasure and looked out over the grounds. From this distance he could see the deserted archery butts where he had drawn his first bow under the archery master's watchful eye. The tenant farms beyond the meadowland looked snug and well-kept beneath their thatched roofs, but up close he had seen the crumbling walls of the whitewashed wattle and daub. He had seen the bony-ribbed cows in the weedy pasture and the wan children playing listlessly in the dirt. He was angered to the marrow.

He gazed out to his left, past the formal shrubbery and the yew maze, where he had slain imaginary dragons in his youth. Those had been happy times, when his father was far away, fighting in Calais. Times that ended abruptly with John of Rathborne's return.

And there was the belvedere where his mother had lain upon brocade cushions during the summer of her last illness, reading aloud to him or softly strumming her lute. Just beyond it, swans floated like white flowers on the glassy green river. The remembered beauty of the scene smote him to the heart.

All this to be sold for a pittance or put up on the auction block. His pride, his memories, his very manhood were tied up in Rathborne. Salvaging it would take a miracle; he had none at his disposal.

Francis joined him. He understood well what dark thoughts raged through his friend's mind. "I've always known you to bring your craft safely about. You will not founder this time."

"You are no prophet today. Rathborne is lost. I can no more change a duck to one of those swans than I can turn my outlaw maid into the semblance of a lady."

Francis smiled. "Not a duck, but a cygnet, as you said before. Methinks you are going about this wrongly. You, who know so much of women."

"What do you mean?"

"You have been too long in the rough company of men. Women are gentle creatures. They respond more quickly to soft words than to shouts and curses."

Giles turned to him. "But that is what she is used to, raised as she was."

"Aye. That is exactly my point. In order to bring out her feminine qualities, you must treat her as though she were a lady born. Have you not noticed that you feel and act differently in court clothes than you do on shipboard?"

His friend made sense. Giles tugged at his beard, digesting Francis's advice. "My way has gotten me nowhere. I will try yours. And," he added with an odd twinkle in his eye, "I shall take it one step further."

Francis mistrusted that curious gleam. "More tricks. I swear, Giles, that you will lead us all to the block or the gallows!"

Vera was happily polishing off a dish of thick mutton stew when Giles knocked and entered her room. She glanced at him from the side of her eye and frowned—but she continued to mop up the gravy with a chunk of bread. When she finished, the pewter trencher was clean as a whistle. Not a crumb remained.

He folded his arms and leaned casually against the wall. "Since you are now my honored guest, Mistress Vera, you will sup in style at my own table. Once you are suitably attired, that is."

"I would much prefer my own garments, if you please."

He laughed. "They have not been boiled long enough to kill the lice. Another day or two, mayhap."

Vera bit her lip. Lice, indeed. "There was naught on my garments but a bit of dust and good clean sweat."

And, she amended silently, a few spots of capon grease. The clothes *had* needed a good rinsing in the brook; if things had not gone awry she would have had a swim in them that very afternoon.

"If you would move in higher circles, lady, you must give more thought to your appearance—as I already have."

He gave her a short bow and opened the door. Two serving wenches entered carrying woven hampers. Inside them were gowns of silk and velvet and embroidered linen, ruffs edged with gauze and gold or silver lace, and an assortment of silk stockings and dainty shoes.

Vera goggled as the maids spread them on the bed. Giles smiled. The poor creature had never seen such finery in her life. Well, he was glad to see the stuff put to good use. The gowns and accessories had been culled from the chests and coffers of his late father's mistress. Much as Giles had despised the haughty strumpet, he was forced to admit that she had dressed with exquisite taste.

But Vera was not speechless from wonder. She eyed them with contempt. "Take these frivolous garments away. I am not a puppet, to be decked out in furs and feathers, my lord."

Giles drew his brows together. "Nay, you are a lady. And should be dressed as such."

The servants were staring, openmouthed. He dismissed them with a wave of his hand. When they were gone he approached Vera with determination. She backed away, searching his face for anger or lust, and found neither.

Giles stood before her, arms akimbo. "I think, sweeting, that you will be inclined to do anything I say."

"And I think, my lord, that you will rot in hell first!"

"We have a bargain," he said curtly. "I will return shortly. I expect to find you properly gowned, coiffed and shod."

She laughed in mockery. "I have not the faintest idea of how to begin."

"Then I will send Irme to you." He spun on his heel and walked out. He found Irme in the still room and asked her to assist Vera. "Bring her to the Long Gallery when you are done."

Francis was asleep in a window embrasure with the sun on his face. Giles went out to confer with his head groom and tried out an engaging mare. More than an hour passed in a twinkling. He went to the gallery to view Vera in her splendor. She was not there. The gallery was deserted. Cursing, he strode off to Vera's chamber again—and found a scene from a farce in progress.

Gowns and vests and ruffs and embroidered jackets were strewn across the floor. Bits of feathers drifted in the drafts like colorful dust motes and the air reeked of expensive oils. He spotted a broken unguent jar near the base of the wall.

Vera, still in her baggy brown dress, and Irme, with her cap askew, had squared off over an open wooden chest. It was difficult to tell who looked the most hunted of the two.

Giles stepped into the fray. "By the saints in heaven, what is this?"

"I will not put on that horrible muslin-and-bone contraption. It squeezes the air from my lungs until I feel faint. No wonder ladies are so insipid. They are too weak from lack of air to do more than sit and fan themselves."

Irme wrung her hands in dismay. "Oh, my lord, you see how it is with her. I have tried and tried to reason with this wild creature, and all I have gotten in turn is stubbornness and words so rude they would make a stable lad blush to hear them! If you wish the dressing of this ungrateful chit, you will have to do it yourself."

"Very well, if that is what it takes. Leave us."

Irme made her escape. Giles bolted the door after her and carefully stripped off his gloves. Vera eyed him warily. "What do you mean to do with me?"

"Why, dress you, of course."

"You would not!"

Giles smiled unpleasantly. "At the best of times I am not a patient man. And you, my lady, have tried my patience too far." He advanced on her purposefully.

Vera backed up and still Giles came on. "We will start," he said, "by removing that gown. The color ill becomes you."

She bumped into the wall. He advanced steadily. Vera placed a hand on her breast. Her heart was beating erratically. "Come no farther, my lord, or I shall—"

"What? Talk me to death?"

He reached out toward her sleeve. At the same instant her knee came up sharply. Giles dodged the disabling blow, and twisted her around until her arm was bent behind her back—not enough to do her any hurt, but enough to make her aware of his strength.

"Here is your first lesson, my girl. Do me no harm and I shall do you none in turn. Do me ill and you shall suffer the consequences. Do you understand?"

Vera hesitated. It was not that she lacked courage, but there was a certain look in her adversary's eye that brooked no further arguing.

Giles smiled dangerously. "I will not repeat myself. This is your last chance, sweeting. Either dress yourself or shall I do it for you."

"I revoke my part in our bargain," she said through clenched teeth. She was ready to fight, and although her dagger was gone, she still had her teeth and nails.

He took the wind out of her sails. "Nay, sweeting. You still wish to see your friends cleared of charges and their lands restored, do you not?"

Her face changed, all the fight and fire dying at once. Giles released her. "I will leave you to your toilette, Mistress Vera. You will sup with me tonight and you will be not only suitably dressed, but on your best behavior. Do you understand?"

"Perfectly. I am not deaf." She went to the door and threw it open. "Leave me and I shall dress myself."

"No tricks, you little heathen." He gave her a speculative look. "I believe that you will look very well indeed."

Once he was gone Vera went to the pile of garments and began sorting through them. Peacock colors! And look at these fabrics—why, they were so dainty they snagged on the rough spots on her hands. She wanted very much to disdain them, but something strange happened.

She discovered that the nap of the velvets was as soft as a kitten's fur, and equally pleasing to the touch. The shimmering silks and satins flowed like water through her fingers, catching the light in a fascinating way. This lace with a design of wild roses and marguerites... how did anyone conceive of a pattern so intricate and airy, and then fashion it from spools of fragile threads? Surely it was the work of faeries, and not of mortal hands. Beside the wondrous fabrics, her borrowed dress was dull and drab and her former garments seemed as coarse as sacking.

And the colors! Greens as soft as spring and as deep as the shadowed forest. Sapphire, cerulean and midnight blue. Primrose and topaz and mellow gold. Scarlet and plum and a wonderful deep red shade exactly the color of claret wine. She spread the garments out atop the bed, bewildered by the many choices.

A serving girl entered and bobbed a curtsy. "I am called Audry. Mistress Irme sent me to help you dress."

She had bright red hair and merry blue eyes. Vera remembered the girl from the night of her arrival. Audry had been there to witness her transformation from an urchin in boy's garments to a young lady. Here, at least, was someone with whom she need not pretend.

"Thank heaven above," Vera told her, "for I have not the slightest idea of what to wear or how to go about donning it." She indicated the assortment of finery. "Which should I choose, Audry?"

"Ooh, my mind fair boggles! Garments like these are not for the likes of me."

Vera grimaced. "Nor for me." She would feel like an imposter, dressed in such apparel. By the time she had discussed the possibilities with Audry she felt overwhelmed.

She finally made her choice by closing her eyes and pointing a finger at the bed. "That was not so bad," she announced and dressed hurriedly, with Audry's assistance. Then she sat impatiently while the maid did what she could with such short hair, a few jeweled pins and a pretty velvet cap. When they were finished she waited anxiously for the serving girl's opinion. Audry merely stared at her, openmouthed.

"It cannot be that bad, surely!" Vera exclaimed. Then she sighed. "Or perhaps it can at that. I feel like mutton dressed up as beef."

Audry found her voice. "Oh, no! You look beautiful . . . my lady."

The awe in the girl's voice upset Vera. An hour ago they had been equals. "I am the same person I was when I first came to Rathborne in my boy's garb," she reminded the maidservant.

Audry bobbed an awkward curtsy. "Yes, my lady...I mean, no, my lady. Mistress Irme explained to us about you being the Lady Verena, restored to Rathborne after all these years."

It was plain that the maid had not believed the tale at first, but that she had been rapidly converted—by seeing her in a few yards of lace and velvet. Vera sighed again. The trap was closing in around her, cutting off her breath more surely than the horrid corset she had discarded earlier. "I suppose I had best get on with it."

Audry hurried to open the chamber door and Vera swept out into the corridor in a rustle of silk velvet, feeling very much alone.

Giles and Francis were already below and had repaired to the spacious Great Chamber together. The freshly polished paneling glowed with deep lights and the rich red chair cushions had been beaten of their dust accumulation and plumped up. Late sun angled through the enormous windows, highlighting each small pane and making the colored glass that fashioned the Rathborne crest glow like a fortune in jewels. This, Giles mused, was how he remembered it in his earliest days.

The table had been buffed to a high gloss with oil and beeswax. The beautiful silver plate and the branching candelabrum had been liberated from their tarnish, and their lustrous gleam reflected back from the table's surface. Low bowls of flowers were set at either end, in the latest fashion adopted from France. The setting looked fit for a king. Or a lord, Giles thought wryly.

The men were as elegant as the room. Giles wore a doublet of white silk brocade, hose trimmed with gold, and a collar of gold and rubies. He had a ruby-and-pearl earring hanging from one ear. Francis had chosen tobacco-colored velvet that set off his fair coloring and had decked himself with a chain studded with sapphires.

The two men took their places and presently Irme joined them. She had taken pains with her appearance in honor of the occasion and wore her best gown of figured green silk. A circlet of garnets adorned her thin bosom. "What splendid company we are tonight," she murmured, more to herself than to them. "I am glad the lady warned me to dress well."

"Who is this lady of whom I've heard you speak?" Francis asked, but Irme had already turned to Giles with a comment. He was frowning at the fourth chair, still empty. He signaled a servant. "Advise the lady Vera that we await her pleasure."

"No need, my lord."

Audry had entered. She threw open the door to the corridor, beaming. Giles looked up. Francis's jaw dropped in awe as a vision in black velvet drifted into the chamber. Vera paused on the threshold, nervousness changing to triumph when she saw the reactions of the men. So, they had not really believed that it could be done!

Suddenly she began to enjoy her effect on her audience. Her tight-fitting bodice was cut low and embroidered with gold thread and pearls. A frilled ruff of black lace edged with gold framed her throat and shoulders to stunning advantage. Her fair hair seemed almost white-blond in contrast, and was held back with an almost invisible net of gold thread, studded with tiny pearls and brilliants. Petal-shaped earrings of white enamel with ruby centers and a matching necklet completed her attire.

Francis made her an elegant bow as she approached the dais. Giles stepped down to meet her. Taking her hand, he bent low over it, as if she were the Queen of England herself. As his lips brushed her fingers a shock of warmth traveled up her arm and she felt a curious weakness in her limbs. She wanted to snatch back her hand, but he held it clasped too securely.

I suppose I should be used to that by now, Vera thought wryly. She glanced up at Giles through her lashes. He was looking at her wonderingly, as if she were some fair and magical creature. There was no mistaking his admiration. His dark eyes were eloquent with it. Vera blushed in confusion. No one had ever looked at her this way before. Not even Garvin or Hewe.

Giles's words were meant only for her. "Lady," he murmured softly, "you grace my humble dwelling with your beauty."

Her blush deepened, and she was suddenly breathless. Lord Rathborne, who had done nothing but scold, insult or threaten since the moment of their first meeting, had called her beautiful! That, too, was something no one else had ever done.

He smiled at her with such warmth and intimacy that Vera almost felt herself to be a knowledgeable and sophisticated woman, able to pass muster before ten queens. Then Giles helped her onto the dais. "Come sit beside me...*Lady Verena.*"

The brightness faded from Vera's eyes. Audry had curtsied to her borrowed finery earlier. Sir Giles was not bowing to her now, but to the counterfeit Lady

Verena, great heiress and ward of the master of Rathborne. Something—some*one*—she was not.

Her brief giddiness hardened to angry pride. Her violet eyes took on an icy glare. What a fool she had been to be blinded, even for a moment, by a pretty phrase and a false smile! She made a vow not to be so naive ever again. And no matter what she wore or where she went, no matter what name she answered to, in her heart and soul she would remain true to herself.

Still seething inwardly, she took her chair next to Irme as gracefully as possible. Unaccustomed as she was to her voluminous skirts, it was not an easy task. With the slightest twist or turn, it seemed that she had to rearrange everything. The situation was intolerable.

She was wrestling with her skirts, which had caught on a knob at the corner of her chair seat, when Giles leaned toward her. "Why are you fidgeting?" he demanded in a very different tone from the one he had used earlier. "A lady must be still, serene and seemly."

"My cursed skirt is caught on your cursed chair."

"God's teeth, woman! Mind your tongue or I shall be forced to wash out your mouth with a bar of lye soap!"

He reached over to free her skirts and Vera recoiled sharply. In her haste she knocked her goblet over with her elbow. The claret spilled into Sir Giles's lap, a lake of crimson staining his white satin doublet and hose.

He jumped up with a roar, cursing as he daubed at the spreading stain. "By God, wench, look what you have done!"

Vera smiled wryly. That was more like it. For a moment she had lost her head, lulled by soft words and her first heady taste of admiration. When Lord Rathborne swore and shouted she knew exactly where she stood—in opposition to him on every suit.

Except where Tal and the others were concerned.

Giles was still roaring like a gored boar. "I have not worn this doublet and hose more than twice, and already they are ruined beyond hope by your infernal clumsiness."

Vera lowered her eyes and spoke meekly. "It is not kind of you to point out my lack of grace, my lord. As to your garments, the problem may be rectified quite easily."

Giles glowered at her. "That I should like to see!"

Her lashes swept up to reveal a lambent violet gaze. "And so you will."

Quick as a flash she grabbed up the wine jug and splashed the rest of its content over him, until his garments were splotched entirely with great gouts of wine. While surprise rendered him speechless, Vera rose and dipped him a hasty curtsy.

"You were handsome in white, my lord. But indeed, I believe I prefer you in claret!"

Before he could react she lifted her skirts and scampered from the hall, laughing merrily, and not caring a whit that her behavior was most unladylike. As she hurried up the stairs she could hear him bellowing behind her. In a trice she was in her room with the door shut and a chair wedged in place to keep it so.

She was disappointed when he did not come after her, raging like a bull. Curse the man, he never did quite what she expected of him! But Lord Rathborne was a worthy adversary, and she was beginning to enjoy locking horns with him.

In fact, she quite looked forward to it.

Chapter Seven

Dawn came slowly to the forest. The topmost branches of the trees were outlined against a rosy pink sky, but the inner precincts of the wood were deep in shadow. Tal and his men, steeped in gloom, sat near their rude shelter of sticks and hide discussing Vera's predicament. Wolf lay at their feet.

"I cannot believe that Vera has stayed at Rathborne of her own choosing," Garvin said for the hundredth time. "He has somehow forced her to comply." His big-knuckled hands clenched at the thought of exactly how that might have been accomplished.

"Aye," Ferris agreed quickly. "Otherwise she would have driven a dagger through his ribs at the first chance." He chewed on a peeled stick as his empty stomach growled. "Or mayhap she has truly been lured by the soft beds and rich foods. Vera does love to eat."

Tal was silent for a few minutes, turning over in his mind the last glimpse he'd had of Vera. He brought out the crinkled letter from his jerkin and smoothed it against his leg. The light was still too dim for him to read it, but he knew the words by heart. There was not so much as a clue in the note to guide him, nor had she given him the slightest sign when she had looked down from the latticed window.

No, he decided. She was a clever little thing and would have managed somehow to signal him. He knew her well enough to realize that she had some definite reason for remaining at Rathborne. Perhaps the new lord was not the monster he had been thought to be all along. The fact that he had freed them instead of hanging them from the Druid's Oak proved that there was more to Giles of Rathborne than had been guessed.

And he himself had seen the villainous steward, Heslip by name, brought to Rathborne in chains from Turnley by his master. That action spoke well of Lord Rathborne—although Garvin had argued that it might mean nothing more than a falling-out among thieves.

Tal did not think so. He had solid instincts and he felt that no danger would come to Vera through Giles of Rathborne.

Another thought had been circling in his mind. Perhaps her time at Rathborne would make her realize that this rough life was no place for her. She had been born to better things.

"Keep up the watch on Rathborne," he said aloud, "but do nothing to interfere with any of them, unless either Vera or I give the command. She has some plan in mind. But what game she is playing I cannot yet tell."

Reluctantly the others agreed to bide by Tal's decision. All but Hewe, who stepped back into the shadows to hide his misery, and then quietly left the camp. Only Wolf noticed. The dog yawned, showing a curling pink tongue, then rose and padded after Hewe.

At first Hewe tried to send Wolf back. The hound refused. Hewe shrugged and let the dog come with him. They both missed Vera very much.

It was late when Vera awakened the next morning. Audry brought her fresh bread and ale to break her fast. "Lady Irme is in the still room," the maid said with a twinkle in her eye. "Trying to find something to remove a stain from Lord Rathborne's best doublet and hose."

Vera flushed guiltily. She was to meet Giles for more dancing and deportment lessons shortly. She wondered if he would be very angry over his ruined garments. They had been costly and elegant. It really was a shame that he had worn white, rather than a red that might have matched the spilled claret more closely.

But she had to admit that, with his sun-bronzed skin and dark coloring, he had looked quite handsome in the white. Rather splendid, actually.

It had been even more of a shame that she had had to go to bed without eating a morsel of the excellent supper—but it was not the first time she had slept with an empty stomach and, on the whole, Vera was pleased with her night's work.

When the last crumb was gone, she set aside her tray and rummaged through the garments that Audry had put away in the wardrobe. She eschewed the satins and velvets and heavy brocades, for they would only remind her of how foolish she had felt the previous evening. And how could she learn intricate dance steps when her mind was distracted by the possibility of tipping up her skirts or tripping over them?

Her problems were suddenly solved. She found a simple cambric dress with a low neck and long sleeves, like those that Audry and the other serving girls wore. The skirt would be easy to manage during the lesson, and the style suited Vera's tastes as well. Pearls and velvet were for Lady Verena. For a few hours today she would be only Vera, plain and unadorned. And she would not have to put on that asinine farthingale, which was rapidly becoming the bane of her existence.

Vera entered the gallery a quarter hour past the appointed time, expecting to find Giles awaiting her with his customary impatience. She was prepared to argue the merits of her dress with him, but she needn't have troubled herself; the chamber was deserted. She heard an unintelligible whisper and turned around quickly, but found herself quite alone, except for the images of long-dead Rathbornes staring down at her from their heavy frames.

She glanced quickly at the portrait of Allys and Verena, half-expecting them to look censorious; but their painted smiles were gentle and unconcerned. She did not see the resemblance that Giles and Francis found so striking. Vera went to the window and studied her reflection. She looked only like herself. No one else at all.

Half an hour passed as she examined the paintings and still no one came. Perhaps Sir Giles and his friend had not returned from their morning ride. Vera went to the east window and looked out.

Morning sun kissed the formal garden beds that were laid out between the broad terrace and the lawn. In the clear, uncompromising light she could see that everything was terribly overgrown—late roses choked with thistles and coltsfoot and the knot garden tangled with oxeye daisies and bindweed. The ornamental pond was so smothered with duckweed that the water lilies could barely be seen. Despite the neglect, she guessed that it must have once been incredibly beautiful.

Beyond the lawn something caught her eye—a strange wall of impenetrable green, in the shape of an enormous hexagon. Vera had heard of Rathborne's intricate maze, its boundaries and pathways formed by a living yew hedge. Once the corners of the maze had been trimmed into fanciful forms, but now the shapes were obscured by ragged new growth. Nonetheless, the sight fascinated her.

Vera stood on tiptoe. Vague outlines of the pathways were visible from her vantage point, but not enough to see the full design. She could make out the roof of the tiny summerhouse in its center.

Egad, but she had been cooped up inside too long! Sir Giles had ordered her to stay indoors at present, and she could understand his reasoning—but Vera had been her own mistress too long to let a man who was almost a stranger tell her what she might and might not do.

The temptation overcame her. In a few short minutes she was out on the weedy lawn, eagerly picking her way past clumps of purple thistles and the lacy off-white blooms of wild carrot. A blackbird trilled as she was about to enter the maze. Vera cast a soulful look at the woods beyond. Her signal had been a blackbird's call, repeated twice. She whistled and strained her ears, but there were no echoes.

Then the bird burst upward from behind the hedge and flew away into the brilliant blue of the sky, and Vera felt as if her heart might break. A wild longing ran through her veins. The yearning for release from constraint was so strong it almost overwhelmed her. She wanted the freedom of the forest, of the life she'd led until only a few days past. She needed simplicity, and the sense of knowing who she was and what her path would be.

Instead she was trapped in a world that was as unknown to her as far Cathay—trapped by frilled neckbands as wide as coach wheels and by clumsy farthingales, by dancing and deportment lessons. And by her own promise to the master of Rathborne.

Vera stepped into the maze and followed the path to the first turning. This was what her new role was like, she thought: stumbling down unknown paths, never knowing if she had made the right choice until it was too late. But if she carried out her role successfully, Tal and the others would no longer be outlawed, and all those dispossessed would regain what they had lost.

Tears filled her eyes as she went deeper into the maze. She blinked them away angrily. *I must not feel sorry for myself,* she said. *This is the course I have chosen, and I shall carry out my obligation with my head held high.*

She came to a blind alley unexpectedly. Vera realized she had not been paying her usual attention to her surroundings. She dried her eyes with her sleeve and looked around in dismay. She had no idea of how far she had penetrated the maze, nor of where either the center or the exit might be.

The puzzle had been designed most cleverly, with straight passages and curving ones, the paths frequently doubling back upon themselves. Vera had no fear of losing herself inside the maze. For more years than she could count, she had charted her way about by wind and sun and sound; by a crushed leaf, trampled grasses or crumbled earth. It was not difficult for someone with her skills to figure out where she had been or get to where she wanted to go. In no time at all she had found the heart of the maze.

It was an enchanting place, a wide, grassy square with grape arbors and stone benches and a pear tree at its center. The fruits were ripe, yellow as dandelions, and no one had been by to pick them. Vera sat on the grass and ate two pears. They were delicious. She wiped the juice from her chin with her sleeve and stuffed her pockets with several more to eat later.

She stretched out on the ground, face to the sun, and basked in its warmth. After a span of minutes she shifted. The ground seemed harder than she had remembered. Vera sat up. She had slept in a feather bed for only four nights, yet already her body was turning traitor. What would it be like after six months of soft living? Would she forget how to walk through the woods, as quiet as a shadow, or have the patience to tickle a trout from a stream with her bare hands?

Suddenly her pleasure in the bright morning evaporated. Vera rose and brushed the bits of leaf and twig from her skirts. There were smudges and grass stains everywhere. She would have to scrub them out with strong soap before returning the dress to Audry. And she would have to be more careful the next time.

Until today she had never minded where she sat or what effect it might have on her garments. The front of the gown was stained with juice from the pears, as well, and Vera sighed. She almost wished she had never made her pact with Sir Giles. Being a lady was a much harder task than she had imagined.

Suddenly a dark shape came hurtling toward her. Her first reaction was an instinctive one to protect herself. Then she recognized the intruder.

"Down, Wolf!" The warning came too late. The dog had already launched himself at her, and they went sprawling in the grass. He woofed and licked her face as she tried to sit up. Vera pushed him off and sat up. Wolf rested on his haunches, regarding her with an expression that was the doggy equivalent of a smile.

Vera reached up to scratch beneath his jaw, and found something that had not been there before—a bowstring, tied around the beast's neck. She traced it through the dog's fur to find a hollowed-out reed, which had been used for a tube to carry a broad leaf. Crude symbols had been scratched on the leaf's surface: a rayed circle, a crescent and a zig-zag shape she did not recognize at first. Then Tal's message made sense. She was to meet him tomorrow at dawn, in the maze.

Carefully shredding the leaf, Vera scattered the pieces in the breeze. She slipped the reed into the bushes behind her and rose. "Come, Wolf. You will be rewarded."

The shaggy beast gave a bark of excitement, then loped along beside her toward the kitchens. After begging a handful of choice scraps from the scullery boy, Vera left Wolf in the garden, enjoying his feast. She entered the house through the vast kitchens and ran lightly up the servants' stairs to the west wing.

Then she took off her shoes and moved more quietly into the main corridor. Best to get out of this ruined dress and into another before she got a scold. Audry would tell her how to remove the stains.

It was rather dark at the top of the stairs and Vera suffered a terrible start when she almost collided with someone. The pear she was munching fell from her hand and went rolling across the corridor floor. Her heart thudded until she saw that it was only Francis Finch.

Francis was equally startled. His mouth gaped, as if he meant to say something, then closed again.

She dropped him a curtsy, as she had been taught. Two pear cores dropped to the carpet. Vera pretended not to have noticed. "Good morning, Master Finch."

"And . . . and to you, Mistress Vera." He seemed to fix his gaze on the newel post beyond her. "Sir Giles has been searching for you, fearing that you had come to some harm."

At the sound of their voices, Giles strode out of Vera's room. He did not look worried at all. He looked furious.

"Where have you been, you ungovernable wench? We searched the house from top to bottom."

"I was not aware that I was a prisoner here, my lord," she snapped. "I waited for you in the gallery, but you failed to keep our engagement. The day being fine, I went out to explore the grounds."

Giles restrained an impulse to throttle her. "I was detained on matters of business which are no concern of yours. I thought—"

"Thought what? That I had broken my vow and run off into the forest?"

She could see that she had guessed aright. She wanted to wither him with a look of aristocratic scorn, but it was hard to achieve the right effect while wearing a crumpled gown marred with grass stains, her pockets bulging with pears. Vera did her best, drawing herself up with all the dignity she could muster.

"I am made of sterner stuff. A *lady* does not break her word," she replied coolly. "And a true *gentleman* would never doubt that she had."

Francis laughed aloud. "By heaven, the lass learns quickly."

Giles was not amused. He stared pointedly at her slender ankles and shoeless feet. "Not quickly enough in some matters. Ladies do not run about like barefoot beggars."

He was ready to go on when his eyes narrowed in disbelief. Then he came closer and drew Vera out of the shadows and up to the recessed window. The strong light streamed through the fabric of her outfit, outlining her splendid figure. For a moment Giles was speechless. He found his tongue soon enough.

"Egad! What in God's name possessed you to wander about the gardens like this, in full sight of anyone?"

She flushed. "I am sorry to have spoiled the dress, and—"

"Dress? *Dress?* By God, madam, you are not wearing one. That is a nightrobe you have on!"

Vera felt the blood rush to her face. "Oh," she said in a small voice. That explained the look on Francis's face when he'd first seen her, and the way he had averted his eyes. She wanted to shrink into the wall. Pride demanded otherwise.

"How was I to know? The thing was in with the other garments you had brought to me—and appeared to be the only sensible dress among them. I cannot help it if the fine ladies of the court choose to have their ribs strapped into rigid corsets and tight bodices, or their nether limbs caged in cumbersome wire hoops. If *I* ruled England, I should outlaw such ridiculous garments!"

Giles tried to hide his smile. "What a passionate little termagant you are. Fortunately for England, you are not in a position to dictate fashion."

Vera bridled. She wanted to insult him or call him names, as she would have done with Hewe or Ferris. Instead she struggled valiantly with her temper, and conquered it. "You, my lord, are entitled to your own opinion."

His smile turned to a grin. Francis was right, she did learn quickly. Intelligence plus courage—a necessary combination if they were to pull off their ruse. There was a twinkle in his black eyes as he favored her with a bow.

"As you say, lady. And now, unless you wish to cause further embarrassment to us all, you will change out of that shift and into something more appropriate for your dancing lesson."

Vera's stomach rumbled, a most unladylike sound. "Dancing? It is time for the midday meal, and I am like to starving," she exclaimed.

Giles raised his eyebrows. "Unless my eyes deceive me, you have polished off two pears from my garden quite recently, and were applying yourself to the third with vigor. I doubt that you are in imminent danger of wasting away."

She gave him an innocent look from those deep violet eyes. "I am so hungry, my lord, that I have not the strength to argue with you. I shall go to my chamber and dress, praying that I do not faint from weakness in the process."

Without another glance in his direction, she dipped a curtsy to Francis and walked, or rather, *glided* to her room.

"Your lovely ward has a mind of her own, as well as a sharp-edged tongue."

Giles grinned. "Aye, and the wit to put them both to use." He tugged the bell and gave instructions to the servant who answered.

In the safety of her room, Vera had shucked off the nightrobe that she had mistaken for a dress, and was still struggling to settle a proper one over the hoops of her farthingale. Unfortunately, a bit of the skirt was caught between two pieces of the framework. The more she pulled and tugged, the more the contraption tipped and twisted. Remembering that Giles had threatened to dress her once before if she did not hurry, Vera was anxious to subdue the unruly farthingale. It seemed to be an uneven contest, with herself on the losing side.

She heard a soft scratching at the door, then watched as it opened a crack and a black, shiny nose poked through. "Wolf, you should not be here," Vera scolded. She could imagine Irme's screams of fright if ever the two should meet. The older woman was a kindly, if vague and timid, creature.

Wolf wagged his tail and looked properly humble. Vera grinned. He was a most discreet animal when need be. "Very well. You may stay—but if anyone enters you must hide beneath the bed. And keep very quiet."

Vera bit back an oath as the door again opened. Wolf flashed past her legs and vanished beneath the high bed an instant before Audry came in with a loaded tray. "Sir Giles said as how he thought you might be feeling peckish and in need of some light refreshment," she said in a puzzled tone.

It looked more like a hearty repast to her. Audry shook her head in wonder. Where Mistress Vera would put all this food, after the enormous breakfast she had finished not two hours earlier, was more than she could imagine.

"Is that fresh bread I smell?" Vera attacked the far- thingale with renewed vigor. "If I were queen," she said between clenched teeth, "I would most certainly outlaw these ridiculous things."

Audry disagreed. "They are so lovely and graceful- like," she said wistfully. "If I were queen I would wear a new gown every day of the year."

"I would gladly give you this one," Vera replied. "Corset and all." She gave a sharp tug and was able to yank the dress into place at last. "There."

She removed the towel from the tray, revealing a small loaf of bread still warm from the oven, a crock of sweet butter, a tankard of ale, half a roasted chicken and bread pudding with a dollop of honey. "Now, this is more like it!"

The meal was really far more than Vera had wanted, but she would not let the master of Rathborne call her bluff. After Audry left she whistled. Wolf came out from beneath the bed and rested expectantly on his hind quarters, as if he had guessed a treat was in store. She shared the chicken with him, but ate the pudding and half of the bread. The rest she crumbled and threw out the window into the garden for the birds. Vera rang for the maid while Wolf went back under the bed, tail wagging, and closed his eyes.

When Audry returned for the tray, she was aston- ished to find the dishes empty. It did credit to the ap- petite of a field laborer, it did. "Will there be anything else, mistress?"

Vera dabbed at her mouth daintily with the linen napkin. "Yes. Would you please deliver my thanks to Sir Giles for his thoughtfulness," she said dulcetly.

"But tell him that he need not be so stingy with my portions in the future. I am not nearly as delicate a creature as he seems to think."

After Audry left, Vera tiptoed to the railing over the hall to watch his reaction to her message. If she had expected Giles to be angry she was disappointed. He only tipped back his head and roared with laughter. "By God, did she?"

He had seen the huge dog slip up the stairs and into Vera's room earlier. Two could play this game. "Very well, Audry. Take the lady another tray immediately—and tell the little minx not to feed any more to that tame beast of hers. I doubt the creature is used to such rich foods, and he will grow far too fat."

Vera went back to her chamber laughing. Sir Giles was a worthy adversary. As she straightened her gown and tidied her hair for the dancing lesson, her face was pink with pleasure.

As far back as memory could take her, no one had ever called her little before.

She did not know why such a silly remark should please her so well. Perhaps it came of all the teasing she had endured from Hewe and Ferris while growing up. For several years she had towered over them in height. They had seemed to take this fact as some sort of personal affront. It had been a source of mutual relief when the two youths had finally topped her.

Vera moved to the looking glass to check her appearance. The gown of deep gold velvet with an underdress of primrose brocade suited her well. "If I am to dress the part I had might as well look it," she told herself.

The skirt was cut open in front to leave a vee of brocade showing and the fitted sleeves had small puffs embroidered with gold threads in diamond pattern at the shoulders. She rifled through a bandbox and found a stiff frill of goffered linen tipped with gold lace. It fanned out gracefully to frame her face. Much as she deplored the necessity for such confining garments, she had to admit the effect was pleasing to the eye. Sir Giles would find no fault with her outfit this time.

She went out into the upper hall and along the corridor. She was almost looking forward to the dancing lesson. Tall as she was, she always felt rather small when Sir Giles was near. It was not only his height, but his breadth of shoulder as well that caused her to feel so, and something else, something unnameable that was beyond her limited experience.

Vera heard a man's voice and glanced over the rail to the hall below. Francis Finch lounged against the frame of the open door. He was dressed for riding and his short cloak was thrown back over his shoulders. In the courtyard beyond, a groom stood holding the bridle of a dainty dun-colored mare.

Vera detoured to the staircase and descended it. Her velvet slippers made so little sound that she was halfway down before he realized it. "Ah, Mistress Vera!" He doffed his cap and made a charming bow. "You are as graceful as an aspen leaf in autumn, drifting lightly down upon a breeze. How cruel of you to look your loveliest when I must take my leave."

She paused at the foot of the stairs, hoping she had heard incorrectly. "You are going away?"

"Of course. I thought that you knew." Francis took her hand in his. "Alas, my father has need of me and I have already tarried too long."

Vera did not know what to say. She had never expected to be left alone with Sir Giles. "But you have not been at Rathborne even a sennight."

"I never meant to stay above a day or two." He smiled as he looked deep into her eyes. "Only the charm of Giles's unexpected guest has kept me from my home these past days."

Vera thought she heard a snort of disgust from the shadows of the minstrel's gallery overhead. She was sure she recognized its source, and favored Francis with a blinding smile. "Very prettily said, my lord," she responded with an arch look, "but my poor charms are not enough to keep you at Rathborne."

"Indeed, they were all that lured me into prolonging my visit." He looked a bit sheepish as he patted the letter he had received before leaving court. "My father writes that he fears I have forgotten the way back to Finch Hall."

Vera blushed rosily. As she was about to reply, Giles leaned over the railing of the gallery. He was wearing hunting clothes of soft butternut leather slashed with black and a jaunty cap with a pheasant plume tucked into the band. His dark brows were drawn together in a forbidding line.

"If you've forgotten your way back home, you invidious blackguard, I shall gladly draw you a map."

The tone of his voice surprised Vera and she snatched her hand away. Francis only glanced up at the gallery, laughing. "You wound me, Giles, indeed you do. Less than an hour ago you urged me to stay on yourself, and now you are anxious to see me on my way."

Giles leaned against the rail. "Yes. Goodbye and Godspeed."

Francis merely laughed the more. "I can only attribute this change of heart to jealousy. You are afraid that I shall cut you out in the lady's affections."

Giles came down the stairs and faced him, hands braced on his hips. "What the devil are you up to, Francis, simpering over her as if you were a pimply choirboy in the throes of first love? Remember that I will hold the purse strings to the Lady Verena's fortune. She'll marry if and when I say—and to whom."

There was a gasp from Vera. "*If* and *when* I decide to marry, it shall be to a man of my own choosing. You will certainly have no say in the matter."

Giles glared at her. "You'll call a different tune when that time comes, you impudent wench. Not because I will override your wishes, but because I shall arrange for you so fine a match that you will be delighted to admit that I know what is best for you."

Vera's temper flamed. Sir Giles was taking his assumed role of guardian far too seriously. Once their bargain was completed, he would have no say over anything she did. Especially not over a matter as personal as marriage. She drew herself up in the way that the mother superior had done when her hackles were raised. That good dame would have been very surprised to realize how much of her tone and vocabulary her former pupil had picked up. Vera's voice dripped scorn.

"I find you insufferable, sir. Your rudeness is exceeded only by your arrogance."

Francis rubbed his cheek thoughtfully. Only the telltale quiver at the corner of his mouth divulged that he was fighting a smile. "No," he announced. "I have known Giles far longer than you, my lady. I am sure that his rudeness is greater."

"Oh, is it, you measly toad?" Giles roared. "Then what do you call having the effrontery to be standing beneath my roof while holding my ward's hands clasped in yours?" He took a step closer, eyes narrowed menacingly. "I should be surprised. I had always supposed that your tastes ran more to serving maids and tavern wenches."

Francis shed his languid pose. "By God, Rathborne, the part of jealous guardian does not suit you. Or is it the tone of a jealous lover I hear?"

That did it. Giles strode forward until they were almost nose to nose. "For a ha'-penny's encouragement, you young popinjay, I would rip out your lilywhite liver and force-feed it to you."

"Have at me, then!"

In the flash of an eye their small swords were out and engaged. They lunged and parried across the floor in a dangerous dance. Vera was staggered by their sudden belligerence, but she had been raised among men, and knew enough to stay out of their quarrel. She was unclear as to exactly what had led up to this fight; perhaps they had argued earlier.

The room was filled with sounds of the men's heavy breathing, the clash of their swords and the thudding of her own blood in her ears. Then Giles carried out a risky maneuver that caught Francis's blade and spent it spinning away. It fell to the floor with a clatter. Vera gasped. "Do not kill him, you fool! He is your friend!"

"Hah!" Giles advanced upon Finch, sword raised. They circled each other like wild dogs as she watched, aghast. Giles lunged. The tip of his sword lifted Finch's hat from his head. Giles laughed and threw down his sword. The next thing she knew the two men were wrestling across the floor together, rolling and tussling and dodging punches. She was horrified. Dear God, unless she acted quickly, someone would be killed....

"Stop! Sir Giles! Stop, I say! Oh . . . !"

They had rolled into Vera, almost knocking her off her feet. The scuffle went from one side of the room to the other, the men banging into a carved chest and sending the wrought-iron candelabrum off balance. Vera caught the stand before it could crash down on the combatants. When she straightened up she heard a terrible gurgling sound. She turned to find Francis lying on his back at the foot of the stairs with Giles atop his defenseless body, apparently choking the life out of his erstwhile friend.

The muffled gurgling sound came again, then changed to a whimper. She could not stand by without doing something. Snatching up a stoneware jug from the table, she ran toward them. Halfway there Vera realized that the strange sounds were something she had heard many times before, but never in such a setting, or from such elegantly dressed fellows.

Her whole body tensed with anger. They were laughing! Laughing and wrestling with the good-natured aggression of two bear cubs from the same litter. She expected such behavior from Ferris and Hewe, who were little more than boys—but not from these strutting, bejeweled courtiers.

Men!

She started up the steps in disgust. Irme came out on the landing. "Good heavens, child, what is all the commotion?"

Vera shrugged. "Some idiot's game, which I do not pretend to understand. The master of the house and his guest are wrestling and pummeling each other like drunken fools.''

Irme relaxed. ''Ah, is that all it is? I thought from the sound of it that we were under attack. Caution them not to break anything this time.'' She stepped back into her room, unconcerned.

Shaking her head in exasperation, Vera continued up the stairs, accompanied by more shouts and laughter from below.

''A flaunting popinjay, am I?''

''Aye, and an ugly one at that!''

When she reached the top, she realized that she was still gripping the ale jug in her hand. And it was quite full. Temptation called and Vera answered. She owed them something for frightening her. If they were going to act like silly children, she would give them a taste of their own medicine.

Vera had a good eye, whether for sling and stone or for bow and arrow. It proved true again. She leaned over the rail and waited. In another moment or two they would be directly below her. Almost...almost...*now!*

She upturned the ale jug with marvelous accuracy. The cries and sputterings from the hall below were most satisfactory. As Giles struggled to his feet he was suddenly knocked to the floor by a dark, hurtling figure. Wolf, delighted to have joined in such a fine game, pinned Giles down, barking happily and laving his new friend's face with his rough pink tongue. Giles's oaths were muffled by the dog's yelps of joy and Finch's shouts of laughter.

Vera stifled a giggle. There was no need to waste time in watching any longer. Setting the jug down, she ran and bolted the door. Then she leaned back against it and laughed until her sides ached.

But at the sound of departing hooves a few minutes later she sobered instantly. One of her windows looked out over the long front drive. Francis, mounted on his mare, reined in to wave farewell to Giles, who was standing on the lawn. They had rinsed their hair and changed their jackets, but were still in a frolicking mood. Francis waved to Vera, then called out goodbye to his host with high good humor.

"I shall be back when you least expect me," he added in mock warning.

Giles lifted a hand in farewell. "I shall hire an extra guard to keep you away, popinjay!" But when his friend wheeled away, he called out a hearty "God-speed!" to see him on his way.

When Giles turned back to the entry his smile was already fading. He stared up at the house a long time, frowning.

Vera stepped away from the window. A shiver ran through her. It occurred to her that she would be dining alone with Sir Giles from now, as Lady Irme had taken to bed with an ague, but that was the least of her worries. With Francis Finch and his merry spirits gone from Rathborne, everything would change. And not for the better.

She could feel it already.

Chapter Eight

"You do look lovely, my lady." Audry gave a final tug to Vera's skirt of mulberry velvet. Her chapped hands smoothed the soft fabric reverently.

Vera mumbled an acknowledgment, feeling like the imposter she was. This gown was even more gorgeous and costly than the one she had worn the previous evening. It glittered with beads of gold and silver, and the frilly band of lace that framed her face and neck was studded with rose-colored garnets. The whole ensemble made her feel uncomfortable. She was no more accustomed to such finery than was the serving maid.

Less, in fact.

But she had to admit that she looked her part to perfection. Her close-fitting jacket was collarless, of matching velvet embroidered with gold thread. She could not help wondering about the clothing's former owner. "Why did the lady not take such wonderful garments with her?"

"Lady?" snorted Audry. "She was nothing of the kind. And since she went by dead of night, it would have been difficult for her to smuggle out huge chests of clothing. She took her jewels—as well as most of those that had belonged to Lord Rathborne's mother—

and every small trinket of value she could get her greedy hands upon."

For a moment Vera wished she could put on her own clothes. She wanted nothing to do with the treacherous woman. Audry divined her thoughts. "Not to fear, my lady. These gowns and such were delivered from the seamstress after she had already run off."

That news made Vera feel better. She wanted to be dressed well for her first dinner alone with Giles. She'd donned the most dignified gown she could find in her new wardrobe. She had done so both as a measure of apology for the ale-drenching she had given him and as a talisman against his retaliation. If she looked the part of a gentle lady, perhaps she would be spared any repercussions.

Audry had been about to leave, but stopped at the doorway. "Oh, I almost forgot, my lady. My lord has ordered the meal to be served in his private study rather than in the Great Chamber tonight."

She slipped out, leaving Vera alone with her elegant reflection. An uncharacteristic nervousness fluttered in the pit of her stomach. She already missed the leavening influence of Francis Finch. No, she admitted to herself, the other man's absence was not the sole reason for her wariness.

What bothered her most was that she had never really been alone with Giles for any length of time. Somehow the prospect was daunting. And now, learning that she would be supping privately with him instead of at the high table with the entire household in attendance, she was even more leery.

At the appointed time she made her way to the study. Rush tapers had been lit at intervals along the corridor in deference to the early darkness brought on by a summer rainsquall. Their light was not enough to dispel the gloom that seemed to permeate the house. The atmosphere preyed upon Vera's nerves. She was used to the night sounds of the forest. The silence of the corridor was alien and eerie. She thought she glimpsed a woman's figure ahead. "Audry?"

There was no reply, and when she drew closer, Vera saw a portrait of a dark-haired woman in old-fashioned robes. On the painted hand was a ring with a blue stone enfolded in wings. It seemed oddly familiar. She smiled wryly. No doubt the ghosts of ancient Rathbornes walked here on stormy summer nights. Despite her bravado, she turned the corner and quickened her pace.

The door of the study stood open, throwing a triangle of cheery light across the floor. Inside a fire burned merrily in the hearth and branches of candles chased away the gloom. Vera took a chair and awaited her host. Rain spattered impatiently against the windowpanes. The wind whistled and moaned. The flames dipped and then flared in a shower of bright golden sparks from a sudden downdraft.

The tall draperies had not been drawn and from time to time lightning illuminated the gardens and distant maze. Vera wished that Giles would hurry. Much as she had wanted to postpone being alone with him in such an intimate fashion, his company would be most welcome. "Oh, if only Francis Finch had stayed on!" she muttered, rising to close the draperies. "Or if Lady Irme had not succumbed to the ague . . . !"

As she struggled with the heavy velvet panels a voice spoke behind her. "Allow me."

Vera jumped. Giles stood less than a foot away. By the wry twist of his lips it was apparent that he had overheard her. Stepping forward, he wrenched the heavy panels away from her nerveless fingers. She was incredibly aware of his height and strength, of the play of strong muscles beneath his fine clothes. In one fluid motion he yanked the draperies easily into place, shutting out the rainy night world. Shutting them in, together.

He stood so near she could feel the warmth of his body. The sound of Vera's heart seemed so loud in her ears that it drowned out the distant thunder. His hair and beard were carefully groomed and he had dressed himself with some formality. Tonight his doublet was black and gold. His eyes matched the coat—dark as jet, yet reflecting the mellow gold of candlelight in their depths. A collar of gold and rubies matched his cabochon ring and the small earring that dangled from one ear. He looked, Vera thought, half pirate and half king.

She had never seen a man so splendidly masculine. And certainly she had never been alone with one. Vera felt suddenly constrained in his presence—she who had spent most of her life in the company of men. The fact both infuriated and frightened her. What was it about this man that shattered her self-control and threw her into confusion?

Vera spied a brass box studded with rock crystal and carnelian and picked it up to examine it, as if it and not Sir Giles were the focus of her attention. She was appalled to find her hand trembling and she set the box down immediately. Had he noticed? If so, she did not dare let him guess at how shaky she felt inside.

He was too busy with his own thoughts. When he had ordered a private supper, he had not been thinking clearly. It had seemed like a good idea at the time, but he could not remember why. His senses seemed disordered tonight, perhaps an effect of the wild storm outside. Or it might have something to do with being at sea for three violent but lonely years, followed by a scant few days of merriment with the court at Greenwich.

Or, and this seemed the most likely, it might be due to the fact that his "ward" was not only a woman of spirit, but one of considerable allure. That she was unaware of the fact only added to her charm.

"Come," he said, waving her toward the table. Vera took her seat, arranging her cumbersome skirts gracefully. Giles sent her a smile of approval. "You learn quickly. Now, if I can prevent you from wolfing down your food, we shall convince the servants that you are indeed the Lady Verena."

She flushed and averted her face. Her profile, Giles thought, was captivating. Her brow was high, her nose straight with finely chiseled nostrils, and her mouth was soft and rosy. A kissable mouth, if one was not daunted by her firm little chin beneath. Although her face was not that of a classical beauty, it had something equally compelling. Intelligence. Humor. Passion...

Vera frowned. "Why are you staring at me, my lord? It puts me out of countenance."

"You must become used to men looking at you. It is the curse of a comely woman."

"I do not like to be looked at so."

"The interested glances—and the amorous imaginings of men—are out of your control, dear lady. There is nothing you or any other beautiful woman can do to change that."

As their gazes met and locked, Vera felt her heart skip a beat. *Amorous imaginings?* A shiver tickled along her spine. The air was charged with something

new: an understanding that they were not only part-
ners in a rash scheme that could lead them both to the
Tower, but that they were also male and female. Man
and woman.

And he had called her beautiful. It did not matter
that she did not believe him. Tal had called her his
bonny lass and once Hewe had told Vera that she
looked as fair as a spring morning. Neither compliment compared to this. She had grown accustomed
over recent days to seeing her reflection clothed in fine
satin and velvet; but the person inside was still the same
creature who had come to Rathborne as Giles's prisoner. And she was well aware that he knew so.

Giles gazed at her, fascinated. Every fleeting emo-
tion showed in her face, from pride to touching vul-
nerability. It was like watching the play of light on
seawater: a shadow here, a gleam there, a swift scattering ripple. And beneath it all, shifting colors and
unfathomable depths.

He suddenly saw what a fool he had been, what he
had been trying to ignore all along. From the first, he
had tried to convince himself that Vera was only a tool
with which to save Rathborne. Francis had warned him
earlier, and Francis had been damnably right. Vera was
not an unruly urchin, nor was she only a pawn in his
game to restore Rathborne. She was not even the young
girl he had first imagined. She was a desirable woman.

And he wanted her. Jesu, he wanted her.

He was acutely aware of her pulse beating at the base
of her slender throat, of the sound of her breathing and
of the way her breasts rose and fell with every breath.
Of the swift pull of desire in his loins.

His eyes burned with dark lights. Vera tried to meet his gaze with hers, but faltered. She was the one to look away.

A servant arrived with the first course. Giles was relieved. The spell had been shattered and he had no intention of invoking it again. Complications would doom his chance of saving Rathborne. He had to find a way to set a lighter tone. He dismissed the servant. Vera gazed at the man's departing back wistfully. She really wished that he would have stayed with them. Her host laughed, but the sound had a hollow ring to it.

"Do not be concerned, Lady Verena. He will soon be back with more viands to tempt your taste buds."

She did not reply. Earlier he had scolded her for taking such huge portions. Mindful of his warnings over heaping her plate, Vera declined the dish of mutton and took half a squab. It was roasted to a turn, crispy without and juicy within. She viewed it with disfavor. It looked ridiculously small on such a large plate. Why, she could have eaten four of them easily and had room enough left for a feast.

Her stomach growled. She tried to nibble on a piece, but became aware that Giles was looking at her and dropped the entire squab. It bounced from her lap to the floor. Vera's cheeks burned with embarrassment. He did not say a word, only placed the other half of the squab on her plate.

She felt the blush deepen as she blotted up the grease and tried to think of something to say, anything to get through the awkward moment. "Do you think Francis reached Finch Hall tonight?" she asked as offhandedly as she could manage.

He shrugged and speared a chunk of mutton. "I had not given the matter any consideration. Finch Hall is not far away. I have stayed there frequently with Francis and his sister, the lovely Lady Anne.'' He frowned thoughtfully. ''It might be wise to pay a visit to Finch Hall. You can observe Lady Anne's behavior. She is a paragon of womanly virtue.''

Vera scowled. She had no desire to meet Lady Anne. She clung to the original topic as if it were a lifeline. '''Tis a good night to be inside. Listen to how the wind howls! It will be cold and wet traveling. I do hope that Sir Francis has reached Finch Hall or found himself a snug shelter from the storm.''

Giles's brow darkened. ''Do you, by God? Well, I hope that he may be hiding beneath a hedgerow, up to his elbows in mud, if you mean to spend the entire evening talking of him.''

He speared another piece of mutton with his dagger and popped it into his mouth. Vera picked daintily at the squab. There was not much to it besides bones, but if Giles meant to be so unpleasant she would not do anything to encourage him. He tossed back some wine and watched her nibble at a tiny wing. The smile he had been trying to suppress widened into a grin.

''We are not at court yet, madam. I know that you are dying to match me bite for bite. You need not starve yourself while we're alone.''

Her blush deepened. ''If I am to eat minuscule portions I had better get my poor stomach accustomed to such rations now, my lord.''

''The court ladies do not starve themselves,'' he assured her, ''and the food is good and plentiful. I doubt if even you would find it inadequate.''

Her eyes sparkled dangerously. ''Is that meant to be an insult, my lord?''

He laughed. "No, only a salute to your healthy appetite."

She sat very straight. "No doubt you live in fear that I will disgrace myself before the queen by swallowing a chicken whole—or perhaps an entire roast piglet!"

Giles set down his goblet. "You have a saucy mouth, sweeting, and if you are not careful it will be a bar of Janet's laundry soap that you swallow whole."

Vera sipped her wine, then dabbed at her mouth with a linen napkin. "Idle threats soon lose their terror."

"I never make idle threats, madam."

She met his smoldering gaze with a limpid look. "You would not dare. I am too necessary to your plan's success."

She was reaching for her goblet when he pushed his chair back. In the blink of an eye he was at her side. Vera jumped to her feet, knowing she had gone too far. "If you do me any such trick, my lord...I vow I'll..."

The words trickled to a stop, as did every thought in her head. He came forward. She backed up. He took another step and so did she. Suddenly Vera felt the hard wall behind her. There was no place left to go. Her heart was racing. "My lord..." she breathed.

Giles grasped her shoulders. She looked up at him, wide-eyed and ready to bolt at the first chance. But he seemed to have fallen under a spell.

Giles had only meant to tease Vera a bit and to remind her who held the upper hand; but as he touched her shoulders the tables suddenly turned. Her bones were light and delicate beneath his hand, her flesh soft yet firm. He was intensely aware of her from the tip of her toes to the crown of her head. Tall as she was, her golden hair scarcely reached his chin. From his excellent vantage point the low bodice of her dress revealed not only the rapid rate of her breathing, but a gentle curve of bosom and the soft cleft between.

An ache of desire rose in his loins. He forgot he had ever thought of washing Vera's mouth out with soap. For a moment he forgot that they were, essentially, two strangers playing out a role. He knew only that he was a man, lonely and driven by needs too long restrained, and that she was a woman, warm and tantalizing. And untouched.

Her face and throat had been kissed by the sun but the upper swell of her breasts was as soft and luminous as pearl. Her scent wafted to him, a bouquet of flowers and spice and blooming womanliness. He struggled against the pull of longing.

Vera saw the change in his face. She, too, was caught off guard by the strange intimacy between them. A swift current ran from his hands and down through her body, one that was too strong to fight. She felt herself sinking deliciously into it, carried away by giddy sensations she could not even name.

He lowered his head, and she closed her eyes and lifted her mouth invitingly. She had no doubt that he meant to kiss her, and none at all that she would enjoy the experience.

She had read him rightly. For a few mad moments Giles wanted to sweep her into his arms and lose himself in the madness of the moment. Instead he pinched her chin. "Finish your meal, and no more insolence from you," he said softly, turning away.

Vera felt her cheeks grow crimson with mortification. Nothing had changed. The tension, the delicious pull between them had been the work of her imagination. She was glad that she had not done or said anything to let him know what she had been thinking.

Wanting.

They returned to their seats and tried to pretend that nothing untoward had happened. Giles poured out more wine and drank deeply, as if mere wine could quench his thirst. But it was more than that he needed and the damage had already been done.

His loins ached and his shirt grew damp with perspiration just thinking of what could have occurred before. His hands balled into fists and his gaze swept over her face. Vera's eyes widened, their irises darkening. There was an air of innocence about her that was genuine. He had seen it in the way she had lifted her face to his, like a flower waiting for the first touch of the sun.

Sweet heaven, but he had wanted to answer her unspoken invitation! If she were a lovely wanton he'd have taken her without a thought, knowing that he could pleasure them both to happy exhaustion. Heat rose in him at the picture that evoked. The room was suddenly stifling.

They went back to their meal, but the atmosphere in the room was charged with tension. Vera tried to ignore it, but her eyes were drawn to Giles no matter how hard she tried to turn them elsewhere. His hands were strong and sunburned, and there were small crisp hairs on the back of his knuckles. There was a scar upon one wrist, visible now and then as the frills of his cuffs fell away. The soft textures of his garments only complemented the hardness of the warrior's body beneath them.

For the first time Vera regretted her bargain. She felt as if she had jumped into a cold river, without first gauging its current or its depth. She was being carried away faster and farther than she had guessed possible. And she was definitely in over her head.

When the last course was laid and the servant withdrew, she threw her napkin down and stood abruptly. ''I am weary, my lord. Perhaps it would be better to continue in the morning when we are refreshed.''

Giles had been wondering how they would get through a session of dancing while this urgent mood was still upon him. ''Yes, the gallery will be dark and drafty tonight. I shall escort you to your chamber.''

Vera was both relieved and disappointed. They went into the corridor, following the dimming glow of the rush tapers. When they reached Vera's room on the far side of the house, she paused at her door. Giles held out the candle. ''The tapers will have gone out. You will need this.''

She took the candle, still warm from his hand. There was so much she did not understand. She wanted him to hold her and kiss her, yet she was very much afraid. Not of him, she realized, but of herself. Passion was something new to her. Without another word she pushed open the door and went in.

The room was dark as a cave, the only light coming from the banked fire glowing beneath a blanket of ash. Vera moved a few feet away from the door and stopped short with a small cry. The candle fell and went out. Giles heard her and entered the room, his hand on the hilt of his short sword. ''What is amiss?''

''Nothing, my lord. One of the servants left a chest out of its usual place and I caught my skirts. It merely startled me.''

She took another candle from a box and carried it to the hearth. Giles took it from her hand. As their fingers brushed, a spark jumped between them, invisible yet potent. A draft flew down the chimney and the door to the hallway closed. They were shut away in a small, private world.

The blood drummed in Giles's ears. The only wise move was retreat. He stooped to the hearth and lit the candle, then lit the thick candle in an iron stand beside her bed. "There. Now you can see your way safely."

"Thank you, my lord. Good night."

"Good night, my lady."

Giles was about to pass by Vera when he noticed a small dab of syllabub near the corner of her mouth. "You have missed a spot of something. Come here."

Vera felt a thrill of danger. It did not stop her from moving closer. She could smell the cedar and sandalwood of his clothes and the faintest hint of wine upon his breath.

Giles smiled at her, then brushed at the smear of sweet cream with the ball of his thumb. Heat and cold rippled along his spine. Her lips were incredibly soft. His thumb came back to trace their lower contour, then up and across the delicate arch. Exquisite. Lush and ripe as summer cherries. He knew they would be as sweet to taste.

Once the thought was born it could not be denied. Giles bent his head and touched his mouth lightly to hers. Vera gasped, a small rush of breath that kindled his blood. He pulled her close against him and pressed a real kiss upon those soft, rosy lips, feeling her hand flutter against his chest.

Conscience had held him back before, but now his control slipped its bonds. He had never kissed an unwilling maid, and this time was no exception. She was alarmed—he could tell by the quickness of her breath and the pounding of her heart. And she was passionate by nature. He could tell by the tremor that ran through her and by the way her mouth clung to his.

The tip of his tongue touched her lips. She was every bit as inexperienced as he had judged her to be, yet she did not pull away. He deepened the kiss, awakening something hot and fierce within them both.

Vera felt as if she had plunged into the heart of a whirlpool. She should have pushed him away at the start, but something had prevented her from doing so. It was more than curiosity, it was wonder and awe and then a dark, instinctual need, blood calling to blood. Passion overwhelmed her last vestige of sense. She only knew that she was in Giles's arms and that there was nowhere else she would rather be. Her arms twined around his neck and she stood on tiptoe to kiss him back.

The subtle shift of her body against his sent Giles reeling with the onslaught of desire. Hunger swept through him, sweeping rationality away on its primal tide. He forced her mouth open with a ruthless kiss. His teeth caught at her underlip, and when she gasped, he invaded. Conquered.

Vera was lost in a tempest of sensation. She, who had sworn never to surrender, was delighted to give up control to his masculine strength. She went willingly where Giles led her, opening her mouth to him, arching her back so his seeking hands might find her breasts. His fingers brushed lightly across the swell of her bosom and she shivered with pleasure. They pulled at her bodice, freeing her breasts to his hard palms. She shuddered with longing. She had few defenses against his ardent lovemaking, and none at all against her own, all-consuming passion.

He kissed her throat and his mouth trailed lower. Vera moaned softly. His lips trailed lower still, teasing and taking. The touch of his beard against her breasts was erotic beyond anything she had imagined. The warmth of his mouth was too exquisite to bear. Her legs were suddenly too weak to hold her. She clawed at him for support and his doublet came open.

She felt his skin warm beneath her hands and measured the rapid thud of his heart. A thick mat of hair curled across his muscled chest and down toward his waist. Her fingers tangled in it and held.

With a smothered oath he put her away from him long enough to shuck off his doublet. As he went to draw her back into his embrace, a bolt of lightning lit up the chamber, followed by a horrendous crash of thunder. She looked so wild and beautiful, her mouth all swollen with his kisses, that Giles was consumed by the desire to possess her. He would have taken her then and there. Instead Vera pulled away.

She was frightened of him and of her own actions. Most frightened at how quickly the situation had changed. She was drawn to him. She wanted him. But not like this—without plan, without control, without a single word of tenderness or love.

Unaware that she was weeping, Vera pulled at the bodice of her dress to cover her naked breasts. The fabric did not meet and she realized it was not merely open, but torn. Her breath came in deep, ragged gasps.

Giles started toward her. "Vera." His voice was low and gruff.

She found her own voice with great effort. "We made a bargain, my lord, and I gave you my vow on it. But our agreement was that I play the role of your ward, not your paramour. If you seek a mistress to wile

away your idle hours, you will have to look elsewhere.''

"Vera . . ."

She gave a little sniff and angrily wiped her eye.
"And if you touch me again, I swear I shall bury my
dagger in your villainous heart!"

Thunder rumbled distantly while they eyed one another. In the flickering light of the candle Giles looked
strained and infinitely weary. He had promised Vera
that she would come to no harm within Rathborne's
walls, and then had himself almost been the cause of
the most grievous harm of all.

"You will have nothing further to fear from me."
His eyes were shadowed and his mouth turned down in
bitter lines. "I swear before God and all the saints,
lady, that I'll not step foot into your room again. No,
nor so much as kiss your hand without your leave."

Her eyes did not meet his as she followed him to the
door. Giles stepped outside and Vera shut it behind
him. A second later he heard the thrust of the bolt in
the lock.

A fine thing when a maiden must bolt her door to
defend her honor against the master of the house! He
stared at the door for half a minute, then started down
the hallway. The corridors had never seemed so long
and cold. He returned to his study, filled with self-
loathing.

By dawn he had killed a quantity of his best claret
and any remaining sparks of desire.

Vera had as restless a time of it. After Giles left she
waited by the door a long time, living over and over
again the shattering events of the evening. She had
turned on him like a shrew, knowing in her heart that
she had been as carried away by surprise and passion

as he. Tonight she had discovered secrets in herself that she had never suspected.

She changed into her nightshift and put her torn dress in the bottom of the wardrobe. Sleep eluded her. Every time she closed her eyes she saw Giles's face revealed in that blast of light, filled with savage desire. She had recognized it as the mirror of her own. And that was all that had saved her from succumbing.

Vera rolled over, thinking of Giles. Her breasts still ached for his hands, his mouth, but the fevered heat slowly left her. Tears ran down her cheeks and she shivered with cold until the blood seemed to congeal in her veins. Somehow, in a few short days, he had cast a spell upon her. It was surely magic, although the good sisters at the convent had told her such things were mere superstition. But how else had Giles of Rathborne broken down her defenses so easily?

She must remember who she was and from whence she had sprung. She was no lady, only Vera. And she was at Rathborne for only one purpose, which did not include seduction by the master of the house.

Vera was not ignorant of the rhythms of life. She had watched the pheasants drumming to attract their mates and seen the swans pairing off for life. It was the nature of things. But she had never suspected the raw power of those instincts, nor guessed that humankind was not exempt from them. She wiped a tear from the corner of her eye. Now she understood why Tal had sent her away to the convent.

It was very late before Vera finally drifted into troubled sleep. As she sank down into it thankfully, she hoped and prayed that Giles meant to keep his promise; because if he ever tried to make love to her again, she very much feared that she would have to keep hers.

Chapter Nine

Toward morning Vera awakened. There was a scent of lavender and rosemary in the air. She opened her eyes slowly. Someone was standing just inside her door.

She sat bolt upright, frantically trying to chase the sleep from her benumbed brain. In the half-light she saw it was a young woman in an old-fashioned maid's dress of dark material, with her pale hair caught up beneath a stiff lace cap. It seemed a strange thing to wear at such an early hour.

Something was wrong. It had to do as much with the strange clarity of the air as with the fact that the hairs were rising on Vera's nape and the back of her arms. And that she could see, very faintly, the outlines of the door and wall shimmering through the woman's figure.

Vera shook her head and blinked; perhaps she was still dreaming. She *must* be dreaming. The shiver of alarm was banished by a warm, soothing feeling. Like a mother's loving embrace, Vera thought wonderingly. The woman smiled, came toward the foot of the bed . . . and vanished.

It been a dream after all. Vera's heart pounded and her mouth went dry. The woman had seemed so real!

But the door was closed and bolted from within, just as she had left it last night, and she was alone except for a stray beam of sunlight at the foot of her bed.

She jumped up. The curtains were still drawn, but a chink of light streamed through the part between them. She threw them back. The household must be still abed, since no one had come to rouse her. Unless, she thought with a tiny shiver, that had been the purpose of her imagined visitor. Well, whether dream or apparition, the woman at the foot of her bed had done the trick. She was certainly wide awake now.

Dressing hurriedly in a plain gown of dark blue material, she rifled through the bandbox until she found a small collar of stiffly pleated linen. It was in the old style, and covered her up to her chin. The only parts of her left uncovered were her face and hands. After winding her hair in a simple knot, she checked her reflection.

Neat as a nun—an altogether different effect from the lovely lace and mulberry velvet she had worn the previous evening. Vera was pleased. She wanted nothing to spark reminders of last night's events, in herself or in Giles. Feeling better able to face him, she tucked a final wisp of hair into place and went downstairs. She was not aware that the rich deep blue of the simply cut gown brought out her clear skin and the radiant nimbus of her spun gold hair, nor that it darkened her violet eyes to a startling midnight hue. Personal vanity had had no place in the forest, where one's ability to survive was of more immediate concern.

The hall was empty and she followed the corridor to the sunny breakfast parlor on the south side of the house. Her heart beat a little faster as she approached the entrance, and her palms felt damp. Vera paused in the shadow of a carved screen and gave herself a talking to. She had ridden breakneck across furrow and field, slept alone in a ditch and on a platform high among the oaks of Rathborne Forest. She would not let herself turn into a shy little mouse just because a man had tried to make love to her. Taking a deep breath, she went in.

The parlor was empty. A flood of warm morning light varnished the long table with a mellow glow. The tray of bread and cheese and smoked ham was untouched and the pitcher was still full to the brim. Vera took a seat facing the door. She did not want to be caught at a disadvantage.

Much as she would have preferred to wait, she was hungry. Vera cut off a thin slice of ham. It only whetted her appetite. And what was that delicious smell coming from the napkin-covered basket? She pulled off the linen cover to find a loaf of bread twisted into a braid and browned to a rich gold. Propriety warred with necessity and came out the loser. Vera hacked off a thick slice of ham and spread a chunk of pale butter over the still-warm bread.

It melted in her mouth. When the masquerade was over and she returned to her former life, she would miss the luxury of crusty loaves, hot and fresh from the oven. Truth to tell, she would miss a soft pillow and the warmth of the fire in her bedroom each night.

Her musings were interrupted by the pounding of hooves. She pushed back her chair and ran to the window. A horseman galloped across the park, his black hair tousled by the wind. She need not worry about Giles after all. From the look of it, he planned to be gone all day. A swift pang of disappointment caught her by surprise. She fervently wished that she had never tried to prove herself to Tal by attacking Giles that fateful day. The daring feat had turned her whole world topsy-turvy.

Her appetite deserted her and she decided to visit Lady Irme. Outside the door to Irme's chamber she paused, thinking she heard voices. Then there was only silence. She knocked and entered. Lady Irme was quite alone, propped against her pillows in the high bed, with a lap desk across her knees. She seemed in good spirits and her color had returned.

"How are you this fine morning?" Vera asked as she shut the door behind her.

"Very well indeed, child. I am only resting this morning at Giles's insistence. You know how he can be when he takes the bit between his teeth."

"I have been talking to my ladies. The ghosts, you know," Irme added conversationally. "They visit often."

Vera blinked. Perhaps Irme was truly mad, although harmless, as some of the servants claimed. Ghosts indeed! Vera didn't want to believe in hauntings; but the memory of her waking dream—it had seemed so real—lingered to plant seeds of doubt.

Irme held up a sheet of paper, crossed with lines of elegant script. "I have prepared the household inventory while I've been kept abed, and tomorrow I will begin overseeing the making of fruitcakes and Christmas puddings. But first I must check our stock of sugared lemon and orange peel."

"But Christmas will not come for weeks yet!"

Irme gave her a puzzled look. "But the cakes and puddings must be soaked in spirits and sealed away for more than a month, you see. I vow, the nuns at the convent may have seen to your spiritual instruction, my lady, but they have sadly neglected your basic education."

Vera chuckled. "I think they have at that."

There had been no rich cakes and sweetmeats at the convent, nor much meat or fowl. Vera, coming from withy huts hidden in the forests, had never tasted a Christmas pudding in her entire life. The thought of sugared lemon and orange peel made her mouth water. "May I help you in their making?"

The old woman laughed. "Never fear. I am a simple woman—daft, some would say—but I can dress a joint better than the queen's own cooks and make a mince pie fit for angels. I will teach you all I know and you will soon be a good housewife. Perhaps one day soon I shall be handing over the keys to the spice cupboards and the linen stores to you."

Vera was alarmed. "You must not say such things! You shall be chatelaine of Rathborne another thirty years and more. Why, look how improved you are after a few days rest."

"You misunderstand. I was thinking, my lady, that perhaps you would make your home at Rathborne permanently." A sly smile crept across her face. "It would not be unusual for a man to marry his ward, heiress or not."

Vera was appalled. Had one of the servants seen her with Giles last night? Her face was flaming. "Nay, Lady Irme. I have no wish to step into your shoes as chatelaine, and no desire to wed any man. Least of all a criticizing, domineering one like—like..."

Irme's smile broadened. "All that will change, my lady. As you will see. Giles is as fine a figure of a man as any maiden could wish for. And once he takes an idea into his head there is no shaking it out."

"You are talking nonsense," Vera responded. Her lips felt stiff. "You have no reason to think that he fancies me."

"Time will tell, my lady. We have a saying in my family concerning heiresses. 'A man, a maid, and a fortune to be made. Wedding bells will ring before the fire is even laid.' "

Vera rose. "There is another, plainer one. 'Do not count your chicks until they hatch.' "

Irme gave her a toothy grin, then went back to her lists as if she were alone. Vera watched her in dismay. The servants all said the old woman was daft, although Giles insisted she was not.

But that, Vera thought as she left the room, would not be the first mistake he had made.

Giles tried to counter the effects of a sleepless night with a hard cross-country gallop. Physical action had always been his way of releasing the tension of roiled emotions. Before the sun had cleared the distant line of trees, he and Caliph were far from the house. But as they thundered across the meadows and fallow fields, he could not outrace his problems. They awaited him at Rathborne in the guise of a fiercely independent female. That he was attracted to her and that she held the key to his future in her small, capable hands rendered the situation more than disturbing; it was intolerable.

He thought of going into Halford, the nearest town. There were women aplenty there who would be willing to ease the ache in his loins. That plump and pleasing armful who pulled the taps at the Fiddler's Three Inn was a lusty wench.

Or if he had a mind for more elegant company, he might call upon a certain widow of his acquaintance.

Unless, of course, she had taken another husband in his prolonged absence. He threw back his head and laughed. No, Mistress Jenkins was a wealthy woman in her own right, and the freedom of widowhood suited her too well to give it up for a ball and chain.

He set his direction for the town road, thinking fondly of these ladies and several more, but somehow found himself headed up the drive to Rathborne a short time later. He reined in abruptly. There was no use in trying to fool himself. The woman he wanted was waiting there within the walls of his own house. A sudden heat stirred his blood.

In his grandfather's time—even in the days of his own father—things had been quite different. If a Rathborne had wanted a woman, he took her and damned the consequences. No one had thought the worse of either of them, and many a child born locally had carried some hint of Rathborne blood.

And when a man had wardship of a young heiress, it was not uncommon for him to press her into marriage by the simple expedient of getting her with child.

But Vera was not really his ward, and he was not a ruthless scoundrel. He had even sworn a solemn oath to do her no harm. Giles was angry with himself for kissing Vera. How could he have done such a stupid thing? One taste of her lips and he had been like a tippler with his ale, parched and avid for more. There must be no repetition of last evening.

Giles took out his linen handkerchief and mopped his brow. By St. Michael, a vigorous conscience was a terrible cross for any man to bear.

He turned off the drive and spent the afternoon hearing the complaints and problems of his tenants. That effectively put all thought of Vera from his mind.

The sun was long past its highest point when he turned homeward. After stabling his horse, Giles repaired to his study, careful to avoid a chance meeting with his "ward." He carefully put all memory of the previous night aside and drafted a letter. An hour later he watched from the window as a messenger rode out, bearing his sealed missive.

He was about to send for Vera, but decided that the setting was too dangerous, and went looking for her instead. He found her down in the kitchens, up to her elbows in flour. There was a dusting of white powder across her left cheekbone and her eyes were alight with excitement, which drained away when she looked up and saw him.

He put his fists on his hips. "Have you no better way to fill your time than playing at scullery maid?"

She brushed back an errant lock that had fallen from her chignon, leaving a floury trail through her hair. "I am used to a more active life, my lord. Surely you do not expect me to sit upon a cushion and embroider knots of flowers all day, or whatever fine ladies do," she snapped saucily, "while you ride out as gaily as a lark?"

He glowered at her, ignoring the stares of interested servants. "If you wish to ride out with me, you have only to say so."

"Very well. I wish to ride out with you tomorrow, my lord."

"Tomorrow," he said shortly, "I will remain within doors."

"Then I shall ride out alone."

He stepped down into the kitchen. "No, you will not. You shall be plying a needle in the parlor instead. Audry says most of the garments are too large for you and must be redone to fit. However, she has other duties and cannot be tied up with taking in your garments when she is needed elsewhere, so you must see to the task yourself."

Vera cast him a look of pure amazement. "Surely you are not serious!"

"Indeed I am. If you are to mingle with the ladies and gentlemen of the court you must first learn to be at ease among company. I have sent a message to Finch Hall. We are going to pay a visit to Sir Francis and his sister, Lady Anne. She will be a good influence and serve as a model of ladylike decorum for you to emulate."

A mulish expression settled on Vera's face. "If you expect me to prepare my garments before going to Finch Hall," she announced roughly, "you will likely wait forever. I have not the least notion of how to go about it. I cannot sew a proper stitch to save my life."

Giles leaned across the table and glowered at her. "What nonsense is this? All women sew."

"Not I, my lord. I have tried and I have no talent for it."

He smiled. "Then from where did obtain your clothing?"

"I bartered for it or st—" She stopped abruptly.

"Stole it?" He slapped his hand down on the polished surface with the sound of a thunderbolt. "By God, woman, I thought you were a *noble* outlaw, not a common thief!"

Vera gasped aloud and rose so quickly that she almost overturned her chair. "If you will recall, my lord, I have never pretended to be anything but what I am. It is you who are trying to make a lady out of me."

"Fool that I am!"

Vera's cheeks reddened and her eyes snapped with anger. "And, if I may point out, my Lord of Rathborne, if you do not call taking an inheritance that is not yours thievery, then you are a greater scoundrel than I thought."

"I am doing it for Rathborne," he countered through clenched teeth.

"Yes," she replied sharply. "*Lord* Rathborne."

Her withering disdain struck him like a blow to the face. He fought back a hot retort. How dare she doubt his motives! Vera waited for his rebuttal of her charges. When none came she felt greatly disappointed. That did not stay her wicked tongue. "I see the truth renders you speechless," she murmured and spun around on her heel.

Giles let her stomp away, unanswered. She might think what she would of him; he would be damned before he ran after her with explanations. He was still too angry to reply without saying things he would regret later, and the urge to curl his strong fingers about her fair white throat made them fairly itch.

Giles left and made his way to the stables. Another brisk ride would clear his head. He hoped it would clear it of Vera. She seemed to have taken possession of his thoughts in an alarming way. He had Caliph saddled and rode out across the park in a dark mood. A flight of geese soared across the autumn sky, but Giles was too absorbed in his own thoughts to envy them their freedom.

Perhaps he should have taken Vera into his confidence from the first, he thought. In the beginning he had not wanted to share his family history with her, for fear she would use it against him in some way. He had not realized what an innocent she was then. And was still.

That was a part of his black mood. It was her very innocence that drew him to her. That, and the passion he sensed in her, untried yet awakening. The man who first roused her slumbering sensuality would be fortunate indeed. The reward would be well worth the effort and ...

Giles suddenly noticed his surroundings. The land had gradually slanted upward, and the wind now ruffled his hair and sent his cloak winging out behind him. God's teeth, he was halfway to Briarton Ridge and he had not managed to stop thinking of Vera for a single moment. What power had she over him that she could bend his thoughts her way, waking and sleeping?

He removed his jeweled cap and raked his fingers through his thick curls. There was no help for it. He had to get her somewhere where there were people around them. The serving wenches were of no use for that. He knew that if he swept Vera into his arms right now, they would all fade away into the shadows like any well-trained servants.

He had to get her to Finch Hall in short order, where the presence of Francis and his sister and all the attendant activities would put these thoughts of making love to Vera from his mind.

God help them both if it did not.

With Giles gone and time on her hands, Vera decided to familiarize herself with Rathborne. The house was huge and, to her, a veritable palace. She wandered up and down staircases and in and out of empty rooms. She discovered state rooms and boudoirs, storage cupboards and sewing rooms, and rows of empty servants' quarters beneath the eaves. A few of the bedchambers were intact, with massive canopies or hangings about the carved beds, and intricate linenfold paneling. On the end of the center wing was a library complete with globes of the world and maps of the heavens. She examined them idly, wondering what their patterns signified.

Her favorite of all was an old-fashioned solar, with comfortable window seats and an embroidery frame next to a tapestry-covered chair. It looked to be just the place to curl up with a lute or a book of poems. Vera sighed and went to the window. The glass panes reflected her gown and the goffered band that stood out around the square neckline to frame her face. "I am a sparrow in swan's feathers," she said aloud.

She pressed her fingers against the glass. It felt cool and smooth, but was filled with wavy lines, and minute bubbles like clear and perfect seeds. Looking beyond the glass, she scanned the drive for signs of Giles's return. Then her glance fell on the maze. Wolf lay stretched out by the entrance, his noble head resting on his paws. Vera uttered a quick oath. By the saints, she had been so upset that she had completely forgotten Tal's message! She was to have met him in the maze at dawn, and here it was well past the time.

Now that she had the layout of the house committed to memory, it took only a few minutes to work her way down and out by the nearest door. She flew across the lawn, praying that Tal had waited. He might be worried sick by now.

Without looking left or right, she ran between the high green walls of the living maze. The hedge was ten and twelve feet high in places, and it cast long shadows in the morning sun. In some places where the gardeners had not yet trimmed it, the new growth reached out from either side to form a shifting canopy of leaves. Vera felt as if she were in the corridors of a dim, forgotten world at the bottom of the sea.

The first time it had taken her almost an hour to work out the pattern. Her memory had let her down regarding the message, but it served her well in finding the secret court in its green heart. In no time at all she had penetrated to the center. A figure stepped from the green dimness where the hedge walls met at right angles and she ran eagerly toward it.

Vera laughed and opened her arms wide. "Oh, I was so afraid you had not waited!" She flew across the grass and almost into his arms. "Pray forgive me!"

"I would forgive you anything," a low voice replied. "Only tell me that bastard has not harmed you!"

She jumped back with a squeak. "Hewe! What in God's name are you doing here? Where is Tal?"

He shifted his weight from side to side nervously. "'Twas I who sent that message to you, Vera. I have come to rescue you from the foul clutches of Sir Giles."

"What?"

The youth dropped to his knees and grasped her hand between his two sweaty paws. "Come away with me, quickly. I have two mules hidden in yon woods."

Her heart plummeted. "Is it Tal? Oh, tell me quickly! Is he ill . . . dead?"

"Nay. All are well."

Vera peered down at him. His face was pale and tinged with green, although that might be a trick of the dim light. His eyes were goggly and there was a distinct odor of strong drink on his breath.

"What ails you, Hewe? Have you been quaffing too many tankards of home-brewed?"

"Nay, sweeting. If I am drunk, then it be with love. But Hewe Purdy will not let you be sacrificed to the lust of that foul . . . That foul . . ."

He frowned with the effort. Hewe was not a man of words. He struggled back to his feet, aware that he had made a tactical error, and tried to pull her into his arms. His lips, moist and trembling, caught the corner of her mouth. "One kiss from your sweet lips and I will willingly die for you."

Vera smacked him. "Have you gone daft? Leave hold of me, you cloddish lout!"

"But you do not understand. I have come to take you away. . . ."

She shook her head. "I cannot go with you. I do not wish to leave. Get that through your head once and for all."

He was about to importune her again, but Vera saw there was no use in arguing. "I am sorry I cuffed you, Hewe," she said contritely, "but you must not carry on so. I have given my solemn oath and I must remain here at Rathborne."

Vera saw that he did not—or would not—understand. She turned and ran back the way she had come.

Hewe stared after her. He could not divine why she had refused the chance at freedom. Oaths were made to be broken, especially oaths to tyrants. But that was what came of having truck with nuns and convents. They put flighty ideas into a young girl's head. Vera, Vera. . . He would have cared for her tenderly. More so than Tal and Garvin had, selling her into slavery to the Lord of Rathborne.

He would have to find a way to convince Vera before it was too late.

* * *

As Vera went back toward the house, she heard a horseman coming along the village road. Surely it was Giles, she thought in panic. If he noticed her coming from the maze, he might see Hewe leave it, too. She did not want to have to explain what they had been doing there together. Hewe was a fool, but a good-hearted one, and he had been her friend as long as she could remember. She would not let anyone harm him or hold him up to ridicule.

Vera stepped behind the tall wall of rhododendrons, then gathered her skirts and ran pell-mell down an alley of ornamental trees. She turned at the dovecote and made her way through the formal shrubbery at a more decorous pace. If anyone saw her from the park now, it would appear she had just come in from a sedate walk.

Smoothing the folds of her skirts, she rounded a corner—and ran right into Giles. It was like running into a stone wall. "Jesu!" she exclaimed, to cover her astonishment. "Pray look where you are going."

His hair was rumpled and his eyes were dark as sloe berries. "I am going nowhere at all, madam. I have been standing here this past quarter hour, watching you and that skinny-shanked stripling come and go!"

Her eyes grew wide in alarm. How large he looked, and how fierce. She took an involuntary step backward. Giles caught her by the arm.

"Is he your lover? Is he?"

"I have no lover," she protested. "Nor do I want one." A diversionary tactic seemed in order. "You men are all alike, telling me what to think and what to do. I am sick to death of it!"

She broke away from him and ran into the house, wishing that Hewe and Giles were both a hundred miles away. Or that she was.

Vera was late coming down to the evening meal and Giles went up to her chamber. She was sitting at the table in a gown of cerulean silk trimmed with silver. Her eyes were reddened as if she had been weeping.

"You are late to the table," he said.

"I do not wish to sup with you tonight," she answered curtly.

Giles chewed his lip. He was as reluctant as she; yet there was a need for her to spend as much time learning to be a lady as possible. Tension filled the room until it seemed that something soon might snap. It was his temper.

"You will come with me or I shall carry you down. You are about to make your debut to the world at large and we have much to discuss. We shall be joining Francis and his family at Finch Hall for several days. He writes that his sister is eager to make your acquaintance."

"God's teeth, have you gone mad?" Vera exclaimed, knocking her hairbrush from the table with her elbow.

Giles retrieved it absently and set it back in place. "Are you so unsure of your part? I am not. You will do very well, you know."

"I know nothing of the kind. I am not ready."

There was a catch in her voice and Giles saw the rapid pulse at the base of her throat. "Do not be overly concerned. We have already gone over the list of possible guests, of how you are to conduct yourself with them, and—" A glint came into his dark eyes. "—of which topics, regardless of what *you* might think, are totally unsuitable for the conversation of a lady."

She rose, surprised once more by how much he towered over her despite her height. How could she explain to him the panic she felt at the very thought of going to Finch Hall? Especially when he had told her that he admired her courage?

Vera shivered. It would go wrong, she was sure. Somehow she would give away their scheme and they would both be ruined. That was a burden she did not want to shoulder. Against her sudden pallor, her eyes became the deep color of sapphires. "Do not make me do this, Giles. I beg of you. Not so soon."

A strange thing happened to Giles. He was filled with a sudden urge to comfort her. Cupping her chin, he tilted her face up to his. "This is no formal affair. There will be no grand balls or twenty-course suppers. And you are not alone, sweeting. I will be by your side."

That helped. It seemed odd that a few words spoken in a low, concerned tone could ease her smothering panic. What he said was true—they were in this together. And Francis would be there as well. Vera closed her eyes and sighed in relief.

Giles thought she was swooning. Instantly he put his arm about her waist to support her. He was surprised at how light she was against him. How warm and soft and feminine. There was no time for more. Her eyes flew open and she jerked free of his embrace. Her skin, so pale a moment earlier, was becomingly flushed, but she was rigid with anger.

"How dare you!"

He stepped toward her and she stepped back. "Are you afraid of me, Vera?"

"I am not afraid of any man!"

"Little liar." He came closer and clamped his hands down lightly on her shoulders. Her mouth trembled and he wanted to kiss it. He intended to kiss it.

Until she stopped him with her sharp tongue. "Remember your promise, my lord. Otherwise I shall gut you like a hog!"

Giles refused to play her game. He pulled her close and pressed a chaste kiss upon her forehead. Even that light touch sent tremors through her body and raised an ache in his. He pretended not to notice it. "I will have Audry bring up a tray."

When he was gone she sat down again and picked up the fabric she had been trying, most inexpertly, to hem earlier. Lady Irme had spent an hour showing her how to ply the needle, before throwing up her hands in despair and asking for a headache powder.

Vera looked at the seam in the piece of heavy brocade. It had seemed a simple task in the older woman's hands; but the line of tiny stitches begun by Irme had turned into drunkenly wavering tracks of thread in a dozen different sizes. At the moment, the needlework was the least of Vera's problems.

She had been certain that Giles was going to break his promise and kiss her on the mouth again. If he had done so, she doubted that she would have had the willpower to stop him.

She jabbed the needle through the brocade and into her thumb and muttered a number of angry phrases that no real lady would have even known.

The lessons continued daily and now included geography. Giles told her of his adventures in far-off lands as part of her education. How she envied him!

After each lesson he would help her find the place upon his globe and maps: Italy, India, Africa; Virginia and the unknown lands of the New World. Geography became her favorite subject. Giles showed her his compass and astrolabe and even taught her something of how he navigated by the stars.

One evening before supper Vera had time on her hands and went off to the library to spin the globe and dream of voyaging to such wondrous lands herself someday. Outside the oriel window rain fell in sheets. In her mind she stood upon a tropical shore beneath a blazing sun. She was so lost in her imaginings she did not hear Giles enter until he was right behind her.

"Your supper grows cold, Vera."

"Oh!" She jumped and turned around. He was dressed in scarlet and black and looked so handsome he took her breath away. Belatedly she realized that she was staring.

"How—how fine you look, my lord." She groped in her mind for a comparison. "Like...like Lancelot...or perhaps Roland."

Giles was startled. He wondered where she knew of such heroes. Vera's knowledge of history seemed scant. In his grandfather's time the old stories had been widely told; since then they had fallen out of favor. Vera might be familiar with tales of King Arthur's knights, but a French hero like Roland was not likely to be well known in the countryside—at least, not in the company that she had kept.

He walked to the fire and turned to face her. "And where did you learn of these heroes? At your convent school, mayhap?"

Vera frowned as names and bits of story filled her head. "No, my lord. It was a poor place devoted to prayer and good works, and not endowed with grants or noble patronage. These scenes that flash before me are pictures on cloth. A tapestry, I believe.''

Giles went stock-still. ''Tell me about them.''

Her eyes were closed now as she tried to bring the colorful images into focus. ''There were banners...a whole field of them with the French lily in silver and gold and others bright as poppies. And the helmets of Roland and his men were embroidered with golden thread...their swords, also. There were flowers in one corner. Red and blue and yellow, shaped like six-pointed stars. And King Arthur's sword was surmounted with a jewel of red glass, which glowed like the rubies that you wear tonight.''

That was all. She tried to hold on to the memory but it was elusive as smoke. The more she tried to grasp it, the less substantial it became. ''I cannot remember more,'' she said regretfully. ''It was very beautiful to me and I loved to look at the tapestry. But I cannot remember where I saw it.''

Thunder rumbled as Giles stared at her thoughtfully. The disquieting idea that had flitted through his head had come back again even stronger. First, her ease in finding the heart of the maze, and in finding her way back as well—and now the tapestries. He rubbed his jaw. There was one way to find out.

''Come with me.''

Taking a taper to guide them, he led the bewildered Vera out of the study and up a flight of steps to a small room near the top of the house. Lightning flashed three times in rapid succession, filling the room with a blinding white light. A tapestry hung on the far wall, stirring slightly with the draft from the open door.

She went to it, amazed, as Giles held the taper near.

There were Arthur and Galahad, Gawain and Lancelot mounted on their destriers. And, just as she remembered, there was Roland against a background of banners. The armor of men and war-horses was embroidered with thin silver filaments, tarnished with time; but the helms of the men gleamed with thread of purest gold, as bright as the day it was sewn there.

There were also figures of St. George fighting the dragon and of tragic King Harold meeting the Conqueror. Vera examined the tapestry carefully.

"How curious. This is very like the one in my dreams." She pointed to King Arthur, the mighty sword Excalibur gleaming in his brawny hand. "Even to the jewel in his hilt. But there are many more figures here and the hanging seems to be much smaller in size."

The tension drained from Giles. Vera did not recognize the tapestry that had once hung in the minstrel's gallery above the Great Chamber. He was oddly relieved. For a few minutes he had been swayed by an insane notion. He had almost believed that he had really found the missing heiress.

Giles came from the stables dressed in his favorite riding garb. The brown leather doublet was soft and supple from wear and made a pleasing contrast with his gold shirt and hose. Everything was ready for their departure from Rathborne. Everything but Vera, Giles realized. He left the courtyard where the party was assembling and approached the house.

"Where is the Lady Verena?" he asked a passing servant.

"She is still in her chamber, my lord."

Giles gritted his teeth. What now?

But as he started into the house Vera came down the staircase. She was dressed in a riding habit of dark blue silk with a red velvet cap and gloves. Her short cloak was of the same silk and trimmed in red so that she looked as if she had been born to a life of privilege. Giles shook his head in wonder. It was uncanny! If Verena Stanton had survived, he imagined that she would look exactly like this.

He gave Vera a deep and formal bow. "My lady, will you ride out with me this fine day?"

She lifted her chin. "I shall be delighted to accompany you, Lord Rathborne."

He took her arm and was amazed to feel the fine tremors that shook her. He leaned down, brushing her ear with his lips. "Have no fear. You look as much a lady as the queen herself."

Vera laughed and felt more at ease, although she did not quite believe him. She was glad that they were trying out her masquerade at Finch Hall first, rather than at court. She had only four months to practice and polish and learn everything she needed to know to pass as a lady of birth and breeding. Four months did not seem nearly long enough.

Giles tossed her into her saddle. Vera would have liked to ride astride rather than sidesaddle but he had prevailed on that score. Still, it was good to be riding again on a lovely, crisp morning.

They set out for Finch Hall in fine style, accompanied by servants, a cart with chests of clothes and their feather beds and pillows, and a dozen of Giles's men. They had not gone five miles when a groom from Rathborne came riding hell-for-leather after them.

"A message for you, my lord. Lady Irme said to seek you out and deliver it at once."

Giles was concerned. "Has any accident befallen her?"

"Nay, my lord." He pulled out a thick sheet of vellum, folded and impressed with a wax seal. "This did come for you from Hampton Court."

Giles took the missive and glanced at the seal. From the queen. He broke the wax and opened the letter. "God's death!"

The fury in his voice astounded Vera. "Evil tidings, my lord?"

He did not answer for a moment. A muscle knotted in his jaw as he clenched the paper in his hand. It was with difficulty that he mastered himself. Without meeting her eyes, Giles folded the letter and tucked it inside his doublet.

"It seems you are saved from visiting Finch Hall, my lady. I shall have to send a message to Sir Francis and the Lady Anne with our regrets."

Vera sent a silent prayer of thanks heavenward. The ordeal was averted. She was saved!

Her gratitude was premature. It turned to shock a moment later, when Giles repeated the gist of the letter. His voice reached the entire company, but his real message was for her alone.

"Our gracious Queen Elizabeth, along with other messages, sends greetings to you, Lady Verena. Her majesty, in her infinite kindness, expresses delight and joy that you have been restored to us."

His words were soft, his eyes hard. A ball of apprehension formed in Vera's chest, cutting off her breath. She did not know what was coming, but she suspected it was something bad.

Giles's hands clenched on the reins. "As to the matter of your wardship, my lady, the queen is taking my request to be named your official guardian under advisement. Meantime we are summoned to Hampton Court to join the queen's company there."

"To court!" Vera gasped. The bottom had just dropped out of her world. "But I am not—" She caught herself in time. "When?"

His eyes were blacker than midnight. "We leave immediately."

Chapter Ten

Vera stood at the rail of the pleasure barge as it glided smoothly along the Thames. The late afternoon sun was warm upon her face. Her light wool gown and traveling cloak were a rich, glowing brown and her cream-colored ruff was sprinkled with tiny gold beads. A velvet cap trimmed with gold threads and a jaunty plume topped her hair, which was pulled back at her nape. The outfit was far finer than anything she had worn at Rathborne and bolstered her shaky confidence. If she was to help Tal and her friends she must play her role well.

But in the meantime there were wondrous sights to be seen and no reason not to enjoy them. One of which was the master of Rathborne, magnificent in black and gold beside her. She had noticed the other ladies casting interested glances in his direction and felt a twinge of satisfaction at the envy in their eyes as they looked at her. Truly, he was a splendid figure of a man.

"Oh, look!" she said, distracted from her thoughts.

Another barge, painted blue and gold, sailed downriver past them. It left a shimmering silver wake upon the surface of the Thames. Vera had never been on the water before and was fascinated by the river traffic. Her eyes were alight with pleasure.

"This is what it must be like to be a swan," she announced, to no one in particular.

Giles laughed. It was rather strange to see familiar things through her impressionable eyes. He remembered his first time on a barge and his barely suppressed excitement. Odd how her company took him beyond the bad times and into the softer memories of his past. He wondered when he had lost his own sense of innocence and wonder. Until now, he had not even realized that it was gone.

They drifted gently around a bend. Vera craned her neck in hopes of spotting the palace through the trees. Giles had enlivened their journey by telling her anecdotes of the queen and her courtiers and of Hampton Court Palace. It had been built at a cost of 200,000 gold crowns by Cardinal Wolsey, who had prided himself that it was fit for a king. His words had proved the clergyman to be an unlucky prophet: in a vain attempt to protect himself from the enmity of Henry VIII, Wolsey had given the splendid estate to his liege, complete with elaborate contents. Nevertheless, the gift did not save the former favorite from the king's displeasure.

There was something else in the history of Hampton Court that intrigued Vera even more. It was said to be haunted by the ghosts of Henry's queens. Catherine of Aragon had lived there with him—and later Anne Boleyn. When lovely Catherine Howard had been condemned to follow Anne to the block, she had managed to slip away from her jailors. She had hoped to find the king in his chapel and throw herself upon his mercy.

Before she could reach the door she had been intercepted and dragged away down Hampton's long gallery, screaming in fear and anguish. To this day dozens of servants and courtiers had reported seeing the shade of lovely Catherine Howard running down the gallery leading to the chapel—and many more had heard her ghostly screams. Vera shivered.

As she strained her eyes for a first glimpse, Giles watched her, as had become his habit. Since she had seen nothing of the world, her surprise and enthusiasm amused him greatly.

Suddenly Vera gave a cry of excitement as the red brick chimneys of the palace showed above the distant treetops. She had been disheartened to learn that they would not visit London town on their way. All disappointment vanished as the barge floated around a curve and the towers and turrets and gates came into view. The grounds and buildings covered many acres. In her wildest dreams she had never imagined it to be so huge. Or so splendid. She had thought Rathborne very grand, but it was dwarfed by a single wing of Hampton Court. She felt as insignificant as a mouse.

Giles stepped closer. He had seen the awe in her eyes change to panic. His gloved hand covered hers. "Chin up, little coney. It is not as daunting as it seems."

As he smiled down at her Vera experienced a most peculiar feeling. It started in the pit of her stomach, filled her chest with a pleasant ache and then flew up to dazzle her eyes. And her brain. She could scarcely bear to look at Giles; neither could she tear her gaze away. Every detail of the moment was indelibly imprinted on her mind. The rhythm of the water and the warm breeze that ruffled his curly hair. The ruby-and-diamond earring he wore in one ear caught the sun.

The sweep of his dark brows and the white of his teeth against his tanned and handsome face. The amber glints that lit the depths of his eyes and robbed her of both speech and breath....

Vera felt dizzy and hot, as if struck by a sudden fever. She felt her cheeks burn with the heat of it. Giles seemed as disinclined to look away. He lifted her bare hand to his lips while she stood frozen in place. His mouth grazed her skin and left a tingle in its wake.

"Welcome to Hampton Court...Lady Verena."

The barge bumped against the landing and she lost her footing. She reached out to him instinctively just as he threw his arm about her waist to keep her from falling. The jostle of the other passengers kept them pressed close for half a minute. When they continued on, neither she nor Giles moved. His arms tightened around her until her cheek was cradled against his velvet doublet. She could hear the steady drum of his heart.

She felt safe, protected and yet thoroughly overwhelmed. The heat of his body, the shelter of his arms were more potent than wine. A brief madness came over Vera. She wanted to twine her arms around his neck and stay in the shelter of his embrace forever.

Then someone pushed past them and Giles set her away from him with firm, impersonal hands. Vera's blush deepened and she could no longer meet his eyes.

He looked down at her gravely, a small frown between his brows. He had been a fool to drag her into his intrigues. She did not fully understand the consequences. In the beginning he had not thought of her as a person, but as a tool to save Rathborne and free him for adventure. Things were much more difficult now that he knew and admired Vera. He tried to rationalize by reminding himself that he was doing this for his people, too. It was a small salve to his prickling conscience.

He was suddenly afraid for her. The good Lord knew what might happen to such an innocent within the lofty walls of Hampton Court. "It is not yet too late to end this masquerade. If you lack the heart for it, Vera, tell me now."

Anger replaced her embarrassment. It blazed in her eyes and burned through her veins in righteous indignation. How dare he insinuate that she would go back on her promise! Vera drew herself up haughtily. "My lineage may not be noble, my lord, but my word is as good as yours. I swore you an oath that I would see this scheme through. I intend to honor my vows."

She pushed past him and hurried to the gangplank. As she stepped foot on the dock a thrill of danger ran through Vera. The die was cast. There would be no turning back.

Grim-lipped, Giles caught up with her. "Remember, lady, if aught goes amiss, that I gave you your out and you refused it."

He hustled her along toward the octagonal towers of Anne Boleyn's Gate. They passed through the gate with its famous clock that also told the phases of the moon and the high tides in London, and into the enormous courtyard beyond. There was nothing tender in the set of his jaw or his strong grip bruising her arm. Vera was certain that she had imagined the previous idyllic moment.

Directly ahead loomed another brick gateway almost identical to the first. It opened into a second courtyard. She tilted her head. More spires and orna-

mented chimneys held up the azure canopy of sky.
Astounding!

While Vera turned this way and that, trying to ab-
sorb the massive dimensions of Hampton Court, Giles
took out a square of white linen and mopped a film of
sweat from his brow. If all went well he could turn Vera
over to one of the queen's ladies within the hour.

And not a moment too soon.

Jesu, what had he been thinking of, to pull her
against him in such a way? And within sight of not only
their fellow passengers, but the palace windows as well.
He tried to tell himself that it was only the need of a
man for a woman. Nothing more.

The unacknowledged truth, hovering around the
fringes of his thoughts, was that something wild and
untamed in Vera called to its twin lurking within his
own breast. Like called to like, the old saying went.

A strolling couple glanced their way and the woman
laughed before turning away. Vera's frank admiration
was drawing attention from the jaded courtiers.

"Cease your gawking," Giles said in a low tone,
gripping her arm more tightly. "They will take you for
an ill-bred bumpkin with hayseed in your hair."

Vera rounded on him. "You are bruising me!"

He released her immediately. She rubbed her arm,
scowling up at him. "How can I help but gawk, when
I have seen nothing to equal this in all my life? Unlike
you, my lord, I was not born to such magnificence."

He gave a rasp of laughter. "Nor was I. But that,
madam, is another story for another day."

There was no time for her to question him further.
They had arrived at a splendid archway set with a
wonderfully carved wooden door. Two floors above,
a window was flung wide. A dark-haired beauty in a

gown of yellow damask leaned out the open casement. "Lord Rathborne!" she cried out gaily.

Giles appeared to have gone deaf. He pushed the door open and steered Vera inside quickly. "Wait," she said. "Did you not hear her, Giles?"

"I heard nothing." He steered her swiftly down the corridor toward another door. "And remember—you must call me Rathborne or my lord when we are in public."

"But a lady called out to you. I heard her quite clearly."

"That was Lady Laetitia Lattimore," he said viciously. "And she is a lady only in title, not in character. It would do you more harm than good to make your first appearance at court under her wing!"

Vera mulled that over. "I understand you," she said finally. "I am not a child."

He pulled her into an alcove abruptly. Another small courtyard was revealed beyond the rippled panes of glass. He grasped her shoulders hard.

"Listen to me, Vera. You are less than a child in this game. Where worldly matters are concerned you are an infant . . . a helpless babe in arms."

Her face took on the sulky look Giles knew so well. He wanted to kiss it away. He wanted to turn around and lead her out of there. Take her straight back to Rathborne before her innocence was corrupted by the false flattery and easy virtue of certain circles within the court.

"I wish to God," he said, "that I had never brought you here."

Vera yanked back from him to hide a sudden sheen of tears. "You are a coward," she accused. "You are afraid that I will shame you before your fine friends!"

She stumbled away and he tried to catch her. Giles succeeded only in part, linking his arm through hers as Vera tried to pull away. "God's death," he said, slipping an arm around her waist. "Be still for a moment, woman!"

A clear, commanding voice startled them both. "It seems that my lord of Rathborne has learned no wisdom since last we met. At least at our last encounter the pretty maid in his arms was willing!"

Giles suppressed an oath. Keeping an iron grip upon Vera, he pivoted her around with him. "The queen," he murmured in her ear.

Vera stood stock-still. *The queen!*

Yes, and it was Gloriana in full glory. Elizabeth was above middle height, with a regal and graceful carriage. Her gown was white tissue heavily embroidered with silver and gold, and topped with an overgown of black velvet sewn with the same embroidery and encrusted with rubies and pearls. It was held out with a wide French farthingale and made a striking contrast with her pale, creamy skin and the wonderful red-gold hair that might be a wig. Vera wondered but could not tell.

The queen floated toward them, followed by her colorfully gowned ladies. A necklace of pearls and diamonds wreathed the monarch's elegant neck and a curious diamond brooch, in the shape of a frog with ruby eyes, was pinned to the center of her décolletage. Beneath a coronet of rubies, pearls and gold was a patrician and keenly intelligent face. Eyes the color of topaz scrutinized Vera and her companion. Ice was building behind them.

Giles tugged sharply on Vera's sleeve and bent his leg in low obeisance to his liege. "Majesty."

Vera suddenly found the ability to move again. She dropped in a deep curtsy, afraid to rise without permission. Afraid to even raise her eyes. She had imagined her introduction to her monarch as a much more formal affair than a chance meeting in a corridor. Especially when it appeared that she had been struggling to escape from an overamorous suitor.

There was a long silence, punctuated by a muffled titter from one of the queen's attendants. Giles could have ground his teeth in chagrin. The queen demanded virtue of her ladies and had little tolerance for romantic intrigues carried on beneath her roof. And, no matter how much he wished otherwise, he knew exactly the impression he and Vera had just made.

"Surely, my lord of Rathborne," Elizabeth challenged, "a man of your countenance and station can find a lady less reluctant to share your favors."

Before Giles could reply, Vera was on her feet again. "By your leave, majesty, I must tell you that appearances are deceiving. It was no lovers' quarrel which you have witnessed, but a moment of my own temper when Lord Rathborne admonished me for my rustic manners and tried to improve them with a lecture. You see, majesty, that I am not used to being in grand company."

Elizabeth motioned and Giles rose. "What say you, my lord?"

"Any fault must be mine, majesty, for I have no such excuse."

Giles stood protectively beside Vera. Egad, the wench was honest to a fault. And brave in her ignorance. He knew, as she did not, that her future and his hung in the balance. She must not suffer for it.

The queen moved so that the light from the window fell full upon Vera's calm countenance. "A lovely maid, fresh and fair of face." She eyed Vera thoroughly, raising an eyebrow. Tall as she was, Elizabeth had to look up. "Radiant with health and tall as the Queen of Scots, I vow."

She addressed Giles. "Here is a riddle, my lord. We do not know her yet we do. You think you know her yet you do not. Who is she?"

Giles let the tension ease from his powerful frame. It was going to be all right. "Majesty, I beg your gracious leave to present to you my ward, the Lady Verena Stanton."

Vera did not know what to do. She dipped another curtsy and gave Elizabeth a shy smile. The queen tapped a long finger against her cheek.

"You have the look of Allys, who was lady-in-waiting before her marriage. And you have none of her discretion." She smiled graciously at Giles. "I am glad that you have brought the Lady Verena to us. As to the other matter, my lord, you are too hasty. She is not yet your ward. Perhaps never."

She signaled her ladies, who had been stunned by Vera's boldness. Before they swept away, the queen paused. "Send the girl to Lady Stafford after the banquet tonight. There is a position open for a Lady of the Presence Chamber. Perhaps Lady Verena will be chosen to fill it."

Giles was filled with consternation. He prayed the queen was not in earnest. He heard Vera take in a breath as if to speak, and headed off trouble. "You are very gracious, majesty. As you see, Lady Verena is speechless at the great honor you propose."

Vera wanted to protest, but a nip of her arm from Giles stopped her from speaking. The queen smiled. A glimmer of gold shone in those shrewd amber eyes.

"Perhaps, if Lady Verena pleases me, I shall be inclined to find a wealthy husband for her."

The queen and her women continued up the corridor in a rustle of silk and velvet, leaving Vera in a state of bedazzled astonishment—and Giles in a cold fury.

Vera was weary and more than a little bored. After procuring refreshments, Giles had dragged her around from pillar to post as he made his arrangements. Only her inborn sense of direction had kept her from getting lost in the endless maze of rooms. She wanted desperately to get away from the press of people and lie down in a quiet corner—if there was such a haven to be found within Hampton Court.

But now they were on their way to yet another part of the palace, where he was to confer with Sir Francis Drake. Vera had been excited until she learned that the meeting was private and that she was not to meet England's hero just yet.

Suddenly she stopped and faced Giles with that steady, unwavering look that he was growing to know all too well.

"God's eyes, Giles, but I am tired to the bone. You cannot convince me that in all this great pile of brick and wood there is not one quiet corner where I might curl up and catch forty winks."

Giles was ready to tear at his hair in exasperation. He sent her a quelling look. "Once you get an idea into your head there is no prying it out, is there?" he snapped. "For the last time, there is nothing that can be done until I speak with Lady Stafford. It is she who will assign you your dressing closet.''

To his surprise, Vera laughed. ''Am I being mulish again? That is what Tal calls it. But, my lord, in truth I find this place overwhelming. I am not used to such noise and to having a swarm of people all about me—nor am I used to following you all day like a stray pup. I fear it makes me waspish.''

Strangely enough, he sympathized. He had no liking for being penned up himself. Aboard ship it had been different, with the seas stretching blue to the horizons and the possibility of adventure and danger ahead. But the crowded corridors and anterooms of Hampton Court had the same effect upon him as they did upon Vera. He would be heartily glad to return to the freedom of Rathborne once this business was finished. He stroked his chin. ''I should not let you out of my sight for a moment. However, there is a place where you might rest undisturbed—if you will give me your word to follow my instructions implicitly.''

''Oh, I shall.''

''You are a brazen little baggage,'' he told her. ''The man fool enough to marry you will find himself living beneath the cat's paw, I vow!''

She did not reply. Vera had won the battle, but no good would come of crowing about it. Or crying about it.

Giles led her through myriad connecting chambers and down stairways until they came to the ground floor. He pulled her back into an open doorway rather abruptly as two gentlemen came around a corner ahead. ''Alençon,'' he whispered in Vera's ear.

She was vastly disappointed that she had only a glimpse of the French prince. The Duc de Alençon had come courting the queen, and there was great talk throughout the country that she might take him for a husband. Even deep in the forest precincts she had heard of this French prince. Rumors of an impending marriage had caused widespread concern throughout the country. Elizabeth's councillors were greatly agitated over the matter. Alençon was some twenty years the queen's junior. Still, stranger unions had come about in the cause of international alliances.

When the coast was clear, Giles and Vera stepped out of the doorway. "He is not very handsome," Vera said, "although rumor says he is quite charming. Do you think the queen will wed him?"

"Nay. She likes him well enough, but toys with him like a cat with a mouse. While an alliance with him is rumored it holds off those who would be England's enemies. When he has served his purpose she will send him packing back to France. You will see."

They followed a roundabout path. Giles showed her an out-of-the-way corner off a wide corridor, with instructions to stay there until he retrieved her. Vera sighed with gratitude as she settled herself upon the cushioned bench.

"Speak to no one," he warned. "And draw no attention to yourself in any way. I doubt you will see any but servants while I am gone. I shall return shortly."

Vera wiggled her feet out of her slippers as he strode away and tried to lean back against the wall, but her bell-shaped skirts and their support prevented it. Servants bustled past from time to time, intent on their tasks. The minutes crept by. Vera fidgeted. She was unused to having time sit idly on her hands.

After a time she employed herself by counting the sections of paneling along the opposite wall. Then she counted the squares that made up the sections of paneling. She counted the bosses within the carved squares. Then she counted the rosettes within the bosses....

An hour passed, then two. By the time she heard the clock strike again, Vera had counted every pane in the windows at the opposite end of the room, breaking them down by size, shape and color. She was restless and bored. *If I sit another moment I shall lose my mind!*

She rose and felt the soothing coolness of the flags beneath her stockinged feet. Slippers in hand, she moved away a few paces, avoiding the main corridor, since she had given her word to Giles. But he had not said a word about the small area leading off of it. As she paced up and down she discovered a small, windowed door hidden beneath a tapestry. It led to a secluded garden.

Vera glanced over her shoulder. Not a soul was in sight, for once. Surely Giles could not object to her taking some air in the privacy of this sequestered spot. She slipped out into the garden, still carrying her shoes, and walked along the mown grass that edged its quiet gravel paths.

A statue of Diana graced the garden, and a pond, its near edge fringed with oriental weeping trees, lay in its center. Yellow water lilies floated on its serene surface and dragonflies hovered over it, flashing glimpses of deep, iridescent blue. She wished suddenly that Giles were here to see it with her.

Vera was so enchanted by the scene that she did not hear the voices at first. When she did they were already close at hand.

Remembering Giles's stricture, she stepped back beneath the trailing greenery. The ground was damp and the wet earth squished beneath her feet. She hoped fleetingly that she would not ruin her stockings. A branch scraped her head, knocking her cap off. It fell out in the path but she snatched it away in the nick of time. Two gentlemen came around the bend and stopped not six feet away.

"Banish your doubts, Simmier. I, too, can play at games."

"Do not be fooled by her, *Monsieur*, I beg! The Queen has no more intention of marrying you than you have of adopting the Reformed Faith."

"Nonsense. I tell you Elizabeth will have me. She has told me so in private. But first she must prepare her council."

Vera peeked out, startled, when she picked up the thread of the conversation. The last speaker was the same man she had glimpsed earlier. He was small and swarthy, with a wide mouth and large nose dominating his homely face. Crinkles of good humor alternated with lines of dissipation; yet, with his warm smile, graceful movements and intelligent eyes, he had a distinct and captivating charm.

So this was the famous Duc de Alençon, who was brother to the King of France and had come to England to woo Elizabeth. She leaned closer for a better look at him through the screen of leaves.

The little white dog that trailed behind the two men sniffed and ducked under the cascading branches. He was so small that Wolf would have gobbled him up in a single bite. He stopped and gave a yap of discovery when he came upon Vera. She stood as still as possible, ignoring him. The dog refused to take the hint. He had found a likely companion and wanted to play.

Tail wagging, he picked up a tiny stick and dropped it at her feet, barking encouragingly. *See what a fine stick I have brought you, lady. We shall have a game, you and I. Come, throw it. Throw it!*

Vera found herself in an exceedingly awkward position. If she stooped to pick up the stick they would surely see her. If she did not, this miserable yapping creature would give her away. She tried to shoo away the dog, praying that the *duc* and his minister would move on before her presence was revealed.

It seemed that they meant to stay on the spot forever. Monsieur picked up a bit of gravel and chucked it at a lily pad. A fat frog leapt away in a blur of green and splashed into the water.

Simmier sighed and waved his hands in a show of Gallic dismay. "She merely toys with us by dangling her hand and throne as a glittering prize, but she does so only to keep Spain at bay."

"Have no fear. My eloquence will win the lady's hand, as it has her heart." Alençon favored the statue of Diana with an elegant bow, as if it were the lady in question. "If I had the will I could melt even this stony heart."

He gave his friend a wry smile. "Elizabeth loves me. Am I not her 'dear Frog'? She wears my diamond favor pinned to her breast and praises my poetry. It is all a matter of time. And of perseverance in the cause of Eros."

Simmier shrugged in exasperation. "I waste my breath."

"Indeed you do. And your time, as well. If I am not mistaken, you have an appointment...."

Their voices trailed away as they started toward another door on the far side of the garden. Vera heaved

a sigh of relief. The dog had discovered a bow on her
slipper and was trying to eat it. She stooped and waved
him away.

"Shoo, you fiendish mutt!" she whispered. "Off
with you!"

As she straightened, Vera discovered that stooping
had been a serious mistake. The hoops of her collapsible farthingale had nested together, pinching a quantity of fabric and a slender branch between them. The
more she tried to free herself, the tighter they were
wedged. She cursed softly and yanked at her gown,
setting it swaying about her feet.

The dog was ecstatic. Vera heard a crunch of gravel
and seized the small beast. "Hush, you little sausage
with legs!"

The slippers fell to the ground and the dog eagerly
licked her face. Vera listened with bated breath. She
heard nothing. Whoever it was had passed on.

Then the curtain of greenery parted and a man
chuckled. With a sinking heart she saw that it was
Alençon. His brown eyes twinkled. "Is this how lovely
English ladies while away their afternoons? Come out,
I beg of you, *mademoiselle*. There is a comfortable
garden seat nearby."

Vera did not know what else to do. She stepped
through the opening he made in the weeping branches,
cradling the traitorous dog against her bosom. The
creature yelped with joy and jumped out of her arms
to greet his master. Alençon waved him away. To Vera's chagrin the dog obeyed and curled up happily in
the grass.

She dropped a curtsy. "I had . . . had lost an earring
here earlier, *monsieur*, and come to retrieve it."

The shrewd eyes surveyed her with humor and just a touch of suspicion. "A strange place to lose an earring, *ma chère*. If I may be so bold, what was a lady of the court doing in such . . . such an *interesting* place?"

"I am not a courtier, my lord, but a simple country maid newly arrived today."

He raised his brows. Her garments were expensive, yet her manner was charmingly farouche. He smiled down at her stockinged feet. Perhaps she spoke the truth.

"Allow me, *mademoiselle*." He retrieved her slippers and led Vera to the garden seat. Without asking her leave, Alençon put the slippers back on her feet. Where other ladies might have chided or flirted with him, she accepted his assistance without question. A most intriguing young woman.

He switched tactics and addressed her in rapid French. "What is your name, if you please?"

Vera did not answer. She had heard someone call her name. It came again. Oh, no. Giles! Now the fat was in the fire.

He came around the corner and spotted her but not Alençon, who was hidden from him by the marble Diana. "God's death, Vera! Where the devil have you been? I distinctly told you to wait for me."

Giles was still five yards away. He broke off, realizing belatedly that they were not alone. The *duc* laughed and winked. "My thinking is not slow. I understand, *mademoiselle*, why you were—ah, searching for your earring, was it not?—in such an unusual place. And I see that I am considerably *de trop*."

He backed away with a graceful bow. "Let it not be said that Alençon stood in the way of a lovers' tryst. *Adieu, mademoiselle*. We shall meet again."

By the time Giles reached Vera, Alençon was gone and the little white dog with him. "Jesu, first the queen herself and now Alençon! With your stockinged foot in his hand! Can I not leave you alone for a single moment?"

Under ordinary circumstances she might have retorted that his "single moment" had stretched into several hours; but this circumstance was most extraordinary. She tried to gather her scattered wits. "Giles," she exclaimed, seizing his sleeve. *"Monsieur*... he spoke to me in French!"

Giles scowled. Another female turned soft for that ugly little lecher. He had expected better of Vera. He pried her fingers from his arm. "Surely that is nothing to become so excited about."

"But Giles," Vera blurted. "He spoke in French and I—I understood him."

He stared at her as if she were mad. *"Mon Dieu, cher demoiselle,"* he said in the same tongue. *"Ce n'est pas possible!"*

"It most certainly is," she said angrily... and then gasped. "You see, Giles? It is true. But how can such a thing be credited?"

"Do not try my patience. You learned the language at the convent where you stayed."

"Nay. 'Twas a poor place filled with good women of simple English stock. The mother superior could read Latin, it is true, but we spoke no French, my lord. So what is the answer?"

Giles narrowed his eyes. He had gone pale beneath his tan. "Perhaps that is something you can best tell me. Perhaps you have been stringing me along with your tales of bandit chiefs and convents." He clamped his hands down on her shoulders. "What is the truth, then? Who are you?"

She was equally pale and her violet eyes looked enormous against the translucency of her skin. "I am Vera," she said softly. There was a catch in her voice. "That is all I know—and all I want to know."

Her eyes brimmed over. With a sob she turned and fled.

The garden door opened and a lady in green came through. She was of middle years, small and thin with faded blue eyes and a gentle smile. "I am Lady Stafford. The queen pointed you out to me. We saw you from the balcony."

Startled, Vera looked up. She thought that she had seen three tall windows earlier, but realized belatedly that they were the arched openings of a recessed gallery on the top floor, open to the air. She wondered with a qualm if her strange meeting with Alençon had been noticed as well. The queen was known to dislike any ladies who dallied too indiscreetly with her favorites; an unmarried woman letting a man hold her unshod foot was certainly in that category.

"If you will come with me," Lady Stafford said with a kindly smile. "I shall show you to your dressing closet."

Vera followed Lady Stafford, glad to escape further questioning from Giles, yet uneasy to be away from his protection. Somehow she had not expected that they would be parted from each other.

Lady Stafford led her up wide stone stairs and through a long gallery with a ceiling so high it dwarfed the huge windows along the right-hand wall. Vera felt very small in this great, sprawling palace.

And very much alone.

* * *

Two gentlemen of the court stood in the shadow of an archway, their tennis rackets in hand, as Vera passed by, accompanied by Lady Stafford. They could not help noticing her wide-eyed wonder as she took in the intricate carvings of the paneled walls and the marvelous tapestries hanging at intervals. When she craned her neck for a better look at the curious gilded knobs that hung down from the ceiling, the men had difficulty in containing their laughter.

The older one, a sophisticated Frenchman, waggled his dark eyebrows in appreciation. He was a noted connoisseur of beauty and in need of a rich wife. Unfortunately, the combination, coupled with the single state, did not occur as often in England as he would have liked.

"Ho, Lumleigh," he said softly. "I believe I have been struck by Cupid's arrows! That face...those eyes!" He sighed. "Tell me, what innocent little lamb is this, brought to the court for shearing?"

Lord Lumleigh's eyes were a curious shade between yellow and green. With his sharp features and red hair, he looked like a cunning fox. "You aim high, De Vigny. That sweet confection is the Lady Verena, heiress to the Stanton estates."

"Ah, Rathborne's ward. A lucky dog, he!" The Frenchman stroked his beard. "Then there is no hope for me, alas."

Lumleigh grinned malevolently. "Look for no marriage banns from that direction, my friend. I have heard from an excellent source that they were seen quarreling earlier today. And when Rathborne laid hands on her, Lady Verena assailed him in a fury.

There is no love lost there. You must try your charm on the lady and win her away."

"You give me hope." They sauntered down the stairs together and went out to the tennis courts. A smile played about De Vigny's mobile lips. To think he had not wanted to come to England with Alençon. Here was a way to satisfy his need for riches and his love of beauty. He grew pensive.

"There is one problem. If a suitor must seek permission of Rathborne, I foresee great difficulties ahead of me. The man has no liking for me since I cut him out in the affections of the fair Jane Lindsey."

Lumleigh laughed. "Since he sailed off on the Spanish Main and left the damsel alone for your plucking, you mean. But you are borrowing trouble unnecessarily. Despite Rathborne's plans to become Lady Verena's guardian, the queen has not yet agreed. The lady, and her considerable estates, will be bestowed on whichever man the queen chooses to favor."

De Vigny rubbed his hands. "Excellent! I am in good standing with her Gracious Majesty and shall make certain that she favors me in this as well. A word in her pearly ear from Alençon will aid my cause."

"Jesu, man! Is this a farce you act for me or are you in earnest?"

"Where love and beauty are concerned, my friend, I am always in earnest. I do not admire your pale English beauties, but that one..." He kissed his fingers. And she had wealth in the bargain. "I shall not rest until I have her."

Lumleigh shook his head. "You seem to think the outcome is certain."

"But I am, *mon ami*. I have a romantic soul and a practical mind. The Lady Verena and her fine fortune will both be in my hands before the month is out. And," he added silkily, "I believe that I shall enjoy the one every bit as much as the other."

Chapter Eleven

Lady Stafford led Vera through some of the state apartments and then along an upstairs corridor. She stopped before a narrow door carved with the Tudor arms.

"Here you are, Lady Verena. This dressing closet has been assigned to you. I hope you may find it snug and comfortable. It is rather small but you will sleep in it only on the nights you are not attendant on the queen. Otherwise you will bed down on the floor of either the Presence Chamber or the Privy Chamber. I shall speak to the queen as to when she wishes you to begin."

"I thank you, Lady Stafford. You are most kind."

Vera curtsied. Her mentor *was* kind, and efficient, but Vera was anxious to be alone for a while. Privacy was a scarce commodity in a human beehive like Hampton Court, and solitude was rare and priceless.

The dressing closet proved to be a small, airless room designed primarily for a modest amount of storage and the changing of one's clothes. Most of the floor space was taken up by the boxes and hampers of clothes she had brought with her from Rathborne. The place was dark and stifling.

The room contained a feather bed fit into an alcove and something that was either a tall stool or a low table. A covered chamber pot was set in one corner and a bowl for washing up was placed in the center of the single shelf.

As her eyes became accustomed to the gloom, Vera found the sliding screen that let light through a hole cut in the wall. She peered through it and found her view was limited to a section of roof and a gap of sky framed by chimney pots. Why any young girl would think it a boon to be made lady-in-waiting at court was beyond Vera's comprehension.

A knock sounded. Vera sighed. No hope of solitude just yet. She thought of not answering, until Giles called her name. She opened the door. "I would invite you into my hovel, my lord, but I fear there is not room enough for us both."

He folded his arms across his chest. "I take it that you are ill pleased with it."

"I would far rather sleep outdoors beneath a hedge," she said flatly, "than be cooped up in here like a rat in a trap. All it lacks are manacles on the wall and a decaying skeleton to make it a perfect miniature dungeon!"

He tilted back his head and roared with laughter. "A thousand women would give their eyeteeth to trade positions with you, and count themselves lucky in the bargain."

"Then they are silly creatures and deserve what they get."

When he peered inside, Giles had to agree. "Egad! I would not kennel my dog in such a place. But cheer yourself up, sweeting, for in a few weeks we shall be back at Rathborne."

He chucked her under the chin and smiled. "I must wait upon the chancellor now. If I am late, meet me in the banqueting hall for supper. At the table beneath the tapestry of Agincourt and the Field of Cloth of Gold. Until then, keep to yourself. But wait, I almost forgot something."

Giles drew out a chamois pouch lined in velvet and spilled a golden necklace into his palm. "A gift to celebrate your first visit to court. Wear it in good health."

Vera picked it up carefully. It was designed to encircle a woman's throat. Links of chased gold flanked the intricate design in the center, an elegant likeness of a bejeweled swan.

"How lovely! It looks very old. Why would you give me such a costly gift?"

There was a tiny pause. "I found it at a goldsmith's shop across the river," Giles said quickly. "It reminded me of you."

She grew pink with pleasure. Giles constantly threw her off her guard; one moment he was shouting at her, the next surprising her with his thoughtfulness.

He took the necklace from Vera and placed it about her throat. He managed to tangle the clasp in her hair and took several moments freeing it—not because it was caught so thoroughly, but because her nearness aroused him. She was flame to his fire.

As Giles's hands brushed the back of her neck, Vera's entire body reacted. Shivers ran along her nerves. Her skin tingled and her breasts ached. Recalling that night back at Rathborne in his study, she hoped, she feared, that he would touch her that way again.

The necklace ringed her throat and she knew he was fumbling with the clasp. When his fingers rested on her flesh again she felt hot and cold and almost sick with

longing. *Hold me, Giles. Kiss me again. Giles...
Giles... Giles...*

The same phenomenon was affecting him. With
every breath, Giles took in the fresh scent of her hair,
and it fairly intoxicated him. His fingers shook as he
worked at the tiny clasp. Silky strands drifted across the
backs of his hands. He wanted to weave his fingers
through the shining tresses. He wanted to turn her
around and pull her into his arms, to cover her sweet
face with rough kisses.

Instead he lifted her hair higher. Another mistake.
The nape of her neck was soft and white. It looked so
tender and vulnerable, so inviting of a lover's kiss. He
imagined pressing his lips against it, inhaling the perfume of her body, reveling in intimacy. Sliding his
mouth along to the curve of her shoulder. Reaching his
hands around to cup her breasts and pull her hard
against him....

"Ouch!" Vera yelped. "You are pulling my hair out
in chunks!"

They were back on familiar footing. "If you would
hold still instead of wiggling like a bucket of min-
nows, we would already be done!"

He gave another tug and the clasp came free, along
with a few strands of her hair. They shone like threads
of spun gold. After slipping the strands inside his doublet, he settled the necklace without further trouble. It
seemed that the only way he could deal with her safely
was when his temper was high.

Thank God he had gotten her away from the iso-
lated situation at Rathborne. Their slightest touch sent
sparks flying. It would take very little more to set it
flaming out of control. Giles frowned. Perhaps he
should pay a visit to Laetitia Lattimore, that most ac-

commodating lady; but even as the thought came into his mind he pushed it away. His old pursuits no longer tempted him. Jesu!

"Turn around," he said gruffly.

She did as his bade her. The necklace was perfect, suiting her clear features and virginal beauty. "You will outshine them all tonight, Vera. I shall have to draw my sword a dozen times, I vow, to keep your admirers away."

"The admirers of my pretended fortune, you mean." She smiled a bit lopsidedly. "I know what I am, my lord. A chicken dressed up in peacock feathers."

"Nay, my lady. 'Tis you who have it wrong. You are a lovely little swanling, a cygnet newly fledged and still unsure of testing your wings. But a swanling, all the same."

He went out, closing the door. The room was dark as a tomb, but at least Vera was alone at last. She sat on the narrow wooden boards in the alcove, which served both as bench and sleeping pallet. Her thoughts were jumbled. It was not only the newness of her surroundings nor the odd discovery that she understood French perfectly well that confused her.

It was Giles.

He had become very important to her in the past few days. She had not realized the extent of her feelings until she was away from him. It frightened her. She was not of his world, nor was he of hers. She had no intention of continuing to live a lie. Despite his impression, once this sorry charade was over she meant to return to her former life. Giles needed her only until—and if— the queen granted him stewardship of Lady Verena's fortune. Once that was obtained, even if "Lady Verena" disappeared for a second time, Giles would still have stewardship of the estates for the crown. He would no longer need her.

Vera could not think past that point. There must be something wrong with her. She did not want the queen to find her a husband; that was the stuff of nightmares. Vera knew that she could not keep up her pretense. She had not wanted Tal to play matchmaker, either. Perhaps some women were not cut out for marriage, and she was one of them.

She dabbed a bit of moisture from the corner of her eye. Vera imagined ending her days as a spinster drudge in some unhappy household, milking the cows at dawn and setting the hens to lay. She hated hens. They were greedy and stupid and mean, and gave painful pecks when you stole their eggs from the nests. She imagined herself yawning over piles of mending and sewing while the household slept, working by the light of a single rush to save expenses.

The doleful picture had an opposite effect. Vera burst into laughter. Her one attempt at hemming had been so disastrous that Irme had picked every single stitch out again. A friendly bird landed on the window hole and cocked its head at her from side to side.

"Well, friend robin, you would laugh too if you could read my thoughts. If I have to depend upon my needlework skills for room and board I shall surely starve!"

The bird chirped and flew away, and Vera took off her outer garments and curled up on the feather bed. In less than a minute she was sound asleep.

When she awakened, Vera was astounded to realize she had slept for hours. Since this was her official introduction to the court, Giles had warned her to wear something befitting her first appearance in high company.

She chose a splendid gown of white silk and an overgown of heavier silk brocade the color of rubies. Her ruff was pleated lace edged with rosettes of tiny gold beads, a red cabochon garnet in the center of each. It was a perfect accompaniment for the swan necklace Giles had given her. After perching a small headpiece of ruby velvet with gold trim upon her hair, she was ready.

Taking a deep breath, Vera opened the door and went down the stairs. She let the steady stream of people carry her along toward the banqueting hall. Many noticed her but more did not, and no one spoke to her at all. As they drew near, music and tempting aromas wafted out through the open doors. Her stomach rumbled; she had been sorely neglecting it.

Still no one spoke to her, but she was the object of several curious glances. When a hand caught her sleeve she jumped.

"Giles!"

Her relief was so palpable he should have laughed. Instead he grew irritable. "Did you think I would desert you? I have been waiting here for you this past half hour." He shouldered his way through the crowd, drawing her after him. "Are you hungry?"

"Hungry?" She sent him a quizzical look. "I am beyond that. I am fair famished!"

Someone overheard and guffawed. Face flaming, Vera let Giles lead her away. She could hear him muttering beneath his breath.

The banqueting hall had been built by Henry VIII. The paneled walls and ornate roof were carved in marvelous patterns. As she took her place beside Giles,

Vera could understand why it had taken five years to build, even with workers laboring by shifts in candle-light.

The room was filled with ladies and gentlemen in silk and velvet and shimmering brocade. The hall was hot, although the doors stood open to the air, and filled with a confusion of scents: cinnamon and cloves, roast meat and fresh bread, sweat and perfume. At one end the royal dais stood empty. Elizabeth, Giles explained in answer to her question, dined in solitary splendor in her own chamber except on feasts and other special occasions.

A page approached with a whispered message for Giles. He made his apologies to Vera. "I shall return shortly. Mind you, keep out of trouble while I am gone."

"As long as there is food before me, my lord, you need have no fear."

She passed the time in eyeing the fine ladies and gentlemen in their elaborately decorated garments. When the Duc de Alençon came in with his party, he glanced casually in her direction, then made her a po-lite bow. Vera flushed to the roots of her hair. She was relieved when he passed by without stopping.

There was no sign of Giles. Vera stopped looking for him when the food was brought out, carried aloft by the servers. The quantity and variety of the courses boggled her senses: jellied eels and poached fish, ven-ison and larded boar's head, mutton and hare pie with onion. Roast capon and duck...and swan, cooked and covered again with its own plumage. Vera's appetite fled when she saw it. Wistfully, she remembered the simpler meals eaten by a camp fire in a forest clearing.

She closed her eyes, wishing she could transfer herself back by sheer longing.

Someone sat beside her. She opened her eyes, expecting to see Giles, but the man in blue velvet was a complete stranger. He was handsome, with swarthy skin and brown hair and eyes that changed from gold to greenish-brown in the flickering light of the tapers. Vera recognized him as a member of the Duc de Alençon's party.

His arms snaked around her waist to support her. "Are you faint, *ma chérie?*"

His English was excellent, his accent intriguing; but it was the friendliness of the man's tone that surprised and cheered Vera. She had been feeling completely alone and invisible, the tiniest speck of sand in this great sea of people. He must be a kind and gentle person to have noticed her bewilderment and hastened to her aid.

She tendered a shy smile. "Nay, my lord. Only weary." Tears were foreign to her nature, but as the gentleman smiled warmly back, they threatened to fall. "You must think me silly, but I am a stranger here and your kindness has touched me."

He kept his arm around her waist and leaned closer, until his mouth almost brushed her ear. "If it is a soft bed and a warm lover that you seek, you need look no further."

Her indignation was real. He saw that he had erred. Court ladies were women of the world, and used to its wicked ways. This maid was as innocent as she looked. "I see that you are new to court and not used to the arts of dalliance."

"Not such vulgar ones, to be sure!"

He recovered his composure quickly. The English miss was an original! His smile was ingratiating and filled with the proper degree of humility. "Forgive me if I have given offense, *mademoiselle*. My nonsense was only an attempt—a very poor attempt—to make you smile."

Vera was poised for flight, but hesitated. His apology seemed genuine. Giles had warned her not to be shocked by some of the warm banter she would hear among the courtiers. She had reacted like a nun to a bawdy joke. Still, she need not let him think she encouraged his boldness. She drew herself up with dignity.

"Indeed you startled me, my lord. I am not used to court ways."

"You are right to scorn me for my forwardness, *mademoiselle*. It is evident that you are a virtuous maiden and that I have clearly overstepped my bounds. I pray you will forgive me for my jest and let me be known to you." He took her hand and kissed it. "I am Charpentier, secretary to his grace, the Duc de Alençon."

Giles stopped in the doorway of the banqueting hall and searched the crowd. He'd been detained by Lord Grenleigh and was later than he'd realized. He spied Vera's bright head in time to see Charpentier lifting her hand to his lips. His blood heated. Charpentier was hanging out for a rich wife. Worse, he had a reputation as a lecher and a cad. Giles could imagine no worse influence on an innocent like Vera.

There were rumors of Charpentier's past. It was said that he had fathered a child on a young Frenchwoman of gentle birth, who claimed they had entered into a secret marriage. Charpentier had repudiated her and her unborn child, saying that she had fabricated the entire story. The truth would never be known. The distraught young woman had been sent home in disgrace and her family had turned her away as well. Three days later her body had been fished out of the Seine.

Vera was no match for a man of such persuasive and polished address.

Moving through the crowded room, Giles cursed beneath his breath, wondering how word of Vera's identity had gotten about so quickly. Charpentier was only the first of many, he knew. A wealthy heiress with no living relatives was a prize too great to resist. And when the woman in question was as lovely as Vera ...

Giles made his way past the tables. It did not matter that she was only carrying out a charade; the danger to Vera was still real. Charpentier was a rake with a winning smile and a reputation where women were concerned. Women like Laetitia Lattimore and Jane Lindsey were sophisticated women of the world—fair game for the amorous court swains. Vera was not.

Giles kept his eye riveted on Vera as he worked his way closer, for fear Charpentier might induce her to leave with him. He could not hear the Frenchman's words, but he understood the message in his eyes as they rested upon her. She blushed and smiled, and still Giles pushed his way through the glittering throng until he reached them. He rested his hand menacingly upon the hilt of his sword.

Charpentier rose to his feet and made a negligent bow. "I am sorry to relinquish your so charming ward to you, Lord Rathborne. I had hoped you would be detained. Indeed, I had dared to hope that you would not come at all. Lady Lattimore had spoken warmly to me of you."

"I do not wish to be discussed behind my back."

The look in Giles's eye was murderous. Vera thought it was because Charpentier had spoken out of turn. Her heart plummeted. First Lady Anne, now Lady Lattimore. She really knew very little about Giles or his past.

Charpentier smiled. "It is difficult not to discuss one of your heroic persuasion, my lord. Your exploits are on everyone's lips. I refer, of course, to your adventures with Sir Francis Drake."

Giles would have liked nothing better than to plant his fist in Charpentier's face. He restrained himself with difficulty. "You have inherited a noble title along with that damned handsome face of yours, Charpentier. If you wish to live long enough to enjoy them both, you had best learn not to practice your wiles upon a woman under my protection."

"Mon Dieu!" Charpentier held up his hands in mock horror. "So fierce is he! I must leave you now, Lady Verena, or your bold champion will run me through with his sword. Adieu, *demoiselle.*"

The Frenchman could not leave without another swipe at Lord Rathborne. "You mistake my intentions, my lord. Had I known this fair beauty to be the Lady Verena Stanton, I would not have even ventured to smile in her direction. It is well known that you intend to keep her—and her fortune—for yourself."

The rush of heat to Giles's face was nothing to the ferment roiling inside him. It was as if the man had read his thoughts. "Step outside, Charpentier, and I'll flay your miserable hide from you."

Vera stood up so quickly she almost overturned the bench. Her long sleeves upset her pedestal cup, sending a stream of wine down the table. She clutched at Giles's sleeve, hoping to ward off an incident.

"Please, my lord, do not brangle on my account. And you need not worry about my virtue. I am not at all susceptible to the blandishments of . . . of smooth-tongued fribbles!"

The astonished look on Charpentier's face was comical. Giles did not laugh. He was too busy fighting the primitive urge to send his fist smashing that visage. Prudence won out. To create such a scene would give him enormous pleasure, but it would bring censure down on Vera's head as the source of the altercation—and too many eyes were already turned in their direction.

He took Vera's arm. "Come away. We will leave this 'smooth-tongued fribble' to his meal. And may he choke on it."

Vera let him escort her outside and into the formal garden. Dusk had fallen while they supped, but the sky was still aglow with a faint purple light that deepened quickly to indigo. The river turned from tarnished silver to jet and crickets sang their scratchy songs along its verge. A wave of homesickness assaulted Vera. If she closed her eyes she could almost believe that they were back at Rathborne. She wished with all her heart that they were.

She sighed without knowing it. Giles saw her face in the dimness, lost and forlorn. "Your first day at court has been wearying."

"Aye. It has been a long day, my lord. If you please, I think that I should like to retire to my chamber."

"You are a gallant little thing, Vera, and I am a knave for driving you so hard." Giles took her hand in his. "But the night is soft and fair. Will you walk with me?"

When he spoke, his deep-timbred voice seemed to resonate in her bones. Vera would have gladly walked barefoot to Rathborne and back if he had asked. "Certainly, my lord. If you do not mean to lecture me again."

They went along the formal paths toward a bench. Strains of music wafted from the banqueting hall on the warm night air. As they passed the open doors she saw two rows of ladies, gay in their rich gowns and jewels, moving in stately rhythm across the floor. The huge circles of their French drum skirts reminded her of something. . . . A vague memory stirred. Hollyhock blossoms.

Vera stopped in her tracks, trying to reel the memory in from the murky waters of the past. A warm summer day. Bees buzzing through the garden. Someone showing her how to make the queen and her ladies from overturned hollyhock blossoms, with smaller blooms for their bodices and fat little buds for their heads. For just a second it was clear as rock crystal, but then the image faded back into obscurity. One detail remained.

Giles had been watching her, frowning. "What is it?"

"I do not know. Suddenly I recalled a pleasant memory from my childhood. Making dolls out of blossoms with a woman. Who she is I do not know— her face is a blur—but she wore a ring with a dark blue stone—a sapphire, I think—on her left hand. The stone had a curious mark engraved in the center and was enfolded in wings of gold.''

A chill wind blew across the back of Giles's neck, raising the hairs along it. His mother had worn such a ring. It was most unusual and certainly rare in England, having been brought back from the Holy Land by his great-great-grandfather. Giles could not remember ever seeing another like it in all his wide travels.

"Where does this memory take place?" he asked, attempting to keep his tone casual.

"Alas, I do not know." Her brow puckered. "It seems long ago and far away, like something from a dream. I recall a brick path leading to a wall with a squat wooden door set into it. Beyond the door lies a small garden with curious little stone figures, and there are cushion plants and hollyhocks and wallflowers blooming everywhere."

Giles relaxed. There was no such place at Rathborne. The frown cleared from his face. "If you meant to avoid my lecture, you must think of something more distracting than hidden pleasure gardens."

Vera smiled. "I was not really trying to change the subject, my lord. If I am to be given a scold, I would as soon hear it now and have it over with."

"It is not a scold but a warning." Giles stopped and took her hands in his, trying to ignore the rush of possessiveness he felt. By God, he would make sure Charpentier kept away from Vera!

"Be careful of those who would be your friend too easily. You must be alert and cautious at all times. And be especially wary of men like Charpentier or Lumleigh. They have charm—when they wish to use it—and the instincts of boars in rut. Men like that, when crossed, will destroy everything in their paths.''

Vera laughed softly. ''You forget, my lord, that I have nothing they want. Since I am not Lady Verena there is no way they can use me to get her fortune away.''

''Jesu, woman! 'Tis not the fortune that concerns me. Even if they knew you were penniless, those lechers would flock to you like flies to honey. There is something about innocence that draws depravity. And when innocence is combined with beauty in a desirable woman, it makes the challenge even greater.''

Beauty in a desirable woman. How easily he said such things. Did he mean them? Her cheeks grew hot and she tried to make a joke of it. ''And what would such villains do? Tie me up in a wool sack and smuggle me to their hidden lairs? I have no fear of such a ridiculous thing.''

Giles was angry that she dismissed his warning so lightly. His grip on her hands tightened. ''Charpentier has no need for wool sacks and moonlight abductions. His weapons are flattery and attentions that lead to seduction. And, from what I witnessed earlier, they appeared to be working their charms upon you well enough!''

''Your anger is unseemly, my lord. I have done nothing to warrant it.''

''See that you do not.''

Vera tried to draw away. ''You are insufferable. Indeed, I would much prefer it if you returned to the banqueting hall and sent Charpentier out in your place!''

''Do you, by God!''

He had felt jealousy before, but never like this. He pulled her into his arms. Restraint had never been one of his cardinal attributes. He was a man of hearty appetites, who went after what he desired and took it.

Vera found herself trapped against his hard chest. She quivered as he drew her closer and her traitorous body yielded against his. His kiss robbed her of breath and sent her pulses pounding. When he finished she was speechless as well.

Giles looked down at her with a light of triumph in his eyes. He ran the ball of his thumb along the curve of her lips. "Well, madam, what do you say now? Do you still wish that I had traded places with Charpentier?"

Vera felt as if he had slapped her. So that was what this was all about—not kisses by starlight, but vain male pride! Her temper flared. After his promises and her threats of retaliation, she had melted like butter in his arms. Fool that she was! Well, she would not add to his conceit.

"I do not know if I would have enjoyed it less or more, my lord. I have not yet been kissed by *him*."

The air hummed with tension, as if before a storm. Before he could reply, he realized that they were no longer alone. Laetitia Lattimore was coming down the path toward them.

"There you are, Giles! I have been looking for you everywhere."

He muttered an oath. Vera took advantage of the distraction and fled. She reached the privacy of her dressing closet after losing her way only once. Pushing the bolt in place, she leaned against the door and wept.

* * *

The next morning Vera was to be given her official audience with the queen. Vera waited outside the Presence Chamber nervously. She had dressed carefully in white silk, having learned that white and black were the queen's favorite colors. At the last minute she had added the swan necklace and a belt of gold links. She might be angry with Giles, but there was no reason to bite off her own nose to spite her face.

The antechamber outside was thronged with ladies and gentlemen. They whispered together, discussing the latest foiled assassination plot, planned by the Queen of Scots against Elizabeth. The words *poison and gunpowder* caught Vera's ear. Several looked her way and two or three stared. She did not recognize one of them. She was almost glad when Giles came on the scene. They glared at each other across the length of the room. He made his way through the crowd toward her.

"I would like to know why you ran off last night," he said in a low, tense voice. "Half the court has heard of it."

She turned a cold shoulder to him. "It is no fault of mine that Lady Lattimore is such a gossip! You should choose your companions more carefully."

Giles's face darkened. "God's death, Vera! If we were anywhere but here I would turn you over my knee."

Her eyes flashed danger. "I am not a child, although you insist on treating me like one."

"No, you are not." He was angrier than he could remember. "And that is more than half the trouble. You are an inexperienced girl in a woman's body!"

"Then mayhap I shall seek more experience." She flounced away.

He started to catch her arm, but Charpentier wedged himself between them. "The lady seems in no mood to speak with you today, Rathborne. I suggest that you leave her in peace."

"God's teeth," Giles thundered, "is it you again? I am damnably tired of you intruding in my affairs. Let us step outside and settle this matter for once and all."

Before Charpentier could reply, the door of the Presence Chamber opened. The Countess of Rutland announced that the queen was ready to receive her courtiers—and was especially happy to meet with Lord Rathborne and the Lady Verena Stanton.

The crowd parted. Charpentier offered his arm to Vera. "Allow me, my lady."

With a brilliant smile, Vera took his arm. "Thank you, sir. I shall be glad to have your escort."

There was nothing for Giles to do but follow them in. As they entered the chamber, Charpentier noticed the swan necklace. "A unique jewel. Lady Stafford tells me that the queen gave such a necklace to her maid-in-waiting, Allys de Breffny, who was your mother."

Vera stiffened. "That liar! Giles told me he bought it yesterday from a goldsmith!"

Charpentier was not a man to let the advantage slip from his court. He leaned close to Vera's ear. "A word to the wise, *chérie*. It is bruited about that Lord Rathborne's coffers are empty—and that he means to replenish them by forcing you into marriage with him. If you need a friend, *mademoiselle,* you may count upon me."

Vera sent him a smile of gratitude. "Thank you, *monsieur.* I hope that I shall not have to call upon your good offices."

The room was rectangular, with a fine carpet from the Orient upon the floor and many tapestries hung between the latticed windows. A single chair with a high back sat empty upon the dais at the far end. Vera took up her place next to Charpentier while Giles glowered at them from across the room.

Elizabeth came out through the other door, followed by her Ladies of the Presence Chamber. Her attendants were gowned in wonderful garments, but the queen put them all in the shade. With her fine, porcelain skin she looked half her true age. Her attire was indeed fit for a queen of England.

She was magnificent in black velvet worked all over in gold in a pattern of mulberries and leaves, with sleeves embroidered with wavy lines to represent the silkworms that had brought wealth to the English silk industry. She wore a stomacher of gold, pearls and diamonds upon her bosom and a matching coronet crowned her red-gold hair. Her long fingers were covered with jeweled rings of every sort and the diamond frog that Alençon had given her was perched upon her shoulder.

The ladies swept their sovereign deep curtsies while the men fell to their knees. "God save our gracious queen!" "Death to the Scottish queen!" came the salutations.

Elizabeth smiled at them. "It is good to know that our loyal subjects are incensed on our behalf. As you see, we stand before you today, healthy and whole. We hope it may alarm the Scots to know that we fully intend to remain so."

There were cheers and relieved laughter. Vera wondered if she were the only one to notice the lines of strain and fatigue beneath the queen's eyes. The assassination plot and its aftermath had obviously caused Elizabeth a sleepless night. Perhaps it was the glitter of gold and jewels that blinded the others to it—or perhaps it was because Vera had also spent a troubled night that she recognized the signs in the queen.

Elizabeth was seated on her dais. She spoke first with Sir Christopher Hatton, her chancellor, who had loved her and served her for many years. That he was deeply enamored of her was a well-known fact and his loyalty was legend. Elizabeth listened to him and smiled.

"English beef is good, but we are thankful that we have our good Mutton to look after our affairs."

The chancellor blushed with pleasure and the courtiers laughed; "Mutton" was Hatton's nickname. The queen bestowed such pet names on her favorites. The Duc de Alençon was her dear "Frog," the Earl of Leicester her "Eyes." He and Hatton had been adversaries for years, jealous rivals for the affection of the virgin queen. Neither favored the suit of the French prince.

Then it was time for Giles and Vera. As their names were called, they came forward together. "Ah, here is our Hunter and his Swan. We understand you crave a boon of us, Lord Rathborne."

"Aye, majesty. Here is the Lady Verena Stanton, who was my late father's ward. She is alone in the world and in need of a protector. I ask that you appoint me guardian of the lady's person and estates until she comes of age."

Elizabeth looked from one to the other, a gold light dancing in the depths of her eyes. "Come closer, child."

Verena did. The Queen frowned. "How old are you, Lady Verena?"

"I believe that I am near to seventeen or eighteen summers, majesty."

"Hah!" Elizabeth slapped the arm of her chair and glanced at Giles. "Eighteen summers! The lady does not need a guardian, my lord. She is more in need of a husband!"

The crowd laughed, but Vera's heart gave a lurch. She had prayed that the queen spoke in jest before, but it seemed that she was in earnest. Vera did not realize that her features had taken on the mulish look that Giles knew all too well.

Giles was suspicious of the conversation's trend. He tried to signal Vera to be cautious. She ignored him pointedly. He might as well be invisible. Vera lifted her chin.

"If you please, madam, I would as leave not have a husband."

That silenced the room. Elizabeth regarded Giles. His jaw was set and his face was flushed with anger. She knew that he and the young lady had quarreled more than once since arriving at Hampton Court. There was more to this tale than she had been told. She decided to smoke out the truth.

The queen twisted a ruby ring on her index finger as she regarded Vera. "If you had no choice but to wed, Lady Verena, would you expect your husband to be an Englishman of noble birth?"

"I would expect nothing, except that we respect each other and live together in harmony."

"A worthy answer and wise beyond your years." Elizabeth cast her golden gaze over the room. "Would that more of the persons in this room subscribe to your philosophy." She fixed her eye upon Vera once more.

"Many a young ward has married her warder. What do you say to Lord Rathborne as husband, Lady Verena?"

Vera's face flamed. She felt as if she were being coerced into a trap. Had Giles set up this scene in his letter to the queen? Charpentier caught her eye and nodded. *You see,* his look said, *I told you nothing but the truth. Rathborne covets your estates.*

She drew herself up. "Lord Rathborne and I would not suit, majesty. We cannot be in the same room without coming to words. Indeed, I fear a prolonged time together might lead to blows!"

Elizabeth considered. "Perhaps you prefer the company of Monsieur Charpentier?"

"Infinitely, madam."

A mask came down over the queen's features. She gestured and Vera came forward. Another wave of her finger brought Charpentier before the throne. Elizabeth took a hand of each and joined them together.

"Your wish is granted, Lady Verena. Monsieur Charpentier approached us yesterday to favor his suit. We give our royal permission for you to be married to him as soon as the banns are read."

Vera's ears buzzed and her vision grew dim. She would have fainted if not for Charpentier's arm around her waist. He raised her hand to his lips and kissed it. Vera was too sick at heart to snatch it away. "My sweetheart," he said, "I can scarce bear to wait so long to claim you."

Elizabeth rose. "Save your lovemaking for a more suitable time, Charpentier." She sighed a royal sigh.

"It pleases us well to make a union between England and France—especially one so near to my heart."

As the queen swept out, Vera glanced wildly around for Giles. Surely he would find a way out of this terrible coil.

But the place where he'd stood was empty. He was already gone.

Chapter Twelve

Charpentier bowed low over Vera's hand. "You have made me the happiest man in all of Christendom. What a sensation you shall cause at the court of France, my love."

Vera hoped that she had not heard aright. "F—France . . . ?"

"Why, yes. Once my duties are finished here we will return to my home in Paris. I shall delight in showing it to you, *ma chérie*. If the particulars can be settled in time we might lift sail before the month is out."

His eyes glowed as he kissed her fingers one by one. "Would that I could take you into some secluded corner and keep you to myself from now until that happy moment. However I must wait upon *monsieur le duc* immediately. Forgive me, my sweet love."

"But of course," Vera urged. "Go to him at once." Go and never come back.

Charpentier let go of her hand reluctantly. A delicious morsel. He could scarcely wait to sink his teeth into her. Metaphorically, of course. "Until this evening then, *chérie*. I shall wait for you in the pond garden tonight. Do not fail me."

Vera was too distraught to answer. Dear God, what had she done!

She wanted to run after Giles and tell him it was all a terrible mistake and to beg him to extricate her from it. That was not possible, as a crowd of unknown well-wishers were gathering about her.

Laetitia Lattimore was among the first to congratulate Vera. Now that her young "rival" was to marry Charpentier, she could afford to be generous.

"La! You are a fortunate creature to find yourself a rich and titled husband within two days of setting foot at court. I would not have thought that you had it in you, you sly minx." Her blue eyes were bright with calculation. "Now that I know you have no claim upon Lord Rathborne, I wish you well, Lady Verena."

Laetitia left, but others took her place. Lady Scudamore, Lady Stafford and little Ellen Beech hurried to add their blessings to the match. Even the Countess of Rutland and the Countess of Warwick proffered gracious good wishes on the upcoming nuptials.

"You are a clever girl," one countess told her. "I would not have expected such a brilliant marriage from a young lady newly arrived in society."

"Yes," the second concurred. "Charpentier is a favorite of the queen and of *monsieur le duc* as well. You will enjoy the benefits of the French court without having to give up the friendships you have established here. I hope you and your husband will be frequent visitors to England."

By the time they were finished, Vera had a headache coming on. She spent the rest of the morning in a daze, carrying out the duties that Lady Stafford, who was Mistress of the Bedchamber, assigned her, and accepting more congratulations on her betrothal to the Frenchman.

Everyone seemed to think she had trapped Charpentier adroitly, by a combination of feminine wiles and cunning strategy. Vera rubbed her temples. Jesu! How had it happened so fast? A fit of pique, a few words spoken in anger, and she found herself saddled with an unwanted fiancé.

Soon to be an unwanted husband, it appeared.

Giles was right. She seemed to land herself in trouble whenever she strayed from his side. Within four weeks or so she would be parted from him permanently. The prospect pierced her heart like a knife.

When the queen went riding with Alençon and his party, Vera was finally free. At the first opportunity she went in search of Giles. Not that she had much hope of running across him in these miles of corridors! She checked the tennis courts and the bowling alleys, the gardens and the stables. He was nowhere to be found. Weary and discouraged, she sought the solitude of her dressing closet.

Even there she could not escape from her predicament. It was the consequence of her own folly, she admitted readily to herself. She had used her sharp tongue as a weapon to get back at Giles. In doing so, she had cut herself to the quick. Before, he had always managed to save her from her scrapes. This time she had gone too far. She had insulted Giles before the queen and court. It had been hurt pride that had led her astray—but he was a proud man. He would never forgive her.

Vera wept into her pillow. Her tears were hot and hopeless. God's teeth, how had she been so blind? How long had she been in love with Giles without being able to admit it?

There was a soft knock at the door. Vera sprang up, hastily arranging her mussed skirts and smoothing her hair back. She opened the door a crack. "Giles?"

Mary Shelton's voice answered. "'Tis only I, child."

Vera opened the door wider. Lady Mary was a kindly spinster and one of Elizabeth's Maids of the Privy Chamber. "Her majesty wishes you to attend her, my dear. She awaits you in the Privy Chamber."

Vera followed her down the hallway, hoping her eyes were not red enough to be noticeable. When they passed through the Presence Chamber into the room beyond, Elizabeth was playing at her virginals. She was an accomplished musician. Her ladies sat around her, one accompanying the queen upon her lute.

When the melody ended, Elizabeth rose and dismissed the others. "We would speak with Lady Verena privately."

They rustled out in a swish of silk and satin. The queen went to the wide window seat and patted the cushion beside her. "Let us have a comfortable coze," she said when Vera was seated. "Tell me, Lady Verena, are you pleased with your marquise?"

"I beg pardon, majesty?" Vera noted that the queen had dropped her use of the royal "we".

Elizabeth smiled. "Truly you are new at court, girl. I speak of Charpentier, the man to whom you are betrothed. How can you be unaware that he is a Marquise?"

Vera flushed to the roots of her hair. "I have not spoken with him above two times, your majesty."

A jeweled finger poked her arm. "What is your haste to wed, then? Are you with child?"

"Oh, no!" Vera was aghast. "I have not been with any man!"

"Giles of Rathborne is a lusty and well-favored rogue. His conquests are too many to count." The queen eyed her shrewdly. She knew the ways of the world all too well. "Since he found you, Lady Verena, you have lived at his home with only a mad old woman and a few servants for chaperon. What is the truth of it? Did Lord Rathborne not please you?" Another jab of that long finger and a short, bright laugh. "Not for want of trying, I vow."

Vera looked down at her hands. She had them clasped together so hard her knuckles were white. "For all my show of temper earlier, I have naught but good to say of Lord Rathborne. He treated me with honor, majesty. I am still a maiden."

"And well for you! Charpentier has had his amorous intrigues, God knows, but he is adamant that his wife be a virgin. His physician will examine you tomorrow to make sure he is not getting used goods."

Vera blanched. She had not thought that far ahead. "Is that necessary madam?"

"If you wish to marry your marquise."

"Marriage is a serious affair," Vera said breathlessly. "I would not want to enter into that estate too lightly."

"Listen to both your head and your heart, young Verena." Elizabeth sighed. "A subject has more freedom than a monarch. You may marry where you choose."

As the queen spoke, she fingered a locket. The front was set with rock crystal and emeralds and the back held a miniature portrait of the Earl of Leicester. Elizabeth gazed at it. She seemed almost to have forgotten Vera's presence. Long ago she had been forced by circumstance to decide between England and marriage to the man she loved above all others. Her face grew pensive. Then she smiled and tucked the locket inside her bodice.

"I have only one bit of advice for you before you go, Lady Verena. True love is a rare and perfect gift from heaven. It should not be squandered."

Vera knelt and kissed the queen's ring. She was unable to meet Elizabeth's eyes squarely. "Thank you, your majesty."

As Vera backed away to the door, she was aware of the queen's sharp gaze following her. Then Elizabeth turned toward the window, her long white fingers caressing the locket chain.

After she was dismissed, Vera was given several duties by Lady Stafford. The queen's wise words echoed in Vera's head the rest of the long, exhausting day. When suppertime drew near Vera intended to seek out Giles in the banqueting hall. Her plans were foiled when she was assigned to help serve the queen in her apartments. It was near midnight when Vera was finally sent away to retire.

She stripped to her shift and lay down upon the bed, trying to think her way out of trouble. Long ago Tal had told her that there was a time for planning and a time for action. Vera sat up in the darkness. It was definitely a time for action.

The hour was advanced when Giles returned to his bedchamber. He had found no solace in the company of friends and even less in his cup of wine. Vera and

Charpentier! God's death, it made him sick to think of it.

From the moment he had left the palace he had been plagued by visions. He had seen Vera's face in the silvered clouds and the smiling moon, in the heart of a lantern flame and the winey dregs of his cup. The breeze whispered her name, and the river, lapping at the breakwater, echoed her scornful laughter.

He was three times a fool. Once for keeping her prisoner, twice for passing her off as the missing heiress and thrice for letting her fall into Charpentier's clutches. How could a simple girl resist the Frenchman's suave airs and handsome face? The man had an ancient title and considerable wealth, to boot.

Damn the marquise and his insinuating ways to the lowest level of hell!

His most dire curses Giles saved for himself. He had driven her to this with his harsh ways, his constant threats and scolds. He had treated her roughly, unable to acknowledge his growing feelings for her. Jesu, how could he have been so blind? When Vera had announced that she preferred Charpentier, it had been like a sword thrust to his vitals. Helpless rage washed up over him again thinking of it.

He stripped off his doublet and shirt angrily. In the course of his life he had imagined himself in love a dozen times. It always started with a pretty face, a dazzling smile, a delectable figure. Each time it had led to nothing but a pleasant dalliance, a summer love that faded gently into autumn memory. Never once had his heart been truly touched. Never once had he looked back more than a time or two in regret.

He laughed bitterly. Things had changed drastically in the past weeks. It had taken a saucy maid with violet eyes and a dagger in her hand to humble him. And, by God, she had at that!

Giles went to the window and threw it open, hoping the night air would cool his fevered emotions. Try as he might, Giles could not tell the moment when he had fallen in love with Vera. He only knew that he loved her with the depth and breadth of his tormented soul.

His love had blossomed from the seed of reluctant admiration rather than dizzying infatuation, and was rooted in affection rather than the passion of lust. Now, his hopes, his dreams, were all wrapped up in one slender woman—who had snapped her fingers in his face and turned her back, for the sake of rank and title.

It would be so easy to bring her down...to show her up as a false heiress, even if he brought himself down with her. A trip to the block or the gallows would at least end his misery. But Vera would suffer as well. Despite all his rage and jealousy he could not betray her by revealing the truth of her identity. He loved her enough that if the choice came down to her marrying Charpentier—no matter that it would almost kill him to see her in the arms of that suave lecher!—Giles preferred it. He would willingly cut off his good right arm before he would cause harm to even one hair of her head.

There was still one other possibility. He could fight for all he was worth to win her. There was still a chance. Otherwise Charpentier would not be so suspicious of him. More than one friend had warned Giles to watch his back where the Frenchman was concerned.

His ear pricked. Stealthy footsteps came along the corridor and stopped outside his door. Giles listened for a knock, which did not come. The door began to open inward, ever so slowly. So, this was how the Frenchman fought his rivals—stealing furtively by night to plant a dagger in the heart of a sleeping rival! Giles stepped behind the arras that covered the alcove.

The door opened wider and a hooded figure slipped inside; the door shut behind it without a sound. Slowly the assassin drew near the bed, which lay in the darkest pool of shadow. A hand reached out toward the bed with deadly intent.

Giles threw back the arras and leapt at the figure. The instant his hands touched the form he recognized his midnight visitor: Vera. It was too late to hold back. The force of his leap propelled them across the room and onto the bed. He heard her breath come out in a rush as his elbow connected with her midsection, and he rolled off her at once. She tried to sit up and flopped back, winded. He leaned over her.

"God's eyebrows, Vera! I might have killed you!"

"I think you have, my lord," she gasped. "Jesu, but you are as hard as a stone column. I swear I shall be black and blue from head to toe on the morrow."

"And well served you will be, for creeping into my chamber like a murderous assassin!" He frowned and held out his hand, helping her up. "A pretty scandal there would be if anyone saw you enter. What on earth possessed you to come to my room like this?"

"I do not care for scandals. Indeed, I have already created one with my horrid temper. Do not send me away, Giles. I—I must speak with you on a matter of grave importance."

Something in her voice alerted him. He bent to the fire and lit a candle. As he stuck the taper in its holder he saw Vera's face, white and tear streaked. A cold hand grasped his vitals.

"Is it Charpentier?" he said hoarsely. "Has he...did he...?"

Vera looked down at her entwined fingers. "Aye. 'Tis Charpentier...."

He was at her side instantly, clasping her hands between his. "By heaven's might, I swear that he will die for this before morning!"

"Nay, my lord, he has done nothing. Yet." She lifted her face to Giles. "He is handsome and charming and kind to me...and if I am forced to marry him, I—I will die."

Her eyes looked into his imploringly. Giles felt his insides turn to jelly; but even as his body reacted to her nearness, his agile brain intervened. A thought struck him and his mouth firmed to a hard line. What tricks did this little heathen have up her sleeve? He willed himself not to pull her into his arms.

"Why, what has caused this change of heart, sweeting? I thought that you were madly in love with Charpentier. That you were entranced by the idea of being my lady the marquise, and mistress of a Paris town house and a fine French château."

Vera looked down, twisting the fastening of her cloak. "I only said that because you were being so hateful! And because I thought the queen meant it as a jest." Her voice quavered. "And because you lied to me about the swan necklace by saying that you had bought it for me, when I know that it belonged to Lady Verena's mother. Charpentier reminded me of it."

The implications of her confession hit him. He could have throttled Vera. "I did buy it for you. It was not until you asked about it that I remembered where I had seen a similar one before—on the portrait in the gallery. That is most likely why it caught my eye. But I did buy it, Vera. And for you. But if you think back carefully, you will recall that the outer design is different. And that the swan in the painting swims one way, while this one swims another.''

She closed her eyes and concentrated. The Long Gallery at Rathborne hovered in her mind and she let herself drift through memory until she stood before the portrait of Allys and Verena. Previously her main interest had been in their features, and in the character their faces portrayed. But her brain had recorded the entire picture.

"God's death!" Vera exclaimed. "You are right. Oh, Giles . . . !''

Giles faced her, hands on hips, his face as pale as hers. The light glittered on the gemstone in his earring. "So," he said wearily. "It all came about because you misjudged me. Jesu, Vera, this is a fine web you have spun for us with your playacting!''

Her eyes accused him. "You are unjust, my lord. It is all your fault that I am here in the first place. If you had not forced me into playing the role of Lady Verena, I would not be in this predicament.''

Giles paced the chamber. She was right to blame him. If he had not tried to save Rathborne she would not be in such a sorry fix. How ironic, that in trying to save his past, he had bargained away his future happiness. He pounded his fist on the table. "By St. Stephen, there must be some way out of this tangle!''

"There is one, my lord.''

He looked up sharply and Vera gathered her courage. "Lady Mary says that I must be examined by the

French physician tomorrow. . . to prove that I am still a maiden. So you see, it is quite simple."

"I do not see anything of the kind."

Vera looked up at him and swallowed. It was plain that Giles did not understand. She needed to be more explicit. "Charpentier insists that his wife must be untouched. If I were not a virgin, he would not want me for his wife."

"And you have a method to make him think you have lain with a man when you have not?"

Vera's voice dropped to a whisper. "No, my lord."

"God's blood, what madness it this? Are you telling me you intend to give yourself to some man between now and daylight?"

"Aye, my lord. And. . . under the circumstances . . . if you would not mind greatly. . . I would prefer that it be you."

He was so angry he wanted to shake her until her teeth rattled. "Let me understand you, madam. To avoid a marriage with Charpentier you would have me seduce you?"

"Oh, no, my lord." Vera met his gaze levelly. "For a seduction to occur there must be one who is willing and one who needs persuasion. So you see, in this instance, I would be seducing you."

It was now or never. Vera unclasped the neck of her cloak. Beneath it she wore nothing at all. The cape fell around her ankles in a heap of silk. She stepped out of it, naked as Venus rising from the waves. "Will you lie with me, my lord?"

Giles gasped. For a moment he thought she was an illusion, a fantasy creature born of his imagination and need and too much wine. But she was more beautiful than he had even imagined. In the candle glow her skin was the color of cream, tipped with palest rose. He must have seen her like this in his dreams, for he knew how the weight of her perfect breasts would fill his hands, how the warmth of her supple body would fill his aching emptiness. He remembered her scent and taste and touch as if he had lain with her a hundred times before.

His breath shuddered through his chest. He wanted her so terribly it was a physical pain. Instead he snatched up the quilt and threw it at her.

"Are you mad, woman? Cover yourself."

Then he turned away. It was the hardest thing he had ever done. Sweat beaded on his brow with the effort of it. "Return to your chamber, Vera. You need not offer your maidhead as a bribe. If you are this desperate to avoid Charpentier, I will find a way to save you. I give you my oath on it!"

As he spoke his hand went to his side in an automatic gesture, as if reaching for his sword. Vera took one look at his clenched hand and rigid shoulders and guessed what he intended. She shivered with premonition. Tomorrow, on some pretext, Giles would provoke a quarrel with the Frenchman. The quarrel would turn deadly and swords would be drawn in a flash of steel.

And regardless of the outcome, matters would be even worse than they were now. If Giles wounded or killed Charpentier, he would be sent to the tower. Perhaps to the block. If Charpentier killed Giles, she would lose...everything.

She hid behind the quilt and stooped to retrieve the cloak, choking back her despair. "If you mean to do something as stupid as fighting a duel, you may save yourself the trouble. I would just as soon throw myself from the highest tower.''

Giles whipped around and caught her shoulders as she held the cloak up before her like a shield. ''Do not even say such a stupid thing! Life is a precious thing, not to be tossed away so lightly.''

''Is that not exactly what you are planning to do?'' Her eyes were wide and dark as violets in the candlelight. Another tear trembled on her lower lashes, then spilled down her cheek. ''Oh, Giles! I could not bear it if any hurt came to you because of me!''

He was drawn to her like a moth to flame, knowing the danger and rushing to meet it. Knowing, too, that once they were lovers nothing—and no one—would ever separate them. The thought was like a drug in his veins. It swept away all caution and the last vestiges of his restraint.

''Vera, Vera,'' he murmured. ''So foolish and so very wise.'' He brushed away the tear tracks with his finger. ''Do not weep, my love. My dearest heart.''

Her fingers splayed across his chest. The cloak dropped to her feet once more, unnoticed. ''I did not know that love could be so painful...and...oh, Giles! I do love you so!''

He groaned and gathered her against him. ''Vera, my sweet termagant! My dear and only love . . .''

His crushing embrace robbed her of breath. She curved into him as if their bodies had been created to fit together, from the very beginning of time. His blood became fevered with the need to possess her. It was like a sweet madness, carrying him past the bounds of intention. Giles twined his fingers in Vera's hair, sending the ivory pins that held it in place tumbling. The shoulder-length locks brushed against the back of his hands like skeins of silk.

Her breasts brushed against the mat of hair that covered his chest. She caught her breath at the sensation. The room was whirling about them and she clung to him for support.

Her fingernails dug into his flesh when he kissed her again. Her heart nearly stopped when his hand covered her breast, then started again at double speed as he rubbed his thumb over the sensitive tip. She was assaulted by emotions, buffeted by a sudden gust of desire.

Giles was shaken by her responsive ardor. His lips found her hair, her temple, her soft cheek, skimming her flesh until finally they touched her mouth. His kiss was possessive and deep. Vera opened her mouth to him as he explored and teased and tasted. Instinct told her what to do and she felt a sharp tug of joy when he moaned low in his throat.

He covered her face with kisses. There was no false coyness in her. She purred with pleasure and threw her head back as he pressed hot kisses against her throat and down to the cleft between her breasts. She was ready to give, willingly, anything he wanted to take. And to take anything he wanted to give. Her body arched against his.

Giles was caught in the same wild currents. He wanted to take her, to make her his, now and forever. Her hair was soft and fragrant and the bare skin of her back was like warm satin beneath his palms. He hungered and thirsted for her.

They were at the boundary between sanity and madness. Another kiss, another moment and it would be too late to turn back. It took all his hard-honed discipline to hold her away from him. Her mouth was dewy and swollen with his kisses, her eyes languid with desire. "Are you sure, Vera?" he asked huskily. "Is this really what you want?"

"More than anything in the world." She leaned forward and pressed her mouth against his chest. He felt her hot breath and then a nip of her small, sharp teeth. "Love me, Giles. Take me. Now!"

He swept her up into his arms and carried her to his bed. The glow from the single candle painted her body with light and shadow. Her hair spilled across the pillow like spun gold. He buried his head in it and wove his fingers through her silken tresses. Her back arched up toward him as her breasts grazed his chest.

He kissed her mouth, her throat, the elegant line of her collarbone. He suckled her breasts until the nipples were taut and tingling. As he roved lower, pressing his lips against the feminine swell of her stomach and the satin insides of her thighs, she began to tremble, not with fear but with anticipation. He eased her knees up and apart. His light, deliberate kiss sent a spasm through her entire body. His probing touch made her cry aloud. When he withdrew his hand she made a sound of protest and held it in place, moving her hips to his rhythm. "More, my lord," she whispered. "Oh! Yes! Yes!"

His need for her was fierce. Giles groaned. It was an agony to hold himself in restraint. He stroked and caressed and fondled while she whispered endearments to him. Suddenly her voice broke off in a gasp of ecstasy and a series of shudders shook her frame. She was ready for him and eager. He straddled her hips, then leaned down and covered her face with kisses.

There was no shyness in her now. Vera smiled up at him. This was how it was meant to be. His mouth traveled down her throat and he whispered her name again and again. She ran her fingertips over his arms and shoulders, reveling in his masculine contours and strength. He kissed her again, passionately. Then he brushed back the hair from her forehead tenderly. "Sweeting, the first time for a maid may be painful, they say. I will be easy with you."

But it was not gentleness that she wanted. She was wild with delight and the need to possess and be possessed. As he sheathed himself in her warmth, she drove up her hips to meet his. A brief resistance, a tiny pang, and then he filled her. She had liked the touch of his hand, but this was so much better. She felt joined to him, body and soul, whole and entire.

They lay together, unmoving, and savored the joy of their union. She could have stayed like that forever, sheltered in his embrace. Then he moved slowly, gauging her reaction. The initial soreness dissolved in waves of pleasure. With every thrust he drove deeper. His hands cupped her buttocks, bringing her closer yet, and her nails dug into his skin.

Giles lost himself in her. The world vanished except for this bed, this woman, this incredible moment of possessing her. He felt as if his heart might burst with love for her. It filled his being. Whatever the risks, whatever the consequences, it was worth the hazard. His body arched like a bow as he plunged into her. The candle guttered and went out, adding its waxy scent to the mingled fragrances of their lovemaking.

The crescendo came like a clap of thunder and he cried out her name again. Vera felt herself swept away, higher and higher at dizzying speed, then whirling down and down into the softness of the feather bed.

When it was over they lay together in the dimness, pretending that their love and its physical consummation could hold back the dawn.

Giles was almost asleep. Vera's fingers traced a tantalizing design across his chest, then stopped. She suddenly realized that he had never said the one thing she most wanted to hear.

"Giles?"

"Mmmph?"

"You did not tell me. Do you?"

"Do I what?"

She pinched him. "Love me, that's what."

He was fully awake now and wanting her as fiercely as before. He rolled over, pinning her beneath his arm. His other hand cupped her breast and squeezed it playfully. "God's teeth, woman! Did I not just prove it to you?"

"No." She caught his nose between her fingers and tweaked it. "Take your hand from my breast and answer me."

He kissed her mouth. "I do love you, Vera, my own. More than I ever thought possible to love another human being. More than life itself."

A sudden fear seized her. "You must swear to me that you will not seek a quarrel with Charpentier. I would rather marry that oaf than see you dead at my feet or rotting in a prison cell for the rest of your life."

He kissed the tip of her breast, laughing at her soft gasp of pleasure. "We shall do neither, sweeting. A better plan has just occurred to me. This morning, when it is time to ride out with the queen's party for Theobalds, you must claim an indisposition and remain at Hampton Court. I will turn back when I learn of it, concerned for your welfare."

"That is not much of a plan," she said, disappointed.

"Hush, you baggage. I am not finished. Meantime, you will go to the stables and have a horse saddled and ready, as if you meant to join the others after all. I will meet you east of the palace, where the meadows end and the woods begin. Then we will ride hell-for-leather for Rathborne, and be married once we are safely arrived. Before anyone learns of it, it will be done."

Vera was uncharacteristically silent. It puzzled Giles. "What say you?"

"Do you ask me out of love, my lord, or pity? Or perhaps from a longing to spite Charpentier?"

He put his hands around her throat in mock threat. "Neither judge nor jury would condemn me if I throttled you for that. You, of all people, should know that I am 'a hard man, without a drop of pity in me.'"

She blushed at having her words thrown back in her face. "Did that rankle so much, Giles?"

"Like a thorn in my side." He traced the outline of her lips with his fingertip. "But now that I have plucked the rose, I fear her thorns no longer." He followed the words with a lingering kiss.

Vera twined her arms about his neck. "Elizabeth will be very angry. 'Tis said she broke Lady Scudamore's finger when that lady eloped and married without her permission. And she threw Oxford in the Tower for seducing Anne Vasavour."

"Ah, but if I recall correctly, madam, you said that it was *you* who were seducing *me*. I doubt the queen would do the same to you. However, we shall raid my share of Drake's booty for a fine jewel—Elizabeth is fond of rubies, they say. And we shall stay away from court until the queen relents. Forever, if you like!''

Vera laughed up at him. She was so happy she could scarcely comprehend it. "Now that we have settled the matter, there are still three more hours until sunrise, my lord."

He smiled down at her, handsome as a god. "Do you wish to spend them talking or sleeping?"

She drew her nails lightly across his chest and down the V of curling hair. "Neither one, my lord. There is a third choice, if you are so inclined." Her hand slid lower. "And I see," she said softly, "that you are."

He gasped at her bold touch. "Aye, sweeting. Very much inclined."

He took her again, this time slowly, enticing her to follow where he led. Teaching her things that were beyond instinct and into the realm of the erotic arts. She barely had time to wonder where he had learned such things before smoldering passion flared into a wall of raging flame. They were consumed by it, and by the power of their fresh, new love. Then they slept, sated and spent, in each other's arms.

Vera bathed in Giles's chamber with cold water from a brass pan, and hurried away to her dressing closet. Luck was with her, for not even the servants were up and about. She dressed carefully and wondered if the profound change in her was visible to a discerning eye.

She broke her fast with bread dipped in ale and dusted her face liberally with white powder. An hour later she joined the queen and her ladies in the stable yard, where the gentlemen of the court and the grooms and huntsmen were already assembled. When she was sure someone was watching, Vera leaned against the wall and placed the back of her arm over her brow.

Mary Radcliffe hurried to her side. "What ails you, Lady Verena? Have you taken the fever?"

"Nay, my lady. 'Tis only a sick headache that has been coming on since yesterday. My eyes feel like two hot coals."

Lady Mary sympathized, having suffered from the same affliction. "You are pale and your eyes overbright. You must lie down in a darkened place with a cloth upon your head until it passes. I will make your excuses to the queen."

Vera's eyes were moist. She hated to trick this kindly Lady of the Privy Chamber, who had been good to her. "Thank you."

She dipped a curtsy and hurried back inside the palace, aware that Elizabeth was watching her shrewdly. The queen signaled the cavalcade to start off, then turned to Alençon's secretary, who was mounted beside her.

"You are a rogue, Charpentier. The Lady Verena sighs and pines for you like a lovesick girl, while you neglect her. Instead of whispering sweet words, you prattle on of settlements and physician's examinations. 'Tis no wonder she is faint and wan."

The secretary squirmed in dismay. "The lady is a great heiress, your majesty, but so much do I love her I would take her barefoot and in rags."

"Prettily said, my lord. Still, I see that you have not given up your place in the hunt, as Lord Rathborne has. He has turned his mount over to the grooms and gone after his ward, to see to her welfare."

Charpentier flushed deeply and bowed. Whichever choice he made, he would still look bad in her eyes—

and Alençon had a scheme planned for the hunt, whereby Charpentier would draw the others away and leave the *duc* alone with Elizabeth to press his advantage.

He shrugged and spread his hands. "With Rathborne to look after her, there is no need of my presence as well."

Elizabeth gave him a disdainful smile and turned back to the *duc*. "My dear Frog," she told him gaily, "you must give lessons in the art of wooing to your secretary, or he will lose his heiress yet."

Vera watched them anxiously from the window overlooking the stable yard. Her headache was no longer a pretense and it pounded at the back of her eyes like a blacksmith on an anvil. Once the party was clear of the grounds, she closed the casement and hastened down to the stable. She winced at the brightness of the sun, which helped her in pretending to have overslept. The groom saddled a spirited gray mare and brought it to her.

"Griselda is fresh as a daisy, my lady. You will have no difficulty catching up with the rest of her majesty's party." He helped Vera mount, and if he wondered why she brought a large woolen bag to attach behind her saddle, he did not comment.

Five minutes later she was off of the palace grounds and riding in the opposite direction of the hunting party. She nudged Griselda into a gallop and every beat of the horse's hooves urged her on. *Freedom, freedom, freedom,* they seemed to say as she covered the ground. She forgot about her headache in the rush of excitement.

Giles was waiting at the prearranged spot. He thrust a bundle into her hand. "You'll be less noticeable if you change into these garments for traveling. I got them from one of the stable lads."

Vera was delighted to pull out a pair of black hose, a long padded doublet in black slashed with green and a pair of leather boots. With her hair pulled up beneath a woolen cap and a short green cape over her shoulders, she looked like a serving lad accompanying his master on a journey.

"Oh, it is wonderful to shuck those silly garments...at least for a few days." She used a stone for a mounting block and swung up easily into the saddle. "How long will it take us to reach Rathborne if we go cross-country?"

"Half the time it took us to get from there to here. If luck favors us—and if I do not have to stop to feed you ten times a day—we could be at Rathborne by nightfall tomorrow."

"I shall live on nothing but dew and sunlight."

Giles smiled wryly. "You would faint in the saddle before noon. Have no fear, there is food in my saddlebags to last until sunset, when we shall stop at an inn for the night."

They took narrow lanes and little-traveled byways until they reached the highway. Once on the open road they kicked the dust of the palace from their heels, and galloped side by side in the morning sun.

The farther they rode from Hampton Court, the lighter Vera's heart became. When they reached the inn that night, still in the guise of master and servant, Giles procured them a hearty supper and a private sleeping room. They were not being followed and it was probable that their disappearance had not yet been noticed.

Later, when the moon rode high, they retired for the night. They made love in the sagging bed, much to the shock or amusement of the farmers in the taproom below, and slept like stones till cockcrow.

They left again at dawn when the grass was still spangled with dew and the sky still streaked with pink and mauve. The air had a clean, woodsy smell that made Vera feel right at home. Soon the countryside began to look familiar. When she spied the bulk of Rathborne Forest atop the distant ridge, her heart was full. She smiled at Giles. "We made it!"

"Yes, love. Almost home."

They skirted the edge of the cultivated fields and took the road past the forest. The closer they came the more they relaxed.

What could possibly go wrong now?

Chapter Thirteen

As Giles and Vera approached the house the sun sank behind the trees, casting the way before them in twilight. Wind sighed through the treetops, whispering of rain and the coming of winter. Her headache was back, dull and throbbing, and her stomach felt hollow and queasy. She needed a hot bath and a warm bed, with Giles at her side.

Despite the throbbing in her head, Vera was taken by the sight of Rathborne, caught in the last rays of the setting sun. She reined in on the crest. "How beautiful Rathborne looks. All warm and yellow as if it were carved of butter."

Giles laughed. "To me it looks like gold, love, but knowing you I can understand that it would have to remind you of something edible."

"You need not poke fun at me," she said, her smile softening her words. "Your appetites—in all respects—are more than a match for mine." She brushed the fair hair back from her forehead. "The hard ride has made me hungry, but it is well past suppertime. Do you think there will be anything left to eat?"

"There are always eggs and bread and cheese aplenty. If that does not suit you, we will have Irme kill the fatted calf."

They rode on at a gentle walk, enjoying the last few minutes of their privacy. Giles was glad to have reached Rathborne. His heart lifted at the sight of it. He could not help but recall his feelings of dismay upon reaching it the last time. Then it had been a reminder of his father's cruelty. Now it was the place where he had spent his earliest days with his mother and grandfather. More than that, it was the place where he had found his one true love.

Vera was filled with relief. All the way from Hampton Court she had been listening for the sounds that would warn they were being followed. She looked back over her shoulder for final reassurance. The road lay empty behind them as far as the eye could see.

Suddenly she heard Caliph snort and grunt. Giles shouted a warning to her simultaneously. Vera turned in the saddle and gasped. Giles was trying to keep Caliph from panicking. An arrow pierced his horse's rump. Another had grazed its hock and left a bloody trail. The noble beast reared, then staggered and fell. Giles barely managed to jump free.

"Ride for the house!" he shouted to her. "Stop for nothing!"

But his words were drowned out by wild yips and yaps from the forest verge. An arrow hissed past and caught Giles in the shoulder. The force of its trajectory tumbled him backward into the grass beside the road. His sword arm, she saw in horror. He tried to draw it with his left arm, but it proved impossible to pull it from the sheath at such an awkward angle.

Vera jumped down from her mare. Already Giles's tan doublet was soaked with blood. He tried to struggle up. "Leave me!" he cried to her.

"No!" She darted toward him and drew his sword. There was a shout from among the trees.

Another arrow whistled toward them, fast as light. Giles realized it was intended for her. "Jesu, Vera…!" He tried to shield her from it, and took the shaft through his thigh. It held him pinned to the ground, facedown.

Vera struggled up. "Giles!"

He did not answer. Now his garments were more crimson than tan and the grass was stained with an ever-widening pool of blood. A figure hurtled out of the forest toward them and Vera sprang at it, sword in hand. She heard a step behind her and whirled. Too late. Something crashed down on the back of her skull.

"Vera!"

She heard the startled exclamation as she pitched forward into the churned dirt. For a brief instant red light flared inside her head. Then there was a dull ringing in her ears and pulsing, overwhelming blackness.

After that, there was nothing at all.

Giles floated into dull awareness. Cold. So cold. And terrible thirst. Bone-deep pain. Time passed. Weeping and gentle hands. A touch of ointment at his forehead. *In nomine Patris, et Filii, et Spiritus Sancti…"*

Then blessed nothingness.

Voices. A rough hand.

"Wake the villain up."

"I cannot, my lord. He has been like this since we found him by the roadside, wallowing in blood. He is nigh unto death, I fear."

"Either way, lady, he is food for the ravens. If he dies, so be it. If he lives it will be only to face the hangman's noose or the headsman's axe. Thus do his kind end their days!"

Giles floated in a gray limbo of pain. At times he rose nearer to consciousness. Then he felt overwhelming fear. Not for himself, but for Vera. He recognized Irme's voice, although he could not seem to gather enough effort to speak when she called his name. Once or twice he thought he heard Francis Finch speak to him. Other times there were only harsh, unfamiliar voices.

Where was Vera? Sweet God in heaven, what had happened to Vera?

He tried to ask a hundred times. It seemed he had no strength. Certainly he had no voice. There was nothing but pain and fear and the struggle to shake off the chains that seemed to bind his useless limbs. His shoulder itched. He tried mightily to raise his other arm to scratch it. It seemed to Giles that he labored for days to lift it, but it was as heavy as a tree trunk.

"Look," someone murmured excitedly. Was it Francis? "He is trying to move his finger. Giles! Giles, old fellow, can you hear me?"

He wanted desperately to answer. Exhausted from effort, he drifted instead into a dark abyss. After a while the air that he floated on became solid and turbulent. At times the pain was so great he sank gratefully into unconsciousness.

Rough voices. More rough hands. Rocking in a gentle cradle. A lurch and then more pain. Time passed with infinite slowness. *I have it,* Giles thought at last when his brain began to clear. *I understand. I have died... and this is hell.*

It was not the pain that made him realize this. It was the absence of Vera.

An eternity passed. He slept, until voices roused him. He was annoyed. He wanted to sleep forever. "It is no use, Sir Francis. He has been bled every day since coming here, without results." A gusty sigh. "I have seen such cases before. He is like to never awaken from this swoon."

The voice rang in his head like the clang of a great brass bell. Giles cleared his throat. "Go away."

It sounded like a croak.

"Jesu!"

Giles opened his eyes to the stark light. It was coming from a narrow window set high in a stone wall, upon which a crucifix hung. "I have never seen this place before," he said more clearly.

A face swam into view. Francis Finch, grinning like a jack-o'-lantern. "Ah, Giles! I knew you were made of sterner stuff. By God, you have given us a fright."

Rathborne tried to sit up, but his muscles refused to obey. Francis helped him, assisted by a portly gentleman in a barber's outfit. His head swam. When the room ceased spinning Giles knew why the room was unfamiliar. It was a prison cell.

"Is this Swansea or the Tower?"

Francis sighed. "You take your surroundings well. You are housed in the Tower at the queen's pleasure. There are those who wanted to have you drawn and quartered as you lay."

Giles took a sip of water from the wooden cup the barber offered. An array of surgeon's tools lay on a low table beside him, the razor sharp and bright. A guard stood warily watching them. Giles pushed the cup away. He felt as if he were blacking out again and struggled against it.

"Of what crime am I accused?"

The guard answered. "There are several, my lord. Abduction of a maid under the queen's protection, theft of one of the queen's horses and destruction of crown property. And murder most foul."

"Murder? Whose murder?"

No one answered. He turned to Francis, whose face was chalky now. "Either this man is a fool or I have lost more of my senses than I guessed. Of whose murder do I stand accused?"

Francis knelt beside him and took his hand. "They say that you abducted Lady Verena Stanton, to keep her from marrying Charpentier. And that you murdered her when she spurned you."

There was a great roaring in Giles's ears. He tried to stand. *Vera, dead?* "No!"

His anguished scream filled the room. Then Giles fell to the floor in a dead faint, and into the arms of sweet oblivion.

With Francis's intervention, Giles was moved from his cell to a more comfortable apartment within the Tower complex. Two weeks later he was deemed fit enough to stand his trial. Because of Giles's rank and the parties involved, the trial drew a great amount of interest. It was held in Westminster Hall, beneath the magnificent hammerbeam roof.

Charpentier sat in the front row of spectators, staring at Giles with cold hatred. Francis Finch and his sister Anne sat on the opposite side, holding hands and praying. Francis had not been permitted to speak with Giles since that day when he had first awakened.

The rod of justice thumped twice. "Giles, Lord Rathborne, is called to witness."

He took his place, trussed in chains like a common prisoner. His wrists were thin beneath the manacles that bound them. Francis had hired a man of letters to represent his friend, but from the looks of things, nothing would sway the jury. The great earls, Warwick and Rutland, sat in judgment.

Lumleigh, representing the crown, addressed Giles. "My lord, is it not true that you left Hampton Court in secret on the morning of September 8, in the company of the Lady Verena Stanton?"

"It is."

"And, my lord, is it not true that you made this lady to dress in the garments of a groom from Her Majesty's stables?"

"It is."

Lumleigh came closer, jabbing his finger for emphasis. "Furthermore, Lord Rathborne, is it not true that you took this innocent maiden to an inn, where you shared a bed?"

A murmur ran through the crowd. Giles bowed his head. "It is."

"And that you treated her as you would a common whore, abusing her body for your own illicit pleasure?"

Giles looked up, eyes blazing. "It is not! The lady was my wife in everything but the eyes of the Church. We planned to marry upon reaching Rathborne."

A ripple of surprise followed his words. "Liar! Liar and murderer!" Charpentier leapt to his feet, but was dragged back down by his companions.

Giles waited until the room was quiet again. He lifted his head higher. "I loved her right well, my lords. She was heart of my heart and soul of my soul. I would have lain down my life to save her...."

Lumleigh seized his opening. "Ah, but the Lady Verena never reached Rathborne. The cloak and hat and gloves she wore that day were found along the edge of Rathborne Forest, soaked with her blood!"

The thought sickened Giles. The lawyer Francis had hired jumped in. "'Twas Lord Rathborne's blood, my lord. He was sore wounded. An arrow pierced his shoulder to the bone. In trying to shield the lady from attack, he took another arrow in the leg, severing an artery! 'Twas this defense that almost cost him his own life, as well."

Warwick called for order. "You shall have your turn in time, Fielding. Continue, Lumleigh."

Lumleigh paced before Giles. "You speak of wives and marriage vows, Lord Rathborne. Of love between a man and woman. Heart of heart and soul of soul."

Giles knew what was coming. Lumleigh pounced. "Yet this woman, whom you claim loved you in return, told the queen herself—before the Court, I might add—that she would as leave not have a husband at all."

Lumleigh drew a paper from his doublet and began to read. "The queen then prompted the Lady Verena as to her liking for you as a husband. These are her exact words, according to the witnesses I will produce next: 'Lord Rathborne and I would not suit, majesty. We cannot be in the same room without coming to words. Indeed, I fear a prolonged time together might lead to blows!'"

The courtroom erupted at that. The bailiffs had to restore peace. Lumleigh waited for silence. He addressed the jury. "It is well known that the Lady Verena accepted a proposal of marriage from Louis, Marquise de Charpentier, and that they were to be married as soon as the banns were read."

Not a cough or whisper disturbed the tension. Lumleigh turned back to Giles. "I profess, Lord Rathborne, that Lady Verena spurned you. It is widely known that your estates are beggared, and that the wealth of the Stanton heiress would have been most welcome in your coffers. I submit that, either by force or by treachery, you lured the Lady Verena into accompanying you for a ride. That you then coerced her to a lonely country inn where you had carnal knowledge of her."

He lowered his voice. "The lady's pitiful cries were heard by customers in the taproom below, who unfortunately mistook them for cries of passion."

A gasp went up. Lumleigh continued. Giles listened inscrutably as the damning facts added up. It did not really matter. Vera was dead. He had no interest in living without her.

Lumleigh leaned in close. "I say, Lord Rathborne, that Lady Verena tried to escape into the shelter of Rathborne Forest. That, overcome by anger and thwarted lust, you killed her and buried her remains beneath the roots of a tree in the forest on your own estate."

The man for Giles's defense was on his feet again. "My lord, you forget his wounds, which nearly proved mortal!"

Lumleigh ignored his outburst. "You were wounded, my lord, either by the lady during the desperate struggle, or in an attempt to make it seem that the wounds had been inflicted by bandits. Let the record show that no arrows were retrieved from Rathborne after the incident!"

Another protest from Giles's lawyer made clear that the bloody arrows had been removed and thrown into the fire. Giles no longer listened. He was still weak from his terrible ordeal. At times he drifted away from his surroundings, into his own misty world: *Vera, Vera, Vera...*

The defense had its say, but in the end the outcome was inevitable. The following morning Giles was brought back to have his sentence read. He scanned the room. Charpentier, forbidding in black. Laetitia Lattimore, red-eyed and sniveling into her handkerchief. Francis, alone this time. His friend's face was drawn and shadowed, but whether from the outbreak of plague that had stricken him or for his own sake was beyond Giles's knowledge. He wanted to comfort him. *Do not weep over my fate,* he wanted to tell Francis. It seemed he would not have the chance.

The Earl of Warwick ordered the court to rise. "Lord Rathborne, you have been tried by a jury of peers and found guilty of murder most foul of the unfortunate lady, Verena Stanton. As a gentleman of noble birth you would ordinarily be sentenced to be beheaded. Since the victim was officially still a ward of the crown, however, your crime is deemed treason."

That sunk through to Giles. His head snapped up. Warwick rapped for order as the crowd bellowed its approval. "For your crimes, you are hereby sentenced to a traitor's death. You will be hanged and your still-living body drawn and quartered. So perish all traitors.''

Giles was led away through the jeering crowd. Someone spat at him. He stumbled along, hindered by his chains. *Ah, Vera, Vera, Vera...*

A hundred miles away, in the Convent of St. Agnes, a young woman sat by the window, awaiting her visitor. There was a small fire in the grate, this being the parlor of the mother superior. It was the only place within the convent walls where a man was allowed to set foot. Her fair hair, not very long to begin with, had been shorn during the height of the fever. Before, it had been perfectly straight, but it had grown out in a feathering of light curls that haloed her head.

The last thing Vera remembered was leaving the little inn, after a night of making love in Giles's arms. Then she was in a narrow nun's cell with her hair gone, feeling as weak and helpless as a newborn babe. "At first we thought it 'twas the plague laid you low, child," the nuns had told her. "We did not expect you to live a sennight."

Plague. That dreaded disease that wasted families and villages and decimated the countryside. Vera recalled, rather vaguely, that she had suffered a headache for a day or two prior to fleeing Hampton Court. The nuns said the fever had caused the headache, but Vera was sure she had not had such a knot on the back of her head then. Parts of the story were missing and she had no way of filling them in. Perhaps she had fallen from Griselda's back to the road below, overcome by fever.

She could not blame Giles for bringing her here. Plague victims were kept away from populated places and the nuns were known for their charity toward the ill and dying. Some men might have abandoned her where she lay. At least he had seen that she was taken care of. That showed that he had cared for her... did it not?

But she had been at the convent for many weeks. Why had he not come back once she was well again, until now? Whatever his reasons, she was eager to see him. She hoped with all her heart that he meant to take her away from here and back to Rathborne.

If only she could think more clearly.

She heard footsteps outside the parlor and braced herself. Little Sister Jaquetta beamed at her delightedly. "Here is your young man come back to see you, child."

"God be praised!" Vera almost jumped from the bench. She expected Giles's wide-shouldered frame to fill the doorway. Her visitor, however, was a skinny-shanked fellow, still more youth than man. "Hewe!"

Hewe entered and paused just inside the room, his posture a curious mixture of pride and bashfulness. "Vera..." He stood before her, tongue-tied and looking more boyish than she remembered from his last visit. A posey of autumn flowers was clutched in his bony hand.

She peered past his shoulder. "Has Tal come with you?"

Hewe blushed to the roots of his hair. "Nay. I am alone."

His words were like a slap to her face. *Oh, Tal! Could you not find it in your heart to forgive me?* To her dismay Vera felt a prickle of tears forming. Because she had stayed with Giles willingly, her foster father had turned his back upon her.

"You are good to me, Hewe. You seem to be the only one who cares what may happen to me." She had meant to pass it off lightly but a sob wrenched her body, then another. "You see," she hiccuped, "I have turned into a watering pot. I blubber all too easily. But I did so hope they had forgiven me by now!"

His eyes shifted away and back. God's teeth! He had never seen her weep before. It twisted his gut. "Do not shed any more tears, Vera," he blurted. "They do not know that you are here."

"What?"

Hewe heaved a mighty sigh. It was very complicated and he did not want to go into the entire story. "I said that they do not know. I—I did not tell them."

Vera stared at him as if he had taken leave of his senses. Hewe dropped to his knee before her and clutched her hand. "If they knew, they would come and carry you off to the farm where Garvin's sister lives. I heard them speak of it while you were still at Rathborne."

Suddenly he pressed wet kisses on her hands. "I love you, Vera. I have always loved you! But Tal had other plans. He thinks of me as a boy still, and I know that he meant you for Garvin. I could not bear it. As for that evil villain, Rathborne... Well, he has paid for what he did to you!"

She snatched her hand away. "What is this of Rathborne? What do you mean?"

He lifted his face to her, eyes shining with fervor. "He could not fool me with his smooth words, like he did the others. Rathborne told us you wanted to stay with him and learn to be a lady. Hah! I knew that was a foul lie from the start! He may have seduced you with fine gowns and jewels, but I could not let him corrupt you with his wickedness. I had to act against him."

Vera was suddenly afraid. Hewe had been her friend, but he had always been odd. It was in his blood, Tal had said. She tried to keep her voice calm. "Tell me . . . tell me everything."

Hewe was pleased to have a chance to tout his skill and cunning. "I was out hunting alone when I saw him coming from the crest. I knew that I had to kill him. I did it to save you from his foul clutches."

Vera was rigid with tension. A cold hand began squeezing her heart. Squeezing the life from her. Jesu! What had he done to Giles? Her throat was so dry she could not speak a single word.

Her companion failed to notice. "I did not know you at first in your servant's garb. Then you turned your face toward the wood and my heart clenched within me. I had to act. My first arrows missed and struck his gelding. Rathborne lunged for you—even then he was afraid to let you escape him, knowing that once away from his influence you would see him for what he was!"

It seemed frighteningly real to Vera. She could see it all in her mind's eye. Giles! Her palms were damp. She wiped them carefully upon the skirt of her plain brown gown. *Dear Lord, please do not let me faint!* "What happened after that?"

"I put a shaft through his shoulder. It was meant for his black heart!" Hewe frowned. "Then—then everything happened at once. You stumbled and fell. Although he was bleeding like a gored bull, Rathborne still had the strength of a devil. He was about to overpower you. I sent another arrow into him and he lay still upon the ground."

Hewe turned red. "I forgot about the horses. The mare was frightened by the blood. She reared, and as she came down, her foot struck you a blow across the back of the head."

As he relived the events, he began to tremble in every limb. "God's death, Vera, I thought that you were dead. I took you to that empty cottage up by the pasture. You were limp as a herring and cold as a stone. 'Twas two days before I realized that you had the fever, so I brought you here to the good sisters, who have nursed you back to health."

He leaned forward suddenly, aiming an inexperienced kiss at her mouth. It grazed her ear as she jerked away. "Do not be afraid, Vera. I saved you from your captor. I will take care of you now. You do not need Tal and the rest. Marry me, Vera, my sweet love!"

"Marry you!" She jumped up, the words ripped from her heart. "Jesu, but you are mad! I was not Rathborne's captive, I was his lover!"

Hewe blanched. "Do not say such things."

"It is true." Vera rounded on him. "Where is he now? Does he even know that I am here?"

Her importunate suitor was bewildered. He rose slowly. "Why do you care what happens to him?"

"Because I love him beyond life itself." She saw Hewe flinch and took pity. "I cannot marry you, Hewe. You are my friend, the boon companion of my childhood. But he . . . he is the other half of my soul!"

Hewe struggled for dignity. "You will change your mind when he is executed in three days time."

His shot went home. The results were not what Hewe had expected. Vera's mouth dropped open. "Executed!"

"Aye," he said, relishing his moment. "You may well stare. Your fine lord is nothing less than a foul murderer."

"I do not for one moment believe that."

"Nevertheless 'tis true. He was tried and found guilty of murdering his young ward, Lady Verena Stanton, in a fit of jealousy. He is sentenced to be hanged, drawn and quartered."

Vera felt the room spin about her like a top. The whole world had gone horribly, terribly, mad.

Chapter Fourteen

"Do you wish to confess your sins, my son?"

Giles eyed the elderly priest. "I admit to folly and impatience. If you wish to shrive someone of the sin of murder, you will have to seek elsewhere. I am innocent of the deed."

The priest closed his prayer book. His rheumy eyes were filled with mild regret. "It is never too late to change your mind. I will be with you upon the scaffold tomorrow, praying for the salvation of your soul. Remember, you may turn your back upon the Lord, but He will not turn His back upon you until the very end."

He went out and the guard began to close the door. Another figure joined them and Giles heard the clink of coins. When the door closed, Francis Finch stood before him, shaking back the folds of his heavy cloak.

"God's teeth, Giles. You must have thought that I'd abandoned you."

"Nay, I know better." He clasped Francis's hand. "How is your sister?"

"As well as can be expected." Francis shook his head. "She takes this hard for my sake as well as yours."

"She is a fine lady. I regret that I did not have the chance to know her."

Francis did not reply. He had hoped to make a match of it between Giles and Anne. If he had acted sooner perhaps things would not have come to this sorry pass. "Is there aught I can do to ease your last hours?"

Giles walked to the window. From his vantage point he could see a small door leading out to a minuscule parapet. Perhaps it had once been a watch point against attack by water. Beyond, through the chimney pots and turrets, he had a fair view of the Thames.

He suddenly wished his last view could be of Rathborne, with its bittersweet memories. He watched a barge ease its way toward the docks. Dignitaries coming to his execution. He turned to Francis. "There is one thing, if possible. Tell me, will my body be burned or buried?"

Jesu! Francis thought. *He speaks of death as easily as if it had nothing to do with him at all.* "Buried . . ."

"Ah." Giles smiled. "Then I do have one last desire. I wish to be buried beside Vera."

"Er, ah . . ." Francis felt a dull flush creep over his face. Was it better to lie and ease his mind, or speak the truth? While he hemmed and hawed, Giles narrowed his eyes. "What is it? Surely they will not deny me this last request?"

"There is one problem." Francis cleared his throat. "Her body was never found."

"*What?*" Giles did some rapid thinking. "Lumleigh claimed that she was buried among the roots of a tree!"

Francis blinked. "That was his supposition. They found her cloak, hat and gloves. Nothing more."

"Jesu!" Giles's heart filled with blessed hope. If his flash of intuition was right, Vera might still be alive. He took a deep breath. "This is of great urgency, Francis. Recall carefully what you know of me being brought in to Rathborne. Did I have anything of value upon me? Gold or silver coins? My signet ring?"

His friend frowned. Whatever did it matter? He cast back into his memory. "You were not robbed, if that is what you mean. Mistress Irme said that you had a purse of coins on your belt and all your jewelry...rings, necklace and earring. By why is it important?"

"Do you not see?" Giles's face was transformed. "Vera disappeared in Rathborne Forest while I lay in a deep swoon, weltering in my own blood—near the same place where she had once lived in hiding with the members of her outlaw band."

He rubbed his forehead, trying to clear his mind of all confusion. "I thought that we were set upon by robbers and that she was killed in the skirmish, before I could even draw my sword."

He pounded his hand into his fist. He could not believe what a fool he had been. "Think, Francis! If not robbers, who would waylay me on my own land? And who would have reason to remove me and take Vera away?"

Francis whistled. "You think she was taken back to her own people? God's toenails, if that is true, why has she not come forward to save you?"

Giles felt a spurt of fear. "Perhaps she was injured after all. Or perhaps she is their prisoner. But I know Vera. She would have found a way to come to me somehow. No more gallant little soul ever lived upon this earth. For God's sake, Francis, find her! Take care

of her for me. If she is alive and well I can face death
with my heart at peace."

"Idiot!" Francis grinned and punched him in the
arm. "If Vera is alive, there is no reason for you to die
at all!"

There was no time to lose. After listening to Giles's
hurried instructions, Francis left the Tower in good
spirits, to petition for an immediate stay of execution.

Two hours later he rode through the crowded streets
of London town with a heavy heart. The heavy down-
pour of an hour past had washed the filth from the
gutters, and the cobblestones were puddled with dirty
water. Now the sun was out again, and so were the
Londoners.

He did not hear the cries of the merchants and the
food vendors urging him to buy, or of the beggars asking for alms. Not even the saucy remarks of a bold
whore could help penetrate his heavy gloom.

He had not been able to save Giles. The stay of execution had been denied. Lack of evidence, said one
earl. A friend's desperate fantasies, the other had exclaimed. Either way, they could do nothing about it.
Tomorrow at noon, Giles would endure a traitor's ig-
noble death.

Francis passed through the city gates with Lumleigh's harsh laughter ringing in his ears. Cold sweat
beaded his brown. At least Giles had taken the news
well. Extraordinarily well, considering the circumstances. Dry leaves skittered across the road and gray
clouds piled up on the horizon, blotting out the hard
blue sky. The temperature was dropping hour by hour.
Soon the mud would be a thick, half-frozen soup. He
drew his cloak about him tightly.

There was only one faint hope in his effort to save Giles now. He had to find Vera. He had to try, even though it was all in vain. Francis knew that, even if he rode hell-for-leather, there was no way he could locate Vera—if she really were still alive—and make it back to London by tomorrow noon.

Lady Laetitia Lattimore had come with the court to Greenwich, although her heart was not in it. She stared out the window and shivered, watching the wind whip the last of the autumn leaves across the grounds and into the river. Her woolen petticoats and heavy gown of emerald velvet could not keep her warm.

Tomorrow, at high noon, Giles of Rathborne would be executed.

"'Tis too cold here at Greenwich," the queen said quietly, interrupting Lady Laetitia's musings. She had left the rest of her ladies near the fireplace to speak a few words in private with the widow. Elizabeth was dressed in black and scarlet, and her pale skin was whiter than usual. "The chill seeps into my marrow and I like it not! This very afternoon we shall remove to Richmond, my warm winter box, in preparation for Advent and the Christmas festivities."

"Alas," Laetitia replied, "I am in no mood to be festive."

Elizabeth understood her meaning. "Nor I. Lord Rathborne was a prime favorite of mine."

She fell into a brooding silence. What part had her own games had in bringing about the tragedy? She had tried her hand at playing Cupid for once, and it had rebounded against all concerned. "I am a good judge of men, but even I have been fooled before," she added. "However, I did not think it of Lord Rath-borne."

Laetitia sighed. "He could not murder for gain, majesty, but in the heat of anger...?"

The queen turned away from the window. Who really knew the secret heart of a man? If she could have been certain that Leicester had had no hand in the death of his wife, Amy Robsart, the course of her own history would have been drastically changed. She frowned. "Come, let us speak of pleasanter matters. I am told that Charpentier now turns his eye to you."

Laetitia smiled crookedly. "He looks to feather his nest with my widow's portion," she replied. "If your majesty is willing that I receive his suit, I wish that you would tell me."

"I am no hand at matchmaking these days. Do you love him?" The keen amber gaze bored into Laetitia.

The widow sighed. "In time, majesty, I might learn to cherish him well, but... I have always preferred a less-civilized type of man, with a bit of the rogue in him."

Elizabeth tapped Laetitia's arm with a bejeweled hand. Rubies and topaz shone in the firelight. "So have I, Lady Lattimore. So have I. To my deep regret."

The queen looked past the window, lost in sad reverie. Then, with one of the lightning changes of mood that were her hallmark, she turned her back on the mournful scenery. "I shall retire to my Privy Chamber. Pass on the news to my household that we remove to Richmond tomorrow."

Laetitia wished she could be well away before word came that Rathborne's execution had been carried out. "Shall we leave early, majesty?"

"By nine of the clock we will be on the royal barge together. I have no more wish to hear the noon bells ring than you, Lady Lattimore."

Elizabeth swept off. Laetitia spied Charpentier near the foot of the main staircase and hesitated. He had not seen her. She gathered her skirts and went briskly down the hall in the other direction.

I am becoming foolish in my maturity, she thought wryly. Even a year ago she would not have avoided so handsome and charming a man. But she had no desire to leave England. She saw her life slipping into the rut of routine. *If I continue in my ways I shall end out my life as waiting woman to the queen—or alone at Lattimore Manor, surrounded by none but my servants and a dozen yowling cats!*

On the way to her quarters she saw a man arguing with a guard. He was mud stained and travel weary, as if he had ridden long and hard. Something about him caught her eye. It was not just his breadth of shoulder or the character in his blunt, good-looking face. She narrowed her eyes. God's teeth, he was wearing Rathborne livery! She went toward them, curious. As she drew nearer she heard her name.

"...For the love of God, man, I must see Lady Lattimore this very day! A life hangs in the balance."

"I am Lady Lattimore."

The man brushed past the guard impatiently. Laetitia held up her hand to let him approach unmolested. His hair was grizzled at the sides and his face lined and weathered, but he radiated vigor. A man of action, she decided.

Despite the urgency of his matter he managed an appreciative glance at the winsome widow. "Thank God," the man said fervently. "I have brought a letter for you, lady, but this oaf would not let me pass. I was told to give it into only your hands or those of the queen herself."

"Who are you, sir, that you wear a traitor's livery?" And ill-fitting, at that. Why, the seams were in danger of bursting beneath the strain of his brawny muscles.

His face grew ruddy with anger. "Rathborne is no traitor. No, nor murderer either. Read that, my lady, and you will see for yourself."

Laetitia broke the seal and scanned the hastily scrawled lines. The writing was ill formed. It looked like a child's untutored hand. Then her eyes scanned the signature. She read the note again. When she looked up her eyes were filled with tears, but she was smiling through them.

"What is your name, sir, and whence have you come? I deem you no servant after all."

He let his breath out in a gust. There was a jolly twinkle in his eyes. "If I told you my home and occupation, you would not credit it, my lady."

He pushed back the lock of hair from his brow and swept her a courtly bow. "My name is Tal, and I am foster father to the girl, Vera, whom you know as Lady Verena Stanton."

"Faster!" Vera urged. "There is no time to spare." Her borrowed mount streaked down the road to Greenwich, splashing mud in all directions. They were riding into a head wind, and tiny flakes of snow blew upon them, heralding the brewing storm.

"We must rest," Hewe exclaimed. "This horse and I are weary and ready to drop by the roadside."

"Then do so, by God." Vera suppressed a sob. "I shall go on without you."

Why, oh why, had she agreed to Hewe's escort? She should never have taken him with her. He was unused to riding and had slowed her down more than once. Vera left him behind as her tough little mare raced against time. If all had gone well, Tal should have reached Greenwich long before noon. His words might be enough to hold off Giles's execution until she arrived as living proof that he had not murdered her.

Her fear was great, but she could not let herself believe that she would not arrive in time. A world without Giles was unimaginable.

Unendurable.

A sheen of tears blinded her. Vera brushed them away abruptly. She was impatient of anything that might cause her to lose precious seconds. She glanced at the sky. The hour was growing late. She must make it in time to save Giles. She must!

Tal was so tired he shook with it. He knelt on the damascene carpet in the queen's Privy Chamber and waited for Elizabeth's reply. It seemed a scene from a dream to him. He could never have imagined that he would meet the queen nor speak to her in her private quarters. Nor, he admitted shakily, under such circumstances. She was so regal and commanding, dressed all in white and dripping with diamonds and pearls, that she seemed like a goddess.

Indeed, she had the powers of one, for at the moment she held the lives of Vera and Giles of Rathborne in her slender white hands.

Elizabeth studied the weary man before her. "'Tis an idiot's tale you tell me. What proof have I that what you say is true?"

"For first proof you have the note which the young woman you know as Lady Verena Stanton wrote to you, majesty, explaining that she is alive and has been recovering from a severe illness." He put a hand into his doublet and pulled out a small packet. "And this."

The queen opened it. Inside was an old prayer book in the language of France, a miniature of Allys de Breffny in a gold frame and a worn note, much creased and still sealed.

"What is this?" Elizabeth asked, turning the note over.

Tal flushed. "Inside is the truth of Vera's birth, written by a dying woman. That is all I know. I meant to give it to her on her wedding day."

"Why did you not open it?"

His flush deepened. "I did not want to know. My late wife took in a nursemaid and a girl child in the time of plague. The nursemaid died after consigning the book and the care of the child into her hands. My wife took the prayer book and hid it from me. She could not read, but knew that such books often held family records. She feared that somehow public knowledge of the book would cause Vera to be taken from us."

Tal's eyes grew bright with memory. "Those were happy days. We grew to love our foster daughter dearly. Later, when my wife herself lay dying, she told where she had hidden it behind a chimney brick."

A hard look came over his face and Tal's hands clenched into fists. "I, too, feared to discover the truth. Almost immediately I was forced to flee into the forest to avoid John of Rathborne's fury. Vera came with me.

I hid the prayer book in a safe place and put it out of my mind. Until now.''

''God's eyes, did you not think the girl had a right to know who her parents were?''

''My wife and I had no children,'' he said simply. ''We lost our hearts to Vera and raised her as our own. In time I almost forgot that she was not.''

The queen consulted the jeweled watch that hung from a golden chain about her waist. Her hand shook. ''Even if what you tell me is true, it is too late. Unless my pocket clock is wrong again, Lord Rathborne will soon be on his way to the scaffold.''

Laetitia looked at her own watch. ''Eleven of the clock, your highness. I checked this against the clock in the Presence Chamber not ten minutes ago.''

Elizabeth took a quick turn about the room while the others waited tensely. She turned back to them with narrowed eyes. ''You say that he is not a murderer, although you bring me scant proof of it.''

Tal braved her apparent anger. ''The proof will stand before you once Vera arrives, majesty.''

''That is neither here nor there. Giles of Rathborne may be innocent of murder, yet he is by your very words a liar and cheat. He tried to thrust an imposter upon me and steal estates that rightfully belong to the Crown.''

Wringing her hands, Laetitia prayed for Giles and Vera. For them all. Elizabeth was working herself up into a rage; she knew the signs. Two spots of brilliant color flamed in the queen's white face.

She advanced on them like an avenging angel, every inch the sovereign of the realm. ''To lie and attempt to cheat the crown, my friends, is a crime... and that crime is still treason!''

She waited till her words sunk in. "And the penalty for treason," she said angrily, "is still death!"

A patch of light marked the shape of the narrow window on the stone-flagged floor. It faded as clouds obscured the weak sun. The door rattled and opened.

"The time is now, my lord."

Giles looked up. The jailor stood at his door with four members of the yeoman guard. The old priest waited beside them, his stole and prayer book in his gnarled hands.

A shiver ran up Giles's spine. Francis had not returned in time to save him. His fate was sealed.

"It is time," the man repeated quietly.

Giles stood and followed them out. His jailers felt badly. They had come to like Lord Rathborne despite his crime. Who could blame a man for a hasty act committed in anger? Women led a man on and on, then laughed in his face. Jezebels! It had been so since the beginning of time, but nowadays the girls were so bold! Hussies, every one of them!

Even the warder, an insular man who had fought to keep his country free of foreign invasion, felt sympathy for Lord Rathborne. It was a shame that his recalcitrant ward had been under the queen's protection. And who could blame him for his outburst of temper? Turning down an honest Englishman for a Frenchie, by God! What were young women coming to these days?

And look how the poor man carried himself, head high as if he had not a care in the world. That was the aristocratic breeding showing true. Aye, it was a terrible shame.

Giles paused as they reached a certain hall. A heavy door stood at the opposite end. He knew where it led.

He had seen it every day from his cell window. The block stood near one end of the yard, with a basket ready to catch a victim's head when it was severed by the executioner's axe. But Giles had not even been extended the courtesy of death by a sharp, clean sword stroke.

He squared his shoulders and prepared himself for what was to come.

The sound of the drums came to Giles's ears. His heartbeat matched their rhythm. Not much longer now. He saw the guardsmen's sympathetic glances.

"Kind sirs," he said, "I have one small request. Before I die I wish to look out over London town once more."

The jailor looked at the priest. The priest shrugged. "I cannot see the harm of it."

"Very well." The jailor pulled a ring of keys from his belt and selected one. "There is a parapet here with a fine view of the city. But we dare not tarry long."

He opened the door. From below came the slow sound of the drums and the din of the assembled crowd. A guard stepped out first, to prevent the prisoner from jumping, were he so inclined. Giles followed him onto the tiny parapet. There was no room for the others.

For a long moment Giles stood shading his eyes as he looked out over the spires and roofs. They were opposite the green here, and out of sight of the vultures who had gathered for the execution. Giles sighed heavily.

The guard shifted his feet. Finally he leaned forward. "It is time to go, my lord."

Giles slumped forward, shaking with great sobs. "Jesu! Do not force me to my death, I beg of you."

He clung to the edge of the parapet like a ship-wrecked sailor clinging to a spar. The collapse of a man who had seemed so solidly courageous unmanned the guardsman. He looked around uneasily, then stepped back toward the door to ask the head jailer for instructions.

That split second was all Giles needed. His desperate ruse had worked. Quick as a thought, he spun around and leapt at the guard. One push to shove the man through the open door, another to grab the pike from his hand and slam the door shut in his face. Success!

The pike was almost too long to wedge in place, but Giles had regained some of his strength in the past weeks of imprisonment. Using his body for leverage, he managed to break off the tip. With the end against the stone of the parapet and the tip solidly planted in the wooden planking, it became impossible to open the door from the inside.

"My apologies, gentlemen, but I have work to do!"

He slipped out the knife that Francis had smuggled in to him and cut the rope that held a pennant in place. For a man who had spent half his life swinging from a ship's rigging, it was no great feat to clamber down to the ledge of the window below. Then he removed the rope that was concealed beneath his doublet, thanking God that Francis's efforts had secured him such accommodations in the Tower complex where an escape was remotely possible. As he looped a knot to the parapet and rappelled down, he found himself grinning.

No one had expected him to put up a fight at the last. He dropped to the ground and ran along the irregular base of the building, then darted inside. They would not look for him in here.

A short time later a group of guards went rushing past the crowd toward the gate. The jailor stopped a plump young woman who was strolling past with her son. "A prisoner has escaped! Has anyone gone by?"

"Nay, sir. Nary a one."

They turned back. Giles moved away from the center of the throng, stooping inside the enveloping cloak Francis had hidden to help him disguise his height. A small boy stared. "Look, Mama. A hunchback!"

He got a smack for his brashness. "Shh. Poor man, he does not need the likes of you gawking and pointing." The woman sighed. Such a handsome fellow, too.

With everyone's attention on either the scaffold or the gate and milling guards, Giles was able to slink away toward the river. The cloak disposed of behind a pile of stones, he slipped into the water. A man who had done repairs to a hull on the high seas had no fear of swimming the Thames. Luckily, the current was not against him, and the tidal surge had already peaked and ebbed. The waters were murky, unlike the clear blue of the Caribbean, but Giles made his way beneath the water, coming up for air as little as possible.

He kept near the shore but well away from the river traffic. Less than an hour passed between the time of his escape and the time he made his way through London's alleys to a certain hostelry. The search for him had not widened to the city as yet. He wondered how long it would take them to realize he was not hiding somewhere within the Tower grounds—and how much longer before someone guessed he had escaped by water.

The tavern owner led him to a private room. No questions were asked. Giles grinned. Everything was there as he had arranged. Thank God for Francis Finch and his quick wits. By God, he was a prince among men!

The church clocks chimed as he rode out by the same gate that Francis had taken the previous day. One of the clock. Had he stayed in London, he would have already been dead an hour now, by his reckoning. A shiver ran down his spine. Once clear of the city, he let the roan have its head.

Giles thundered down the London Road as he had done one fine summer day. The journey brought back a thousand memories. He remembered leaving the court in high dudgeon and riding into Rathborne Forest, unaware that Fate had a grand jest planned for him among its leafy pathways.

He prayed that this time, too, he would find Vera at journey's end.

Tal and Lady Lattimore weren't sure if they had prevailed or if Elizabeth had been toying with them. The queen was now at her desk, scrawling a stay of execution, and a swift barge was ready to carry it to the Tower. A knock sounded. Lady Stafford entered urgently.

"'Tis Lord Rathborne," she gasped. "He escaped from his jailors as they were leading him to the scaffold."

Tal lifted his hands to heaven. "God be praised! We may save him yet."

Lady Stafford's face was very pale. "If you would save him, sir, you had best find him before Captain Fowler and his men do. Three parties of soldiers have been sent after Lord Rathborne, with orders to bring him back—dead or alive!"

Chapter Fifteen

Within a short time of Lady Stafford's announcement, the queen and Tal had left Greenwich along with Laetitia Lattimore and a party of the queen's own guard. If Dame Fortune was with them, they should intercept Captain Fowler and his men and turn them back. If not...

Tal tried not to think of the alternative. Despite the snow flurries of an hour before, the sun had come out. The air was crisp and fine, but there was more snow in the offing; the smell of it was in the air. He muttered an oath as the road turned bad. He had hoped they would catch up with Rathborne before they reached the place where the road branched. His only consolation was that Giles—and the soldiers riding hard after him— would have to slow down as well.

"You do not speak like a ruffian," the queen said to Tal as they slowed down through a patch of half-frozen mud. "Tell me more of your history."

Her astuteness astonished Tal. "I was not always an outlaw, majesty. Like his father before him, my father was a small landowner and architect. He worked at the building of Nonsuch for Good King Hal, creating the carved panels for the State Dining Room and the Winter Parlor."

"Elmund Carver, who studied with Grinling Gibbons—he was your father?" The queen was startled. He had carved some of the finest decorations at Greenwich.

"Aye."

"And do you share his talents?"

"I apprenticed to him at the age of twelve and learned at his side. By the age of twenty I was a master carver and on my way to becoming a master builder. At twenty-five, I was an archer marching with your army to the northern border." His mouth thinned. "By the age of thirty, I was a fugitive living by my wits in Rathborne Forest—thanks to John of Rathborne, God rot his soul."

Elizabeth was intrigued. "Tell me more, Master Tal. You interest me greatly."

He complied, giving a condensed version of his life. Of how John of Rathborne had coveted his wife and then punished Tal when she had refused to become the man's mistress. He could not stop a sigh. "A good woman, my Winn was. She died in childbed."

Bearing Rathborne's bastard. But Tal kept that part of the story to himself, as he had done over the years. Let Winn rest in peace with her good character intact, God bless her. There was good in the new Lord Rathborne, and that was what mattered now.

Tal glanced at Elizabeth, magnificent in her green velvet habit and cloak, with a jaunty jeweled cap on her red-gold hair. Tudor gold, men called it. *Ah, Winn! If you could have lived to see this day—to see your Tal riding beside the queen herself.*

"We lived in the forest," he went on, "helping the honest farmers raise money to keep their lands and baiting our enemies. We did not know that when Morse of Rathborne inherited, he was ill and sick to dying, and that the steward, Heslip, was running the estate. Nor that Heslip was our chief persecutor once old John and his eldest born were in their graves. We blamed the new lord."

"As well you should," Elizabeth said querulously. "Where would my good and loyal subjects be today if I had gone gallivanting across the high seas? Tell me that, if you will!"

Instead Tal turned his efforts to soothing her. By the time he'd related the cruel injustices perpetrated around Rathborne and how their messages to the queen had never been brought to her, his spirits were even higher. Elizabeth drew him out easily. He found himself discussing hopes and dreams that he had long kept buried. As they reached the first fork in the road, she gave her word that a general pardon would be granted for the "outlaws" who had taken refuge in Rathborne Forest.

"But mind you, there will be no more playing at Robin Hood," she warned sharply.

Tal grinned. "I am too old for it, alas. I shall be perfectly content to have a dry roof over my head once more and a real bed in which to rest my tired bones."

"Hah! You speak as if you were a doddering ancient, but I have seen the warm glances you have been exchanging with Lady Lattimore." She sent him an enigmatic look. "You could do worse."

That remark surprised Tal. He'd expected, if anything, a reprimand, for he had indeed been watching the lady in question with some interest. It appeared that

the queen was quite in charity with him. Now, if only
Vera's story could end happily, his cup would truly be
full.

He trained a practiced eye on the clouds overhead.
Unless they made better speed, that seemed increasingly unlikely.

Giles glanced over his shoulder and scanned the
road. There was a large party of soldiers some distance behind him, but they were gaining quickly. Only
a mile ahead the way branched in several directions and
there was traffic on every road. The churned mud
would make tracking him difficult. If he could make it
there before they caught up with him, he could lose
himself easily enough.

The road was screened on both sides by high hedgerows, preventing his followers from spotting him. It
also made the way blind and dangerous, but it was the
only road that led directly toward Rathborne. Giles felt
a spurt of triumph. Not much farther now. . .

A terrible scream shattered his thoughts a thousand
ways. He came around the bend at a thundering pace
and reined in so sharply his mount reared.

A tall ox cart was blocking the way. It was mired in
mud. The driver was nowhere to be seen, but the broken wheel lying several yards back told its tale. Giles
rode around the obstruction. If the driver had gone for
assistance, the way might soon be clogged with other
vehicles. All the better, for the hedgerows and high
banks would cause the soldiers to turn back or go
around them. Every gain on them even of mere minutes, was precious.

On the far side of the cart he discovered a horse and
rider lying in the mud, innocent victims of the acci-

dent. One of the beast's legs was broken and the lad was partially pinned beneath the thrashing animal. He was in imminent danger of death from the sharp hooves.

Giles faced a cruel dilemma. He could ride on toward a safety he might never reach, or he could help the boy before he was killed by a flailing hoof or crushed by the beast's weight. He swung down from his own mount and ran to the boy. No one else was around and there was no other choice. He would not want some stranger to pass Vera by in like circumstances.

There was nothing to be done for the horse except end its suffering, which Giles accomplished quickly. As he pulled the lad to safety, he swore in astonishment. The mud-stained boy bore a startling resemblance to Vera. God's teeth! It *was* Vera. "Sweeting, are you hurt?"

"Giles!" Vera was weak-kneed with relief. He was pale from the weeks in prison and he had lost weight, but he still had his strength and vigor—and his eyes still had a special glow when they looked at her. She threw her arms about him. "Oh, my love! I thought you were dead!"

He helped her stand and patted her limbs, checking for injury. Except for having the wind knocked from her and being covered with mud from head to toe, she seemed unharmed. He crushed her in his arms. Giles kissed her, mud and all. Then he kissed her again. He kissed her hair, her nose, her eyes.

"Oh, Giles, my dear love! I feared that I would never see you again in this world."

"Vera, my heart, my darling! I would have ridden to the ends of the earth to find you! Thank God you are safe!"

They stood face-to-face, heart-to-heart. The rush of joy was almost too intense to bear. They were still locked in an embrace when Giles felt the prick of a lance in his back. He turned slowly, relinquishing Vera. They were surrounded by guards dressed in the queen's livery, soldiers who knew Giles by sight.

"Lord Rathborne," their leader announced in firm tones, "I am charged with bringing you in, dead or alive. The choice is yours."

Giles kissed Vera one last time. "Alive, of course!" he said. "For now I am a man with everything to live for."

They met the queen's party on the ride back to Richmond. Tal signaled Vera to ignore him in front of the soldiers.

"So," Elizabeth said silkily, "you have found my escaped prisoner, Captain Fowler. A good day's work, for which you and your men will be rewarded."

She eyed Giles and Vera. "You have much to answer for—and, by God, you shall both answer to me before the day is out."

Vera was taken to a small room at Greenwich and told to remain there until she was sent for. Two of the guards took up their places outside the door. The others led Giles away. She watched him go, her heart breaking.

The room was comfortable with wide windows looking out over the grounds. Beyond the diamond-shaded windowpanes the sky was a fierce blue. Vera looked at the sprawling walls of Greenwich and wondered where they had taken Giles. Time hung heavy on her hands as she awaited word from the queen. If only she could see him and know he was safe!

A servant brought her food and drink, but she saw no one until Tal was allowed to visit several days later. "The queen is full angry at your deception," he told her solemnly. "And with me as well, for not getting word to her of the situation at Rathborne when I discovered the state of things."

Elizabeth's ringing words echoed in his head. *A man of spirit and daring would have gotten the news to me, come plague or the devil himself. Had I been a man I should have managed to do so!* Tal had no quarrel with that. She was likely right. Now *there* was a woman!

Vera kneaded a bit of lace at her cuff. "What will she do to us? To Giles?"

Tal took her hand. "That I do not know—yet. He told me of your bargain, and gave me leave to tell Lady Lattimore. The queen loves her dearly and listens to her counsel."

He looked down at his work-roughened hands. "Lady Lattimore is a good woman, and stands friend to you both. She has petitioned the queen for clemency, even at the risk of incurring her wrath. It was she who arranged for this meeting. Before I came in she whispered that you will be summoned to the Privy Chamber this afternoon."

"Thank you, dear Tal." Vera was ashamed of her earlier jealousy. "And please convey my heartfelt gratitude to Lady Lattimore. I was jealous of her once, but now I see that my fears were unfounded."

"I shall give her your message." Tal seemed quite relieved. "She advises that you wear your best finery. I have brought your trunks from Hampton Court."

An hour later word came that she was to be granted an audience at three of the clock. Vera prepared herself carefully, donning a gown of sapphire blue and the swan necklace that Giles had given her. Would Giles be there, as well? She realized her hands were shaking.

At the appointed time the guards escorted Vera to the anteroom outside the Presence Chamber and left her there alone. A short time afterward the door opened and Giles came in. "Vera!"

He went to her and took her hands in his. He was breathtakingly handsome in claret velvet. "How fine you look, my lord. I would scarce guess that you are the queen's prisoner."

"This is my new doublet. I chose it for you—since you once told me you preferred me in this color," he told her.

She smiled, remembering her first supper with him, when she had lost her temper and poured wine on him. "How long ago that seems." A lump formed in her throat. "I wish we could go back in time to that moment."

"Do you?" His eyes were warm and filled with tenderness. "I do not, for at that time I had never once held you in my arms, nor kissed your sweet lips."

Vera glanced over her shoulder at the closed door leading into the Presence Chamber. "What do you think the queen will do to us?"

Giles shrugged. He had a very good idea, but he did not want Vera to worry a minute sooner than needed. Tal had visited him earlier to say that the queen was inclined to dismiss her anger at Vera—but not at Giles, who had been the orchestrator of this mad scheme. A year or two in the Tower was not out of the question. Giles did not mind, as long as Vera was waiting for him when he was released.

The door opened and Lady Stafford stood on the threshold. "Her majesty will see you now."

They went into the Presence Chamber. It was all as Vera remembered, except the throne was unoccupied and the room empty. The queen's ladies came out from the Privy Chamber, casting curious looks at Giles and Vera as Lady Stafford led them through.

Elizabeth was playing at draughts with the Countess of Rutland. She wore ivory satin with a black over-gown embroidered in all the colors of the rainbow, and the diamonds at her throat and in her coronet matched them in brilliance. It seemed a formal outfit for an afternoon alone with her ladies. Giles felt a tinge of apprehension.

The queen rose and dismissed her remaining ladies from the room. "What I have to say to Lord Rathborne and Lady Verena is best said in privacy."

Vera's stomach knotted painfully and she saw a thin film of sweat on Giles's forehead. Defying the queen's anger, he took Vera's hand in his. Whatever the outcome, he would protect her at any costs.

"Well!" Elizabeth said sharply. "You are still as bold as ever, Rathborne. First you play off a deceitful scheme, then you seduce my innocent handmaiden, and now you flaunt your loose behavior in my very presence!"

"It is only love we flaunt." Giles squared his jaw. "I love this lady before God and heaven, majesty, and—"

Vera rushed in where angels would have quailed to go. "Your pardon, majesty, but 'twas I who seduced Lord Rathborne. I did not wish to be forced into marriage with Charpentier."

"Forced? God's eyes, woman, you told me of your own will that you preferred the Frenchman to this knave."

Giles tried to hush Vera but she would not stop. "I had quarreled with Lord Rathborne. The fault was mine then, as it is now."

Giles refused to let her shoulder the blame. "Nay, Vera. I coerced you into playing out the role. If not for me, you would not be in this sorry mess."

The queen raised her beringed hand. "Cease you brangling over who is most to blame. That is not the reason I summoned you to my presence."

She opened a jeweled coffer on her writing desk. Vera glimpsed a bundle of letters and a miniature of the Earl of Leicester in a frame of gold and pearls. The queen took a prayer book and small piece of parchment from the bottom of the coffer.

"I have here something that concerns the two of you intimately. Most especially you, *Lady Verena*." There was an odd light in her topaz-colored eyes.

She flicked the letter with one of her long, white fingers. "I have here a letter that will settle the matter once and for all, as to your true identity and that of your mother and father."

Vera drew in a deep breath. "I have long wanted to know that, majesty. It has pained me greatly that I do not know the roots from which I sprung. But how came you by such information?"

"You two are not the only ones with secrets. Master Tal tells me it was left by the dying woman who had you—and another small girl—in her care."

Earlier, Tal had not thought to mention the other girl until Elizabeth had prodded his memory. That girl had died almost immediately upon arrival at his home and he had not thought it pertinent to his tale. Men, she thought smugly, always leave out the important parts.

"There was a plague over the land," Elizabeth continued. "Half the servants at Rathborne lay dead or dying. The woman, a French girl who was nursemaid to Lady Verena, had lived at Hollyhock Cottage until Lady Rathborne took her in. Henrietta le Brun was deeply loyal to the lady and had grieved upon her death. When the plague struck, she fled the house with the girl to save her life... and took along her own daughter, born out of wedlock."

A log snapped in the fireplace, sending a bright shower of sparks up the flue. It was as loud as a cannon shot in the sudden silence. Giles was still as a statue, but he gripped Vera's hand so hard she feared it would be bruised.

Elizabeth was enjoying the high drama of the moment. Two faces, white and strained before her. Two lives, two futures hanging in the balance. "You see where this is leading, of course. The nursemaid died of the plague and one of the girls died with her."

She addressed Vera directly. "So you see that you are either the real Lady Verena, entitled to all her wealth— or you are the illegitimate daughter of a French nursemaid and a simple miller's son."

Vera's mouth was drier than dust. "Then, madam... who am I?"

"The answer to which one lived and which died is in here." The queen stroked the letter with her fingertip. "And now you must tell me whether you wish to read the letter or put it into the fire." She poked a finger at them. "But remember this: at the moment, the girl Vera and the Lady Verena are officially one and the same. Whatever is in this note might change that... and change the course of your lives forever."

Giles touched Vera's cheek. "I care not who you are, my love. It is Vera whom I wish to marry, not the rank and fortune of the Lady Verena."

"Ah," the queen interrupted, "but what of your beggared estates? Surely Lady Verena's inheritance would clear you of debt and go a long way to restoring Rathborne."

He held Vera's hand more tightly. "I will bring Rathborne back to glory by my own sweat and tears, no matter how long it takes me. I will labor on the roof or in the fields. And I will do it for Vera, and for our future children."

"Very prettily said." Elizabeth turned her light brown eyes upon Vera. "And now, child, it is you who must make the decision." The queen shrugged. "I have not read it myself, so I cannot tell you what it says. If you wish to know the truth, I will give you this to read. If not, I shall throw it into the fire and you will remain Lady Verena to the entire world."

Vera's brain reeled. "This explains everything—the maze, the hollyhock garden, the tapestries and the dim memories of your mother's blue ring. Either child would have seen them a hundred times."

Giles laughed aloud. "Of course the tapestries at Rathborne seemed much larger in memory—you were much smaller at the time."

"God's teeth, so I was!" She cleared her throat. "It is very confusing."

"Vera or Verena, it matters not one whit," Giles stated roughly. He addressed the queen. "Majesty, I love this woman with all my heart. Indeed, I cannot live without her. At the first opportunity I intend to make her my lawful wife."

Elizabeth tilted her head. "And if it turns out that she is a pauper?"

"I will take her barefoot in her shift! I will live with her at Rathborne or in a farmer's cot or in a hut in the forest. The choice is hers."

Vera closed her eyes and took a deep breath. "Nor does it matter to me." She relinquished her past willingly. "In my heart I am Vera, Tal's daughter. And so shall I always be."

She took the letter from the queen and held it a moment. Then, with an inner prayer of *Forgive me, Mother,* she walked to the hearth and threw the note into the fire.

"A wise decision," Elizabeth said. "I did not wish to be made a fool before the entire court!"

Her gown of white and gold reflected the warm light along its gilt thread and scattered jewels. The parchment turned brown and the edges blackened. Then it blazed up in a curl of smoke, leaving behind wisps of ash and a few sparks as red and bright at the rubies on her hands.

"So." She eyed them keenly for reaction. "It is done. Have either of you regrets?"

Giles held Verena's hand more tightly. "Not a one, your majesty."

"Nor I," Vera answered.

The queen's stern look softened into a smile. "Then you may retire. Tonight I shall sup in the banqueting hall. I will ask for a toast to Lord Rathborne and the Lady Verena Stanton—who will be married in the cathedral the day after Christmas. It is all arranged with the archbishop. Master Tal and Lady Lattimore will serve as your witnesses."

Vera gasped and Giles could do nothing but beam. He found his tongue after a moment. "We are most grateful for your kindness to us, majesty."

Elizabeth laughed. "You may show your gratitude by staying out of trouble, both of you! I expect that you will return to Rathborne in the spring, where you will raise a great brood of noisy brats! Now go, and leave me to my business. The affairs of the kingdom are more pressing than your tawdry escapades."

She held out her hand and they bowed and kissed her ring. When they reached the door she called after them, "When you start on that brood of brats I shall stand as godmother to your firstborn child and make it a present of a fine silver cup. You have my permission to bring them all to court—once they are housebroken."

For just a moment a sorrowful woman, deprived by statehood of the man she loved and the children she might have borne him, peeked out of Elizabeth's face. Then Gloriana was back: regal, invincible—and forever alone.

As they bowed themselves out, Vera noticed that the queen was holding Leicester's portrait in her hand. She seemed to have forgotten them completely.

The court had retired to Richmond early for the Christmas season and the halls were decked with yew and garlands of holly. Gilded nuts decorated the candle holders and bunches of mistletoe berries hung in the arched window embrasures. Music and laughter filled the halls and galleries and no one took much heed of the blustery weather. Not when there were masques and mummers, and especially not when there was such juicy gossip to be savored.

The Duc de Alençon had left for France, taking Charpentier in his train. Simmier had stayed behind in his ambassadorial post. Would he advise Alençon to return in January as he'd promised, or had the French prince finally grown weary of the queen's refusal to give him an answer to his proposal? And then there was the sudden betrothal of the Lady Verena and Giles, Lord Rathborne. Add to it the spice of the queen's newest protegé—who had come out of nowhere to gain her royal favor—and there was plenty to chew on.

On Christmas Eve Giles and Vera slipped away from the press of people. There were minstrels in the Great Hall and the music drifted up to them as they strolled decorously along the gallery together, arm in arm. The hem of her rich red velvet gown swept the stone floor. Since meeting with the queen, she and Giles had been on their best behavior. Not that there was the slightest chance for real privacy with the place swarming with courtiers. Furthermore, to keep them from the temptation of anticipating their vows *again*, Elizabeth had been requiring Vera to spend the nights with her ladies instead of in her own chamber.

"I must look after the virtue of those ladies in my care," she had told Giles regally.

Both he and Vera wished the queen had minded her own royal business.

As it was, they had to content themselves with whispered endearments and quick caresses in shadowy corners. It was not at all a satisfactory solution for two such hot-blooded people. As they came down the corridor, Giles took the presence of an empty alcove as a God-given opportunity to steal a few kisses. His mouth was hungry for her and his loins ached with longing.

"This waiting is torture."

"Only two more days," Vera whispered against his shoulder.

"Only! God's teeth," Giles exclaimed. "It seems an eternity to me! I cannot wait another second to have you all to myself."

Vera chuckled. "Nor I, you."

They heard voices and peeked out. A group of courtiers was coming down the corridor. From a distance it appeared that either Lady Stafford or the queen was among them. It was hard to tell which, for the winter light was dim. They were taking no chances, however. Giles and Vera left the alcove and ducked into a small room that overlooked the wintry gardens. He drew her behind the door, where they could not be seen from the hallway.

"I am the most selfish man in England. I do not want to share you with anyone, even the queen herself." He pulled Vera into his arms, kissing her until they were both giddy.

"Jesu, I love you!" they both murmured simultaneously.

A discreet cough sent them apart in haste. Lady Lattimore stepped out of the window embrasure where the heavy curtains had hidden her.

"Laetitia!" Vera cried. "We did not see you. I thought that you were showing Tal more of the palace."

The widow's face looked tight and unhappy. "Now that the queen has made a knight of him for helping clear Rathborne Forest of its bandits, Tal is much too busy for the likes of me. He bustles about from morning to night like a rooster in a hen yard. All his time is spent in conference with the queen. He has none left over for me."

"Who speaks my name?" The door opened wider. "And in such a tone!"

Laetitia blushed deeply as Tal walked in through the doorway from the room beyond. She had no way of knowing that he'd seen her and had taken a shortcut to reach her side. "I did not look to see you here, *Sir* Tal."

His grin widened. He chose to misinterpret her remark. "Ah, so you were looking for me, were you?" Laetitia flushed and glanced away.

Vera was extremely interested in this bit of byplay. The little idea that had been growing in her head over the past weeks blossomed into certainty. This could prove very interesting.

She sent her foster father a look of affection mingled with ripe speculation. Tal was a man still in his prime. She thought that he looked splendid in his doublet and hose of dark blue. Evidently Lady Lattimore agreed.

Vera was not used to seeing him in anything but rough jerkins and trews. She could not remember him ever looking so young and handsome. How little she knew him—except in matters that counted most.

He beamed at the three of them and took Laetitia's hand. "You think me grown up in my conceit, do you? Nay, why should a small matter like a knighthood set me cock-a-hoop? 'Tis something far better that has me crowing."

Tal raised her hand to his lips. "I have not been awooing her majesty, but pouring over charts and plans and costs." The corners of his eyes crinkled merrily. "You see before you the queen's master builder. I am to oversee the restorations here at Richmond during the winter months. If I prove to know what I am about— and I have no reason to doubt my capabilities—I shall have charge of building the Queen's new hunting box near Rathborne.''

Vera exclaimed her joy, hugging him until he begged her to leave off for fear of choking him. Giles offered his congratulations on the royal appointment. ''During the construction of the hunting box you will stay with us at Rathborne, of course,'' Giles added.

''That I shall, my lord, with great pleasure. I only hope that your bedchambers may be more comfortable than your dungeons!''

Laetitia didn't understand the reference. Tal had not quite told her everything. She pulled her hand away and stood off to the side, as if unwilling to intrude on a moment of family intimacy. Tal claimed her hand once more.

''Forgive my impertinence but...'' He cleared his throat. ''...may I hope, Lady Lattimore, that you will come out to view the work in progress?''

''Yes, do!'' Vera exclaimed, clapping her hands together. ''Giles and I shall be delighted to have you as our guest. Please say you will come to us.''

Amid much blushing and hesitation, Laetitia agreed. Tal's smile widened even more. He talked of his plans further, and when he left he had Lady Lattimore on his arm. Although he professed to have been on his way to the enclosed tennis courts to meet Simmier for a set, Vera noticed that they went in the opposite direction. It led to an unused block of rooms and a certain curtained alcove with a comfortable window cushion and a fine view of the river, where a couple could converse for hours undisturbed.

Giles viewed them in surprise. The sunlight fell on his high cheekbones and gilded his dark hair, and he was so handsome and dear that her heart filled with happiness. "Tal and Lady Lattimore have struck up a quite a friendship, it seems."

"I am glad. I was jealous of her at first," Vera admitted. "But I know now that I misjudged her. Laetitia is a woman of heart and great sense." She toyed with the buttons on Giles's red-velvet doublet and sent him a glance from beneath her eyelashes. "And you are fond of her, I know."

"Yes," Giles replied. "But not for the reasons that you suspect, sweeting. Laetitia and I were never lovers." He grinned at her patent relief. "Does that ease your mind?"

"Aye, my lord." She slid her arms around him. "I am relieved to hear it—for I have a strong notion that she may well become my stepmother one day!"

Since that curtained alcove, which Giles and Vera knew well, was sure to be occupied for a while, they fetched their cloaks and went down to the garden. A light dusting of snow covered the ground and the trees glittered like diamonds beneath a sheen of ice. The high walls protected them from the wind, and a little chill could not daunt two hot-blooded lovers.

The shrubbery was more private with its tall yew hedges, and would provide a quiet place for more stolen kisses. As they walked the graveled paths, Vera's skirt snagged on a thorny bush covered with orange berries. She yanked at it sharply and it broke free. Automatically she placed her hands on the sides of her skirt to keep the farthingale beneath from swinging like a bell.

Giles smiled wryly. "You are no longer hampered by your fashionable garments, Vera. Do you still wish to take them off?"

She smiled up at him invitingly. "Nay, my lord. I much prefer it when *you* take them off!"

He grabbed her around the waist and pulled her into his arms. "Two days! No, I cannot endure the wait."

She kissed him. "I shall see that the wait is well worth your patience."

The kiss deepened. They forgot the winter weather. They forgot the evergreen shrubbery in its sparkling coat of ice...and they did not even notice the small balcony that overlooked it.

Up in her private library the queen stood at the window. She was fond of Lord Rathborne and his Lady Verena. A smile crossed her face. Love made fools out of the wisest men and women.

Otherwise they would have surely known that she would never have seen that letter destroyed without having read its secrets first.

She turned and beckoned to her Mistress of the Bedchamber. "Lady Stafford, come and look at the pretty lovebirds I have found in my garden. They are billing and cooing as if it were already spring."

Mary Stafford joined her. "Ah, Lady Verena and Lord Rathborne. So deep in love! I have not seen a more handsome or noble-looking couple in many a day."

"Nor I."

The queen smiled down at them with only a small twinge of jealousy for what they had together that she would never know herself. Her warm breath misted the window and frost formed from it. I am getting soft and sentimental, Elizabeth thought. But Lord Rathborne was a splendid figure of a man and Vera, his beautiful wife-to-be, appeared every inch a lady...regardless of her ancestry.

Elizabeth drew a pattern on the frosted window with her fingertip and peered out through the clear places it had made. Why, looking at young Vera now, who would ever guess that she was no lady by blood—and that she was actually the illegitimate daughter of a poor French nursemaid and a simple English miller's son?

* * * * *

Harlequin® Historical

WESTERN SKIES

This September, celebrate the coming of fall with four exciting Westerns from Harlequin Historicals!

BLESSING by Debbi Bedford—A rollicking tale set in the madcap mining town of Tin Cup, Colorado.

WINTER FIRE by Pat Tracy—The steamy story of a marshal determined to reclaim his father's land.

FLY AWAY HOME by Mary McBride—A half-Apache rancher rescues an Eastern woman fleeing from her past.

WAIT FOR THE SUNRISE by Cassandra Austin—Blinded by an accident, a cowboy learns the meaning of courage—and love.

Four terrific romances full of the excitement and promise of America's last frontier.

Look for them, wherever Harlequin Historicals are sold.

Take 4 bestselling love stories FREE

Plus get a FREE surprise gift!

Special Limited-time Offer

Mail to Harlequin Reader Service®

> P.O. Box 609
> Fort Erie, Ontario
> L2A 5X3

YES! Please send me 4 free Harlequin Historical™ novels and my free surprise gift. Then send me 4 brand-new novels every month, which I will receive before they appear in bookstores. Bill me at the low price of $3.19 each plus 25¢ delivery and GST*. That's the complete price and—compared to the cover prices of $3.99 each—quite a bargain! I understand that accepting the books and gift places me under no obligation ever to buy any books. I can always return a shipment and cancel at any time. Even if I never buy another book from Harlequin, the 4 free books and the surprise gift are mine to keep forever.

347 BPA AJJL

Name	(PLEASE PRINT)	
Address		Apt. No.
City	Province	Postal Code

This offer is limited to one order per household and not valid to present Harlequin Historical™ subscribers.
*Terms and prices are subject to change without notice.
Canadian residents will be charged applicable provincial taxes and GST.

CHIS-93R   ©1990 Harlequin Enterprises Limited

MEN MADE IN AMERICA

Fifty red-blooded, white-hot, true-blue hunks from every
State in the Union!

Beginning in May, look for MEN MADE IN AMERICA!
Written by some of our most popular authors, these
stories feature fifty of the strongest, sexiest men, each
from a different state in the union!

Two titles available every other month at your favorite
retail outlet.

In July, look for:

CALL IT DESTINY by Jayne Ann Krentz (Arizona)
ANOTHER KIND OF LOVE by Mary Lynn Baxter
(Arkansas)

In September, look for:

DECEPTIONS by Annette Broadrick (California)
STORMWALKER by Dallas Schulze (Colorado)

You won't be able to resist MEN MADE IN AMERICA!

**Relive the romance...
Harlequin and Silhouette
are proud to present**

by Request

A program of collections of three complete novels by the most
requested authors with the most requested themes. Be sure to
look for one volume each month with three complete novels by
top name authors.

In June: **NINE MONTHS** Penny Jordan
                              Stella Cameron
                              Janice Kaiser

**Three women pregnant and alone. But a lot can
happen in nine months!**

In July: **DADDY'S   Kristin James
             HOME**   Naomi Horton
                            Mary Lynn Baxter

**Daddy's Home ... and his presence is long
overdue!**

In August: **FORGOTTEN   Barbara Kaye
             PAST**   Pamela Browning
                            Nancy Martin

**Do you dare to create a future if you've forgotten
the past?**

Available at your favorite retail outlet.

COMING NEXT MONTH

#183   THE SEDUCTION OF DEANNA—Maura Seger
In the next book in the *Belle Haven* series, Deanna Marlowe is
torn between family loyalty and her desire for independence when
she discovers passion in the arms of Edward Nash.

#184   KNIGHT'S HONOR—Suzanne Barclay
Sir Alexander Sommerville was determined to restore his
family's good name sullied by the treacherous Harcourt clan,
yet Lady Jesselynn Harcourt was fast becoming an obstacle to
his well-laid plans....

#185   SILENT HEART—Deborah Simmons
In a desperate attempt to survive her country's bloody revolution,
Dominique Morineau had been forced to leave the past behind,
until a silent stranger threatened to once more draw her into
the fray.

#186   AURELIA—Andrea Parnell
Aurelia Kingsley knew Chane Bellamy was her last hope. Only he
could help her find her grandfather's infamous treasure. And the
handsome sea captain was determined to show her what other
riches were within her reach.

AVAILABLE NOW:

#179   GARTERS AND SPURS
DeLoras Scott

#180   TEXAS HERO
Ruth Langan

#181   THE CYGNET
Marianne Willman

#182   SWEET SENSATIONS
Julie Tetel